A NOT SO CONVENIENT MARRIAGE

SECOND CHANCES ~ BOOK 1

SANDRA MERVILLE HART

WILD HEART
BOOKS

The characters and events in this fictional work are the product of the author's imagination. Any resemblance to actual people, living or dead, is coincidental.

Unless otherwise indicated, all Scripture quotations are taken from the Holy Bible, Kings James Version.

Cover design by: Carpe Librum Book Design

Author is represented by Hartline Literary Agency

ISBN-13: 978-1-942265-64-1

PRAISE FOR A NOT SO CONVENIENT MARRIAGE

Reading *A Not So Convenient Marriage* was for me a delightful journey into a simpler time, but a time as complex as ours when it comes to relationships, misunderstandings, and the desires of the heart. Author Sandra Merville Hart has crafted characters who will draw you into their story, capture your imagination, and leave you cheering them on as they face their own shortcomings and follow their dreams. A lovely first book in the Second Chances series, one that leaves me waiting for the next.

— ANN TATLOCK, AUTHOR, EDITOR, WRITING MENTOR

CHAPTER 1

*R*ose Hatfield grasped the picket fence gate, her gaze drinking in the farmhouse on the country lane. This must be the Walker home. The front porch, supported by four strong white pillars and nestled under a high extended roof, fit the description her brother had given her. Passing strangers couldn't guess at the heartache that dwelt within the well-kept clapboard farmhouse. What was she to say that hadn't already been said?

Samuel and Ginny had lived a fairytale romance here for nearly nine years. In her imagination, Rose saw the family lounging against the porch's sturdy handrail on summer evenings. Ivory ruffled curtains at the two front windows suited Ginny's delicate beauty.

Unshed tears scratched at her throat for the grieving family. How she longed to comfort...

She squared her shoulders. Enough of this woolgathering. If Samuel wanted company, she'd stay an hour. Longer if he

1

needed help with something. Anything at all. Not that he would need her. No, he'd accept the food she brought and see her on her way within ten minutes. On Monday morning, she'd be some thirty miles away, back in Harrison teaching arithmetic and reading.

Life would go on as it always had.

Rose gripped her well-laden basket and pushed the gate open. Yellow daffodils bloomed at the base of the home. Ginny would never pick flowers from that tiny garden again.

To her right, a pig ambled through a barn opening leading into a fenced sty. Two horses grazed in a corral that extended some fifty yards from the red barn to the dirt road. Woods hid mooing cows. Spacious open fields lay desolate beyond the barn. Cool breezes blew wispy gray smoke from the chimney.

She climbed the porch steps and knocked on the sturdy blue door. Her heart ached for the two young children who lost their mother, a childhood sorrow she knew well.

Her cloak flapped in the wind. Shivering, she tugged it closer.

Perhaps the family wasn't home and there'd be no need to fill awkward silences with words unable to ease their sorrow.

Taking a step back, she caught a wisp of hair that had strayed from the knot at the nape of her neck and tucked it behind her ear. She must look a sight. Her hat had done little to protect her hair from the breeze that whipped up on her walk there.

No need to prolong this wait. The food could be left on the porch. Still, her feet refused to budge. She'd come so far to speak to Samuel and see how he managed. See if there was something—some little thing—she could do for the family.

Before she'd set the basket down, seven-year-old Peter opened the door. It had been a year since Rose had seen him at church when she'd last visited her brother Richard. Pale blond hair fell across Peter's forehead, almost reaching his blue eyes. His wrinkled shirt and mournful expression pricked her heart.

"Good morning." She smiled. "You may not remember me. Miss Rose Hatfield, a friend of your parents."

"You're Clay's aunt. He's my friend." The door opened wider.

Rose stepped inside, attention riveted on the boy, whose shifted to the pink floral rug.

He shut the door. "My Ma … she's—"

"I know." Rose touched his shoulder to halt the dreadful words. The funeral three weeks ago must be a raw wound for the boy. She'd learned the news of Ginny's death too late to attend. "That's why I came. I wanted to help"—her gaze shifted to a table filled with dirty dishes—"if I can." She stacked dirty bowls to clear a spot for her basket, exposing a fine mahogany dining table.

"I reckon you brought more food." He gestured toward the cluttered kitchen beyond the table. "People keep bringin' stuff. Pa never learned to cook, so he's glad. Says he went straight from eating his ma's cooking to my ma's cooking."

She patted Peter's shoulder, appalled at the chaos that had overtaken the spacious room. Dirty dishes covered a long narrow table against the kitchen area's side wall. A hand pump on a basin under a back window proved that the farmhouse had running water. Impressive.

Open cupboard doors revealed almost bare shelves. Near the back door, a skillet on a black stove contained something brown. That would account for the aroma of burnt eggs that overwhelmed the familiar smell of wood burning in the wide hearth.

A filled kettle sat beside the skillet. She stepped closer and peeked inside to see…yesterday's soup? A basket of biscuits sat on the counter near crusty bread. Her gaze paused when she saw the luxury of an icebox nestled beside the cupboard. Why hadn't the soup been placed inside it?

The jars in her basket only added to the disarray.

Dirty clothing lay heaped close to the fireplace, the pile as

3

high as the checkered shirt on the boy's back. She imagined the family lounging on the uncluttered mauve sofa and matching armchairs.

A log shifted, shooting tiny sparks that did little to dispel the dismal atmosphere. Even though this was her first visit, she was certain the home hadn't been this untidy before.

Ginny's death hadn't only taken an emotional toll on this family.

It seemed Rose had discovered a way to help Samuel's family. "Where is Emma? And your father?" She glanced into one of the three open bedroom doors lining the right side of the house.

"Outside." Peter crossed to the back window and looked to the right. "Pa's planting more apple trees. Can't see him. The orchard's at the end of the field." He pointed to the little girl in the backyard as Rose joined him. Beside her, a medium-sized brown-and-white mutt wagged his tail. "That's Zeb next to Emma."

"What a good dog." Emma's lips moved, apparently speaking to her doll. The girl must be cold sitting with her back against a large trunk of a massive maple tree. The shadowy day felt more like November than March.

"He's my dog." Peter lifted his chin. "I taught him a trick, but he ain't good at it. He's 'sposed to catch the stick in his mouth, but he always picks it up and brings it back to me."

She gave a shaky laugh at the first glimmer of the boy's smile. "Learning a trick takes practice."

"That's what Pa says. Should I fetch him?" His brow wrinkled. "He said not to bother him unless somebody gets hurt or something. Some man delivered trees this week. Pa has to get them in the ground so they don't die. He'd forgotten about ordering them, what with Ma ..."

"Please don't bother him." Peter's grief ignited every maternal instinct. "I'll prepare dinner while I wait." She glanced at the cluttered kitchen, which likely hadn't been cleaned in days. "Maybe wash a few dishes."

His face brightened. "Pa said to clean up best I could. I don't know where to start."

"Well, I do. Play outside if you like."

"All right." After shrugging into his coat, he ran outside and plopped onto the cold ground beside his five-year-old sister. The children were fine for now.

Eying the mess, Rose hung her cloak on a wall hook and tied on an apron hanging by the large black stove. Few people she knew owned an icebox. She marveled at the extravagance as she opened the shoulder-high rectangular box filled with bowls, pie pans, and plates. Her mouth pulled at a sour smell.

Plans for a short visit crumbled. It'd take a hard day's work to make the situation manageable. It was the least she could do for a childhood friend.

Hazel, Rose's sister-in-law, understood her desire to help. She told Rose she'd expect her when she saw her but to come for supper because she planned a special meal to celebrate Rose's birthday.

A glance at the mantle clock above the fireplace spurred her to action. Two hours until noon. Rolling up her sleeves, she set to work.

~

*H*eavy boots thudded on the porch a moment before cool air swept through the house. Rose, heart hammering against her ribs because she knew not how to comfort Samuel, looked up from a skillet filled with bubbling gravy.

The tall, haggard man with shadows under his blue eyes couldn't be Samuel. He appeared older than his twenty-seven years. Wind had tussled his already wavy dark hair. A gap in his coat showed he'd lost weight.

"Rose?" Samuel said, his children at his heels. "Peter just told me you'd come. I can't believe you waited. Sorry I was in the orchard when you arrived."

Any oft-repeated words of comfort fled. She longed to give him a consoling embrace, but their friendship had faded a lifetime ago. She clasped his hand instead, ignoring bits of dirt that clung to his fingers. "I didn't hear about Ginny until after the funeral... I'm so sorry. It seems too impossible to be true."

"Thank you." Pain deepened in his eyes as he sandwiched her hand between his strong, callused ones. "There's mourning for you in this. Our school years seem so far away now." He released her and placed a hand on each child's shoulder. "You remember Peter and Emma."

"Of course." She offered each a smile. Their wind-tussled blond hair and blue eyes reminded her of Ginny, especially Emma. The little girl, clutching a doll against her shoulder, might someday rival her mother's beauty. Sorrow clung to them like a cloak. Rose fidgeted with her apron, fighting a desire to gather the children into a comforting hug. They barely knew her, after all. "Peter and I had a nice talk. Emma, I'm happy to see you again."

She averted sad eyes. Rose glimpsed a ruffled dress underneath her stylish cloak. Why wear a fancy dress to play in the yard? Then she remembered the laundry pile.

A whiff of scorched food snatched Rose to the present. She snatched the wooden spoon and stirred, chagrined the spoon nudged at gravy stuck to the skillet. "Please wash up while I set the table."

"You didn't have to do all this." Samuel's shoulders hunched as he raised and lowered the pump handle.

"I simply washed a few dishes." An understatement. She'd also cleaned the kitchen and tossed out stale food, much of it from the ice box. There'd been no time to scour the stove, a long-neglected job.

"Thank you." He scrubbed his hands under the water's flow. "Children, wash up for dinner. Use soap this time." He winked at Peter.

His teasing lifted Rose's spirits.

Within moments, they sat around the large table. Samuel asked a blessing.

"How is Richard?" He selected two biscuits and offered the bread basket to Peter. "And Hazel and the children?"

"Everyone's healthy. They were happy to pick me up at the train depot last night for a weekend stay." Rose's brother had lived in Hamilton since before his marriage. She hated missing out on her watching her niece and nephew grow up. Gracious, Polly was already four and Clay was Peter's age. "Hazel said to expect a supper invitation so the childen can play together."

"We'll look forward to it." Samuel scooped a forkful of gravy and biscuits, gazing at the spotless kitchen. "I can't believe what you've accomplished in one morning."

Heat spread over Rose's face. She hoped he didn't mind her taking the bull by the horns in cleaning the mess. "I found food near spoiling, including bread and soup, that I dumped into the pigs' trough. I made gravy to use the biscuits before they went stale." She sipped her hot tea.

"Thank you for taking on that task. It means more than you know. Meals from friends have come daily since we lost Ginny." Samuel's loaded fork paused on the way to his mouth. He returned it to his plate. "It's a blessing, considering I can't cook. We ate scorched eggs for breakfast." His chuckle seemed forced.

She appreciated his attempt at levity.

"It'll hurt when folks quit feeding us, though we often receive more than we can eat. That's why there's so much food going to waste."

"I'll see if Hazel can coordinate meals from church families.

Unfortunately, I brought gingerbread." She had enjoyed baking the treat for the children. It was a shame that they already had too much food on hand.

Peter's head shot up. "I want some."

Emma looked up from her plate.

Rose's spirits bubbled as everyone devoured the sticky dessert. She'd bake them again next time she visited Richard.

"I hate to rush away, but I'm planting apple seedlings." Samuel stood, rubbing his stubbly chin. "I ordered enough trees to fill two acres last November. Can't afford to lose any. The sooner they're in the ground, the better the chance they'll flourish. Thanks for the meal." The children stood beside their pa.

"No trouble." She stacked the plates. "I'll wash a pile of clothes before leaving."

Samuel raised his eyebrows.

"I have no plans." She plunged in with her arguments. "It needs to be done. And you're busy. Where shall I hang the wet clothing?" As if the matter were decided, she carried a stack of dishes to the basin.

"That's very kind. I'd be obliged for the help. Every bedroom ceiling has lines. Ginny said clothes hanging in the sitting room depressed her spirits." He lifted open palms. "Are you certain?"

"Absolutely." His appreciation was a balm to her spirit.

"I put the task off too long. Among other things." He spoke softly as he slipped on his coat and hat. "Please don't leave without saying goodbye."

"I won't." She shivered in the cold breeze that whipped through the open door.

He smiled and then looked down at his children clinging to his coat. "Want to help dig holes?"

Their eyes lit up. They left with him, leaving Rose to search for laundry supplies.

The children returned two hours later. "Emma's cold. Pa said for us to warm by the fire." They waited at the door.

"Wonderful idea." Did they feel shy with her? They didn't know she spent more time with children than adults because of her teaching position. She'd just lifted a pile of clothes, and a pair of trousers fell from her hands into the rinse pan and splashed her apron. She set the other clothes aside. "Let's get you warm. I'll throw another log into the fire."

"I'll do it." Peter dropped his coat on the floor and ran to the fireplace.

"Thank you." Rose hung his coat on a wall hook. Her students his age built fires in the school's woodstove. Between furtive glances at the boy to make sure he stayed safe, she helped Emma remove her wraps.

Peter tossed a log on the low flames. Cinders shot up the chimney. He prodded embers with a poker, coaxing a glowing blaze. "I did it." He beamed.

"That you did. Why, that heat warms me all the way over here." She ruffled his hair. "Next time, lay the log on top and watch how much happier the fire is afterward."

Rose boiled clothes in a big pot on the stove while the children played checkers on the rug. Such a simple game brought a sense of normalcy to the home. Their playtime comforted her that, for an hour at least, the children were able to cast aside their sorrow. She changed the water in the wash pot from the stove and added more clothes that required boiling. It was a relief to watch the laundry pile shrink.

The siblings rejoined their pa in the fields after Peter won four games.

Someone tapped on the front door. Rose opened it and smiled at an auburn-haired woman. "Good afternoon. My name is Rose Hatfield. The Walker family is in the orchard."

The woman's bright blue eyes widened. "Hatfield? Any relation to Richard and Hazel?"

"He's my brother. I came to offer condolences and found the home needs attention." She was suddenly aware she was in a widower's home, alone, while the family worked on the farm. What must the woman think of her?

"I've been itchin' to clean over here since Ginny passed." The woman peered at the room beyond Rose's shoulder. "I heard about Richard's sister in Harrison. That's still in Ohio, ain't it?"

"Yes, about thirty miles from Hamilton." She returned the stranger's smile.

"I'm Catherine Hill. From next door." Bright curls bounced as she inclined her head to the left. "That thick line of trees hides my house, but I don't mind seclusion. Reminds me of my Kentucky home." She offered a lid-covered pan. "I brung over ham for supper but I could stay and help a while. My boys are at a friend's house. My oldest, Rennie, will keep an eye on the rest. For a time."

Rose laughed. "Absolutely, Mrs. Hill."

"Call me Catherine."

"If you'll call me Rose." She led her to the washtub and scrub board set up in front of the large room's armchairs. "The first laundry pile already fills lines in Emma's room. I can't stay to iron after they dry. This much will help."

"Seems like you and me are peas in a pod—when we see somethin' that needs doin', we do it." Hands on hips, Catherine surveyed the laundry. "Looks like every stitch they own was dirty."

After setting the ham in the warming oven, Rose simmered green beans in a pot. She scanned the yard and the fields. The children were likely in the orchard. Gray clouds cast a gloom on the desolate land. It was a cold day to work outdoors.

The women took turns at a single scrub board. It was a little strange to scrub dirt from clothing while seated on an expensive armchair, but it was too cold to work on the back porch. She should have asked Samuel where Ginny used to scrub clothes in cold weather.

"No one dreamed that sunny February day would bring

tragedy." Catherine wrung soapy water from a blue shirt and then brushed back red tendrils from her sweaty brow. "It had been cold for a spell. Ginny saddled her horse that first pretty morning. Samuel had warned her about icy patches, but she didn't plan to ride far on these country roads. The horse may have slipped. Anyway, Ginny fell and hit her head on a rock. Samuel rode out when her horse came home without her. The children stayed with me. He found her right off. Trent—that's my husband—fetched the doctor, but Ginny never woke up. Died that evening." Catherine disappeared into Peter's room with a wet shirt.

A lump lodged in Rose's throat. The tragedy was still fresh. She plunged Emma's ruffled dress into soapy water.

Catherine brought back a pair of muddy trousers. "Peter and Emma closed up like clams, right from the first. Samuel don't have help. His family's all dead now, not counting that sister who lives out west. Of course, you probably know Samuel grew up in Harrison since you're from there. Ginny's parents left for their home in Columbus—that's in Ohio—as soon as the visiting was done after the funeral. I ain't never seen two more broken-hearted people my whole life. I felt plumb sorry for 'em."

"I didn't hear about the accident until after the funeral. I'd have come." Rose knew what it was to face tragedy alone. Richard's family were her only kin.

"*Everyone* loved Ginny." Catherine rubbed lye soap on a mud stain. "Seemed like the whole city came. Nobody missed you, that's certain."

Rose flushed at the bald truth as she picked up the next item.

Her hands froze. The green dress must have looked beautiful on Samuel's wife.

"Wash all Ginny's clothes." Catherine sniffed. "Best not leave that sorrow for the family."

Catherine was right. Rose searched the remaining pile for Ginny's garments. They worked on them in respectful silence.

Catherine hung the last shirt in the master bedroom and rejoined Rose in the kitchen. "We got more done than I dreamed. I'll ask friends to iron these with me on Monday. I don't iron on Sunday. The Good Lord took a day of rest, and with eight youngins I need it too."

Samuel had good neighbors. Rose thanked her and watched her walk away.

Not much later, pink-cheeked children entered the back door with their father as Rose removed cornbread from the warming oven. "Catherine Hill brought ham for supper. I'll set the table before I leave."

"I thought you left hours ago." Samuel strode into the room, his gaze on the rug where the clothes pile had been. Striding around the room, he stopped at every bedroom door. He gestured into Peter's room with an open palm. "Now that's a welcome sight." His shoulders relaxed.

Tears pricked her eyes. "We laundered clothes. She and a friend will iron them on Monday." Sniffing, she placed three plates on the table.

Eyeing a steaming platter of ham, the children sat.

Samuel blinked. "You've worked wonders. How can I thank you?"

"I was happy to do it." The wonder in his eyes made all the hard work worthwhile.

He clasped her hand. "Won't you eat with us?"

How she missed Samuel's friendship, once so strong. Then a beautiful girl moved to town. When Samuel began courting Ginny, their friendship became a shadowy memory. How she had yearned for him to look at her the way he looked at Ginny all those years ago. Instead, Rose's heart broke to witness him falling in love with someone else.

It had happened so long ago. A painful memory of what might have been, buried beneath the surface. Still, the look in his eyes at this moment—whether it be gratitude or appreciation—tempted her. If only her sister-in-law wasn't planning a birthday celebration. "I'm sorry. Hazel expects me. Can you manage now?"

"Better now. Because you came." He patted her hand and released it. His gaze slid from hers. "Thanks for everything." He picked up her empty basket and held it out to her. "I'm more grateful than you know."

Her fingers brushed his as she accepted it. "I wish I could do more."

Pain flashed in his eyes. After she donned her cloak, he opened the front door.

After saying goodbye to the children and then to Samuel, she stepped onto the porch. Light faded as the door shut behind her. She turned to stare at the closed door in the gathering dusk. A long-forgotten sadness filled every corner of her heart.

A yearning for their old camaraderie stole her breath away.

Yet that was all in the past. She stepped from the warm glow of their home. Samuel had been too mired in grief to think to offer a ride back to Richard's home. No matter. She was well-accustomed to taking care of herself.

CHAPTER 2

*C*lopping hooves halted in front of Samuel's house. Another meal from someone at church? Good thing the dishes were finished. Congratulating himself on keeping the kitchen clean since Rose's visit a week before, he placed the last dripping cup on a towel to drain as someone tapped on the door.

After opening the door, he greeted the gray-haired woman, who carried an open basket containing a covered pot. "Mrs. Bradshaw, what a pleasant surprise." No one sat in the buggy she'd driven. A horse nibbled tufts of grass beside the dirt road. "Pastor Bradshaw isn't with you?"

"He's napping," the gray-haired woman shook her head with a decisive snap, "just like he does every Sunday afternoon. Claims preaching exhausts him. I tell him I can't understand how talking wears a body out, but he insists that it does. Why, I can talk all day."

Samuel had no doubt that was true. "Please come in." A delicious aroma stirred his appetite. "Can I help you with that basket?"

"Of course." She extended it to him. "You can't expect me to hold it while we talk."

Samuel hid a smile and led the way to the kitchen. "Do I smell potato soup?"

"You do." The short woman removed the kettle from the basket he held and placed it on the stove. "I expect this will be your supper."

"It will. Thank you." Mrs. Bradshaw was one of the best cooks in the church. Having sampled many meals in the last month, he ought to know.

"Are the children in the house?"

She usually stayed only long enough to explain how to heat up a meal. "They're playing out by the cow pasture. Shall I call them in?"

"No." She pursed her lips. "What I have to say is for your ears alone."

That sounded ominous. He gestured the sofa, where the plump woman sat with dignified ease. He chose a side chair. What had he done to warrant her displeasure?

"Samuel, poor Ginny passed a month ago." Scarlet tinged the pastor's wife's cheeks. "You may not want to hear this."

Well-acquainted with her blunt manner, he steeled himself.

"Our women are talking." She tugged at fringes on her brown shawl.

"Yes?"

"You need another wife." The words tumbled out. "Your children need the stability of a woman's gentle guidance."

The words sent churning to his stomach. It was too soon to be discussing remarrying, even to be considering it.

"Now, Samuel, are you too mired in your own grief to notice Peter and Emma wandering around like lost lambs?"

A slap on the face would be more welcome than this criticism. "Certainly, my main concern is for—"

"Then shove your selfish grief aside. Search for a wife." She wagged her finger. "Your children rely on you to do what's right."

Her bossy attitude nettled like a burr in his boots. "Now just a—"

"This must be said. Church women can't bring meals indefinitely." She shook her head so emphatically that a large purple feather on her hat dislodged to dangle over her ear. "Am I right that several spinsters and widows were among those bringing you food?"

It was true. One kind woman had been widowed in the war. She had children a decade older than his own. Surely they'd only meant to comfort him.

"You understand those women are looking to become the next Mrs. Walker," Mrs. Bradshaw said. "You're vulnerable and easily swayed."

"So, in your opinion, I should marry a single woman from our church?" Sarcasm crept into his voice despite his best efforts. Advice delivered as a command set his blood to simmer.

"You could do worse." Her lips pursed. "But of course, I didn't mean that. The right woman will present herself." Her tone softened. "You're a young man. Ginny's gone. There will be someone else."

Her words slashed through his heart like a knife through a tender shoot. He stood and stepped to the fireplace. With callused hands, he rested his hands on the brick wall above the hearth and stared into the flames. Ginny was gone.

"I *am* sorry for your loss," the interfering woman said. "We all miss her. It's hard to believe one so loving…"

Her words faded into the background. Samuel raked a hand across his forehead. How much must he take?

"Pray for guidance." Mrs. Bradshaw stood. "It won't always hurt as badly as it does today."

～

*A*fter listening to his children's bedtime prayers, Samuel cradled a cup of coffee in front of the fire. Apparently, he wasn't helping them navigate through their staggering loss. He vowed to do better. He was all they had now.

Mrs. Bradshaw's advice had shaken him from the stupor that had overtaken him at the funeral. He hated to admit it, but she was right. His children's unhappiness cut deeply. No matter what it took, he'd provide security and a stable home.

He prayed for help raising his precious children and for guidance with decisions he lacked the strength to face.

A caring wife would lift many burdens. The next morning, he awoke thinking about an old friend from his school days.

~

"*D*elicious." A week later, Samuel settled against a high-backed chair at his friend Richard Hatfield's home and smiled at Hazel Hatfield. "A meal I don't have to reheat is a pleasant change. There have been too many of those reheated meals lately. Thank you for inviting me and my family for supper." Rose hadn't strayed far from his thoughts since she left two weeks ago. Come to think of it, her delicious gravy had made leftover biscuits a treat too.

"Our pleasure." The petite woman smiled and pushed back the brown curls sweeping her forehead.

Shouts from Peter and Clay Hatfield, who were climbing a tree in the backyard, drew Richard to the window. "The boys are lounging on a low tree branch." The tall, lanky man rejoined them at the dining table in the Hatfields' comfortable, modest home. "The girls are spinning tops on the porch."

"Good." Laughing and playing were worth more than getting to bed on time. Ginny had been a stickler for maintaining a consistent bedtime. Samuel resolved not to worry about the gathering dusk.

"Rose mentioned the food going to waste in your icebox," Hazel said. "Did the meal schedule help?"

"Very much. Folks bring only one meal daily. And we're managing the household chores, thanks to Rose, who got us caught up."

"We'll mention your thanks in our next letter." Richard rubbed a finger around the rim of his coffee cup. "She wrote that you and your family are in her daily prayers."

Rose prayed for his family. Warmth thawed a chunk of the ice surrounding Samuel's heart. His thoughts had strayed to her so often this week that they'd worn a path. "Richard, can we talk?"

The man's forehead wrinkled. "Let's go to the barn. Time for milking."

Both men were perched on milking stools before Richard spoke again. "What's eating on you?"

"Considering marrying again." No sense dragging it out. Good thing the cow's hindquarters hid Richard from view. "Peter and Emma need a mother. I can't be both Ma and Pa." He concentrated on milking.

"Reckon you're right." Richard spoke in even tones. "A good woman is a blessing."

Ginny had been a good woman. Rose was too. "Things have been difficult." Samuel willed himself to breathe. "The only day I found comfort was when Rose came." Seeing her had been like the first breath of spring, bringing a promise of new life. He had prayed all week for the best wife and mother for his children, and Rose's face had continually crept into his thoughts. Rose was the only other woman besides Ginny that ever captured his attention.

"Hmm." Milk struck Richard's wooden bucket.

"You and I have been friends a long time." Samuel's chest tightened. "Our children play well together."

"What's that got to do with you getting married?"

Samuel's ears burned. "Rose and I used to be friends." The milk level in his bucket grew while he waited for Richard's response.

"My sister's a mighty good woman."

"She is." Why was such a sweet, compassionate woman a spinster? He understood the appeal of hair the color of honey, beautiful dark eyes, and a smile that invited a man to smile back. Were the bachelors in Harrison all fools?

"Don't know if she's keeping company with anyone." Richard stood and put the stool away.

Startled, Samuel finished his task. Was she courting? He rose, his thoughts in a swirl, and stowed his stool next to his friend's.

"Probably not, since she didn't mention it."

Samuel gulped. He suddenly realized how much this meant to him. "Is there a chance for me?"

"She loves her job. Lives in our childhood home. There are many memories there." Richard placed both milk pails beside the door. "It's hard to figure women. She's getting on in years—turned twenty-six three weeks ago."

"What day?" He wished she had told him. She hadn't let on. He likely knew such details back in school.

"Her birthday is the eighth. Thursday of the week before she came. Who knows?" Richard closed the barn door and then glanced at Samuel. "She may agree to marry you."

Samuel rubbed his jaw. Rose enjoyed her teaching job. She'd have to give that up to help raise his children. "Do I have your blessing?"

"You have my blessing." He clapped Samuel on the back. "But this is Rose's decision."

~

*O*n a dismal Friday morning a week later, Samuel guided his team onto the road toward Harrison. Five hours by wagon, unless those gray clouds overhead unleashed the rain that had threatened since last evening.

The last time he'd traveled this route was to attend his mother's funeral five years before, at which point he'd sold his childhood home. Tragic memories followed him everywhere.

His only sister, Savannah, had moved to San Francisco with her husband by the time Ginny and her family had moved to Harrison. Savannah'd never met Ginny, but she'd probably met Rose, who had been twelve when his sister left. He doubted either had made an impression on the other.

Samuel had been reluctant to leave his children at Richard's house overnight while he was in Harrison proposing to Rose. They were thrilled to play with Clay and Polly and they'd love them as cousins, he was certain.

Rose's recent visit had demonstrated kindness to an old friend. Perhaps it was nothing more. He remembered sharing, a lifetime ago, his boyhood dreams with her. Her attentiveness had always made him feel important. He'd never acted on his romantic feelings for Rose. Ginny made her interest in him clear, and he had fallen head over heels before long and relinquished his friendship with Rose at Ginny's insistence.

Samuel didn't doubt his feelings for Rose would rekindle. She was a kind, sweet, and fun companion. What if she didn't want the responsibility of raising another woman's children? And who'd blame her for that?

No one. Clenching his jaw, he guided the horses around an imbedded stone on the dirt road barely wide enough for two wagons. There was the occasional farmhouse with fields that would soon be plowed, but this section of the road was mostly lined by budding trees. Spring approached, bringing a promise of new life. His children needed that promise.

He must marry. Finances prevented him from hiring a housekeeper. Money had always been a source of conflict in his marriage. He bore as much blame as Ginny because they'd never agreed on how to spend surplus cash—not that extra cash came often. Last year's plentiful harvest had allowed him to increase his orchard. Investing in apple trees made sense—to him, anyway.

Ginny had celebrated the additional funds with a shopping expedition—more expensive dresses to wear to dinner parties hosted by wealthy friends. What was left purchased winter supplies. Arguments over spending had shoved a wedge between them.

She'd never been content to live on a farmer's income. That still rankled. Samuel's inability to buy fine furnishings had prompted her to cast subtle hints to her parents, who made several large purchases for the home.

To his shame, his father-in-law had paid Ginny's funeral expenses.

Old feelings of inadequacy smote him. She'd married a farmer. Why hadn't it been enough?

Rain sputtered and gradually increased. He shifted his hat down and urged the horses to a faster pace before muddy roads impeded his progress.

Memories of the woman he traveled to see warred with memories of the one he'd married. Rose had caught his eye first. Other than agreeing with his buddies that Ginny was a beauty, he hadn't spared the new girl a passing thought.

But when Ginny'd showed interest in him, he'd been as flabbergasted as his envious friends. Before long, her beauty and sweet nature captivated him. He'd proposed a few months into the courtship.

After the betrothal, Ginny invited female classmates to

suppers and parties and quickly became the most popular girl in school. She had blossomed under the attention.

Yet Ginny had never been close to Rose. After their marriage, they attended the same Hamilton church as her brother. Hazel often invited them to Sunday dinner when Rose came to Hamilton. Those sporadic lunches had stirred longings to revisit Harrison, but they never did. Ginny's parents had moved to Columbus, Ohio shortly after their marriage, squelching any desire on her part to visit the village where they met.

The wagon lurched over a water-filled rut. Dark clouds loomed without a break on the horizon. An omen?

He rubbed a wet sleeve over his brow. Proposing to Rose was a bad idea.

He'd once imagined Rose felt something more than friend-ship for him—even hoped for it—but that was before his courtship with Ginny. If Rose ever held romantic feelings for him, he had no reason to believe she'd love him again. Should he turn around? He'd made his share of mistakes. He didn't want to add to the pile.

But Peter and Emma needed him. Thinking of them strengthened his resolve.

A marriage of convenience ought to ease the way into the marriage for Rose. And he needed time to grieve Ginny before moving onto another relationship.

Pouring rain pelted him. What did it matter? Misery stuck closer than a friend these days.

CHAPTER 3

*P*encils scratched across slates. Strolling the aisles, Rose's thoughts strayed again to Samuel. She fought the depression that had plagued her since seeing him three weeks before. According to Hazel's latest letter, the meal schedule fixed the overabundance of food, relieving one worry. Yet how was he coping for his children?

Rain drummed against the roof. Her gaze traveled over her students' shoulders to the muddy road outside the window. Dreary for early April. A blade of grass clung to her black skirt. She brushed it off and examined her white shirtwaist. No muddy stains from playing tag with the children before the rain on their lunch break. Circling the room, she went to the desk of a struggling student.

At the end of the day, the children scampered out into the rain. Breathing in the fresh air, she stood at the doorway until they disappeared from sight. Their clothing would be soaked when they reached home—hers too.

What did it matter, though? Every week was the same. She'd finish her lesson plans for the following week. Then she'd trudge home and eat supper with the family who boarded with her, just like every Friday evening. Then she'd pick up her latest sewing project, just like she did every night.

But planning next week's lessons came first. With her chair scooted close to her teacher's table, she set to work. Two hours later, the door creaked.

She looked up at the sound, then rubbed her tired eyes. Was she dreaming?

Samuel stood in the doorway, dripping rainwater onto the wood floor. He removed a soggy hat. "Good afternoon, Rose."

Not dreaming, apparently. "Samuel? What a surprise." A loose tendril brushed against her cheek. She shoved it behind her ear. She must look a sight after playing in the drizzle with her students. She hurried to greet him.

"I'm interrupting your work." Closing the door, he hung his soggy hat on a wall hook and then clasped the hand she extended.

"Not at all." Raindrops from his hand clung to her fingers. "I'm happy you're here."

"I apologize for my appearance." Releasing her, he ran his hands over the black hair plastered to his head.

Wet hair didn't detract from his looks. "You look good to me." Had she really admitted that out loud? Heat seeped up her neck. "I mean, it's wonderful to see you again so soon."

"I'm happy to see you." Water dripped on the wood floor. "Sorry. My coat's soaked." He removed the overcoat and hung it beside the hat.

"This room has seen much worse." She laughed. "Please, sit with me."

"I'd like that."

She gestured to the chair behind her desk.

"How about if I sit here?" He pointed to a large student desk. "I haven't sat in one since leaving school."

She giggled at the way his tall frame engulfed the seat. "Doesn't quite fit."

"No." Samuel chuckled. "Our old classroom was arranged in a similar fashion. Just don't remember these tiny desks." He squeezed his frame out of it.

"They're the same size. We aren't."

"You're as trim as ever." He scanned the room. "How long have you taught at Sand Hill? That's the name of this school, right?"

"It is. Since Papa died. This school follows the farming schedule. We'll break soon for spring planting. An unusual restlessness makes me anticipate a break all the more." A restlessness that began when she visited his home last month. Gladness filled her that he was here with her. There was no one else she'd rather see. "Perhaps it's the weather."

"I feel the same way." His fingers trailed against desks as he wandered around the room. "Where do you stable your horse?"

"Students riding to school use a neighbor's barn. Most walk, as I do." Her eyes drank in his haggard face while his finger traced a name etched in a wooden table. Schoolgirl memories of him tightened her throat.

"Long walk?"

"Not quite three miles." She tucked trembling hands into the folds of her skirt. She didn't often find herself alone with any man, much less Samuel. How she missed their talks, their friendship even after all these years. "I don't mind. This job is a blessing."

"Your pupils are lucky to have you." He shivered.

"The fire died after the children left. No wonder you're cold —your trousers are soaked." She half turned toward the black heat stove. "Shall I build another?"

"Not on my account. Thanks." He rubbed his hands together. "This must be a day for old memories."

"Oh?" Her chest tightened. He must not plan to stay since he didn't want her to light a fire. *Please stay longer. Talk to me awhile.*

"Remember us at school?" He glanced at the teacher's table,

the slates, and the shelves lined with Ray's Arithmetic books and McGuffey Readers. "I sat on the right side." He sat on a bench facing her in the confined space.

His chest was broader than in those school years. Had she changed also?

"You sat between Ginny and me." He stared at an empty desk as if seeing her there once more. "Seems like it happened fifty years ago."

Best not remember days that, for Rose, had been more bitter than sweet. This was the first time she'd been alone with Samuel since he courted Ginny. "It can't be fifty years, considering you're only twenty-seven." She forced a laugh. She looked away, unwilling to admit she had once cherished all the details of his life. "Your birthday is in February, exactly one year and one month before mine."

"You remember my birthday." He searched her face. "We were friends before Ginny came along. I don't remember talking to you much after our courtship began."

Time to change the topic. "Is this your first trip to Harrison since your mother passed?"

"It is." He ran his fingers through his hair. "Will you have supper with me? Market Street used to have hotels with dining rooms. Do any still have a restaurant?"

She blinked. "Yes," she whispered. He wanted her company for the evening?

"Wonderful. Will you join me?"

"That sounds lovely." She remembered long-ago days when she'd desperately desired such an invitation from him. How foolish she had been. A plain woman such as herself indulging in such dreams only invited heartache, as she had learned the hard way. She mustn't allow ridiculous hopes to spoil this unexpected gift of an evening with Samuel. "I must go home to change and tell Celia—my boarder, Mrs. Robinson—my plans."

"We met this afternoon at your home." Crimson stained his

freshly-shaven face. "She explained that you prepare upcoming lessons before leaving."

Her eyebrows shot up. This supper invitation had been planned? He'd gone to her home?

Interesting. "Celia and her husband, Fred, have boarded with me two years. She's more like a sister than a boarder. They have a daughter, Harriet. She captured my heart instantly."

"Mrs. Robinson seems very pleasant, and I met her sweet daughter too. I'm glad you're close to them." He sauntered to the window. "Rain stopped. My wagon's outside." He shook his hat, and droplets splattered the floor.

Rose suppressed an exultant squeal and stacked books and papers on her desk. An opportunity to spend an evening with an old friend didn't often present itself. Thankful for whatever business had brought him to Harrison, she donned her hat and cloak and picked up her basket. "I'm ready."

He took the basket from her and opened the door. White canvas covered the back of his wagon, a good idea when traveling in such weather.

"Spring weather is unpredictable," he said. "Thought I might have to sleep in the wagon tonight." He removed a dry blanket from the back and placed it over the wet seat. His callused hand warmed hers as he held her hand to help her onto the wagon.

"You're welcome to stay with us." A thrill shot through her when Samuel joined her on the wooden seat. She hoped all her neighbors looked out their windows to witness him bringing her home from work.

"Thank you, but Will Shepherd invited me to stay with his family." He guided the horses onto the road.

"My brother visits him every time he comes to town." Now that she thought back, Richard, Samuel, and Will used to ride horseback together on summer weekends.

"Not surprised to hear it. We were all good friends." Samuel steered his team around a rut. "Now, we all have children the same ages."

That began before Samuel befriended Rose, though she recalled watching them ride out on hot afternoons.

The conversation shifted to his concerns for his grieving children. Her heart went out to the whole family. How would they cope?

Once they stepped inside her two-story clapboard home where she grew up, she surveyed the main room that doubled as parlor and dining room. Nothing out of place. She placed her basket on a rectangular dining table near the partially enclosed kitchen. A delicious aroma of freshly baked bread reminded Rose of her empty stomach.

Two rocking chairs faced the fire, her sewing basket nestled between them. Several lanterns scattered around the room gave a cheerful glow. A crackling fire added a coziness that Rose hoped Samuel found inviting.

The front door opened, and Celia's dark-haired husband walked in. Rose introduced him to Samuel, who towered over Fred by several inches. The jovial shoemaker offered a hearty handshake and a welcoming grin.

Celia, beautiful in a blue calico dress matching her eyes, carried a bright-eyed toddler down a staircase. She put her daughter down and greeted Samuel with a sweet smile. "How lovely to see you again, Mr. Walker."

"The pleasure is mine, Mrs. Robinson." Samuel clutched the brim of his hat.

"Good evening, Celia. The bread smells delicious." Rose held out her arms, and two-year-old Harriet flew into them. "Samuel, this is Harriet. She stole my heart and won't give it back."

The little girl giggled.

"A pleasure to meet you, Harriet." His tone was indulgent. "My name is Mr. Walker."

Harriet peeked at Samuel and then buried her head against Rose's shoulder.

She stroked the thin brown hair. "Mr. Walker's little boy is seven. And his daughter, Emma, is five, just three years older than you."

Her legs wiggled until Rose set her down. As soon as her feet touched the ground, Harriet scurried for the safety of her mother's skirt before turning to stare at Samuel.

When Samuel met Rose's eyes, there was an emotion on his face Rose couldn't define. Approval? Tenderness? She spoke to Celia and Fred. "Samuel has invited me to dine with him. I need to change first."

"That's fine, then." Fred spoke to Samuel. He offered to lend his horse and buggy for the evening, and Samuel seemed as grateful to accept that as the opportunity to change clothes. With a friendly clap on the shoulder, Fred ushered him to the barn.

"Mr. Walker is an old school friend." Rose looked at the closed door where he'd gone wistfully. "It was a long time ago."

"He seems nice." Celia touched her forearm. "You seem nervous. Are you all right?"

"Of course." She pushed aside rose-patterned curtains at the front window. The men coaxed the team and wagon into the barn. "I need to change."

"It'll take them a few minutes to settle the horses." Celia lifted Harriet and followed Rose into a back bedroom. "I suppose this is your schoolmate from Hamilton who recently lost his wife?" Pale blond curls bounced to the side as she tilted her face, her gaze fixed on Rose.

"It is." She struck a match to light a lantern. "Brr. It's too cold to change."

Celia set Harriet on the rug in front of the heat stove. "I'll start a fire."

Rose opened her mother's cherry wood armoire. "I don't

know what to wear." None of her dresses compared to the simple elegance of Ginny's plainest frock.

"How about your blue dress? Quite becoming with your honey-colored hair." Celia placed kindling from a wood box into the stove.

The floral gingham was her best dress. She removed it from the armoire. How she longed to appear even passably pretty for just one evening. Her stomach knotted. Samuel was accustomed to Ginny's beauty. Rose must be even plainer by comparison.

"My heart goes out to his little ones," Celia said.

"Mine, too. He worries about them."

"A well-founded concern." Celia shut the stove door and straightened, rubbing ashes from her hand.

A familiar smoky smell seeped into the room as flames engulfed the wood, a cozy aroma to Rose. After she changed into the dress, Celia said, "Let's brush your hair and pin it up again."

Rose peered into a small mirror and brushed the escaping tendrils from her face. Brown eyes stared anxiously back at her. "I shouldn't force Samuel to wait."

The front door opened, followed by the men's voices.

"They just came in. He'll need to change into dry clothing. Why didn't he send a letter to warn you that he was coming?"

"The poor man just lost his wife and isn't thinking properly." Rose removed pins from her thick hair, wishing that she had been blessed with luxurious curls like Celia's to frame her face. "I didn't ask what brought him to town."

"You can ask him at supper."

The question could wait. She wanted to dream—just for a little while—that he came specifically to see her. Rose twisted her hair, pinning it up as quickly as her shaking fingers allowed. Dining with a man happened so seldom that her nervousness was easily explained. She turned and picked up her cloak and reticule. "How do I look?"

Celia smiled. "Pretty as always."

Kind words, but everyone knew she was plain. Did her friend mean to bolster her confidence? If so, falsehoods only delayed inevitable disappointment.

Harriet tugged on her mother's dress until Celia picked her up. "Remember, we travel to Indianapolis in the morning to visit Fred's parents."

"Oh, I had forgotten. Shall I take you to the station?"

"Fred said not to trouble you. We'll board our team at the stable near the train depot so you won't have to feed our horses this weekend. We leave before dawn and may be sleeping when you return this evening. Wake me up if you wish to talk."

"I will." Rose couldn't foresee any reason to awaken her friend. It wasn't as if Samuel courted her.

She opened the bedroom door and stepped into the living room. Her heart fluttered when Samuel turned toward her. He had changed into a dark coat with a white shirt and string tie. He wore the same blue vest as earlier. His hair had been neatly combed. He'd never looked more handsome or more vulnerable.

He gave her a tentative smile and held out her cloak. His fingers lingered over arranging her cloak over her shoulders, and she struggled to breathe normally.

Let the storm clouds come. They no longer mattered.

An evening with Samuel awaited.

CHAPTER 4

*S*itting across from Samuel, a dozen butterflies danced in Rose's stomach. Fire crackled in the fireplace nearby. Five of the ten tables in the restaurant were empty, adding to the intimacy of a meal shared with a handsome man.

Samuel reminisced about childhood friends, and she told him who'd moved to nearby Cincinnati or out west. She shared news about those who raised their families in the village.

"Do you know why my family moved to Harrison?" Samuel speared a roasted potato with his fork, his blue eyes intent on her. Half of his generous portion of roasted beef was already gone.

Shaking her head, Rose ate another bite of her chicken pie. "We weren't friends until later."

"We left Cincinnati in 1861."

"Ah." Her thoughts tumbled back to those tragic years. "The War Between the States."

His finger traced the rim of his cup. "My mother feared a Confederate attack on Cincinnati yet wanted to stay in Ohio."

"She almost didn't." Rose glanced out the window toward

Main Street, which bordered Indiana. "Some of those flickering lights are coming from Indiana homes."

"Never thought of it that way." He chuckled. "My sister was sixteen when we moved. I was eleven. Did you meet Savannah?"

"I never did." Rose savored the joy of having his complete attention, which ignited a smile she couldn't contain. Conversations from occupied tables and the clatter of silverware slipped away.

"Papa opened a carpenter's shop on Market Street right across from the market."

She remembered that an accident had claimed his life but didn't recall details. They were both silent as Mrs. Burke, the owner, delivered a meal to a nearby table.

"Remember the day Morgan's Raiders came to town?" Samuel buttered a biscuit.

Rose shuddered.

"Exactly." He set the biscuit on the red-patterned plate. "We moved from the city to escape battle, and then Confederates barged through our little village."

"Our worst fear. What year was that?"

His eyes narrowed in thought. "Sixty-three. Papa was alive, and Savannah hadn't married yet."

Rose recalled that scary summer day vividly because she had feared for her life. The Raiders had set fire to the Main Street Bridge to slow Union soldiers only a few hours behind and the smell of smoke lingered for days. She peered out the window. "Didn't both armies use the American House down the street as their headquarters?"

"I'd forgotten that."

"They looted our town." The destruction still ignited her indignation. "A senseless waste. Ruined items were strewn about the road outside town."

"I was thirteen, too young for fighting. But that day I wanted to be a soldier."

"I'm happy you weren't."

"That was a day our little village won't soon forget."

"No." She spoke quietly. "It's good that unpleasantness is behind our country."

"Soon to be written in our history books."

A family with children too young to remember the war entered and sat at a table near the brightly blazing fire, dissipating the melancholy mood.

Rose sipped her tea. "Enjoying your meal?"

"Immensely." He smiled at her, a spark in his blue eyes. "And the company. It's comforting to share a common past."

She liked that. If Ginny hadn't moved to Harrison after the war, Samuel might have courted Rose. She lowered her eyes to her nearly empty plate. Some dreams were best left in the past.

There'd never be another evening like this one. She must savor every second.

Samuel shifted in his seat.

Was he ready to end the evening already? She wanted it to last as long as possible. "Are Peter and Emma having difficulty understanding Ginny's death?"

Frown lines deepened across his forehead. "I've explained that Ginny's in heaven with God and He'll take care of her until they see her again. They adored their mother. Everyone did. She was vivacious, fun, beautiful."

Rose's heart ached for them, both so young to grow up without her. "They'll never stop missing their mother. I never did."

"How old were you when she died?"

"Seven, like Peter. Richard was ten." A boy put a log on the fire, and Rose stared into the flames that quickly engulfed it. The aching loss hadn't receded for years. "I still want to talk with her sometimes. I guess I miss Papa more, since he was with me longer."

He leaned closer. "Your father died after I moved away. When was that?"

"Six years ago next Saturday, after suffering three years." As she stared out the window, a light extinguished at the drug store, reminding her of the many purchases she'd made on her father's behalf there. "I bought his expensive medications across the street at Marvin's Drugs." She met Samuel's sympathetic gaze. "And you lost your mother the following year."

"Emma was a baby. Peter doesn't remember her."

"Rose, what a surprise." A short woman halted at Rose's side and fastened her gaze on Samuel. Her much thinner husband trailed her.

"Mr. and Mrs. Cahill, how lovely to see you." She gestured toward Samuel, who stood. "Please allow me to present Mr. Samuel Walker. He lived in Harrison as a boy. Samuel, these are is Mr. and Mrs. Stephen Cahill. Their youngest daughter, Lydia, is my student."

The men shook hands.

"Our dear Bernard left for university last fall." Mrs. Cahill placed a plump hand on her throat. "The rest of our sons are married. Lydia is the only one left at home."

"I enjoy having her at school." Rose smiled at the overindulgent mother.

"Of course, you do. She's an angel, simply an angel." Her glance slid to Samuel. "What brings you out on such a wet evening?"

"It's raining again?" Rose frowned at streetlamps flickering in the inky blackness. She hadn't noticed before that raindrops pattered against the shutters.

"My, yes. I almost decided against going out this evening. But then I wouldn't have met your handsome young man." She tapped Rose's hand with two fingers, inclining her head toward Samuel.

Heat infused Rose's face. "We've been discussing childhood memories."

"We attended school together." Samuel tugged at his string tie.

Mr. Cahill tugged his wife's arm. "We'll leave you to your conversation. A pleasure to meet you, Mr. Walker." With a nod to Rose, he led his wife to a table across the room.

A strained silence fell over them after the couple stepped away.

Rose folded the napkin in her lap. Then she refolded it. "What brings you to Harrison?" How she wished it was only to see her.

Samuel met her eyes. "Rose, I wondered if... How about a picnic tomorrow?"

She glanced at the window, where rain dripped down the glass. "I love picnics, but it might rain."

Samuel swirled his coffee in his cup.

He wanted to spend more time with her? "If you like, I'll prepare a meal at my home. Fred and Celia won't be there." She wondered at the impropriety of entertaining a man alone in her home. It would be the middle of the day, though, and the curtains would be open.

"That will be perfect." Samuel's smile broadened. "Your home will be cozier."

Heat spread to the roots of her hair. Perhaps she'd prop the front door open too.

"Warm. I meant warm. No breeze." He ran his finger underneath his collar.

Rose bit her lip to keep from laughing. His embarrassment made him even more appealing. But she mustn't think about him that way.

"Unfortunately," he said, "I need to fetch my children before dark."

"I understand. Where are they staying?"

"At Richard and Hazel's home. They wanted to play with Clay and Polly."

Interesting. Rose sipped lukewarm tea. "Should we eat before noon to insure an earlier start home?"

"If you wouldn't mind." His shoulders relaxed. "I'll spend the morning with Will and his family since I've barely talked with them."

Her skin tingled. Strange—it almost seemed he'd made the trip with her in mind. He'd even left his children with her brother.

Mrs. Burke removed their plates and brought out the pastry course. Samuel talked about his farm as they munched delicious cherry pie.

He drove her around Harrison after the meal, extending their evening by another hour, almost as if he didn't want their time together to end. It was cozy to listen to the rain fall softly on the buggy's roof. Rose savored every moment.

She'd buried her love for Samuel many years ago. One evening with him threatened to awaken those feelings.

Better to remember he preferred beautiful, vivacious women. She was neither.

~

*R*ose soaked dried potatoes in a kettle of water at dawn. A pie using last season's canned apples had been baked in the oven before breakfast. Celia must have taken the bread to Indianapolis. No matter. Fried chicken went well with biscuits.

On the way to the butcher, a chilly breeze nipped at her face. As a girl, she'd dreamed of picnics with Samuel. Why had he invited her on one today? Years of loneliness had taught her to look at situations sensibly, which prevented her from thinking more highly of herself than she ought.

Not much chance of that. Her sense of worth had plummeted long ago. She'd never been important to any man except her father. That was unlikely to change at her age. Which was fine. She was content, most of the time. And if her nights were lonely, if she longed for a man to share her life and her bed, she refused to dwell on those feelings. She couldn't, or she'd drown in them.

Sometimes, the loneliness was nearly debilitating. Bad enough that she'd actually considered marriage proposals from men she barely knew, men she knew only asked because they needed a wife to raise their children and believed that a teacher would do a fine job. And perhaps she would have, but was it so much to want to be loved and cherished for herself, not just what she could do? She'd chosen not to settle...and had ended up settling for a life of solitude.

Chicken was sizzling in the pan when Samuel tapped on the open front door later that morning. "Good morning, Rose." Inhaling the aroma, he hung his coat on a hook beside her cloak. "Apple pie and fried chicken. Delicious. Nothing so welcoming as apple pie."

"I've enjoyed cooking for you." *More than you know.* "Will you check the biscuits while I turn the chicken?"

Samuel washed his hands from the water bucket at the basin and then retrieved a pan from the oven with a towel. "Golden brown. Beautiful." He set the biscuits on a wooden side table. "I'm famished."

Blushing at his nearness, she was grateful heat from the open oven door could be blamed for her red face.

"My favorite meal." He peered over her shoulder at the chicken. "Thanks, Rose."

"My pleasure." Her hand jerked, splattering grease on the stove. He stood mere inches from her side. *Be sensible. He's looking at the food.* She prodded a chicken leg with a fork. "A few more minutes. Make yourself comfortable."

Samuel wandered around the room, probably restless to be on the road.

She tried not to let the thought sadden her. "Will you light candles for the table?" Flickering light from wall sconces on the gray day didn't reach the dining table, which she'd covered with her best white tablecloth.

"Certainly." He lit all three candles in a candelabra and placed it near plates already set.

She smiled at the intimate glow. Something to remember for his only meal in her home.

They settled across from each other, and he asked the blessing before they began eating. He took a few bites, wiped his mouth, and said, "Best fried chicken I've eaten in a long time."

"Thank you." Rose sipped her water. She needed to come up with a fascinating topic to entertain him. She asked about his crops.

He relaxed against his chair as he spoke of his expanding apple orchard. They talked about it, about his farm animals, and about his other crops until Rose sliced the pie.

While she scooped slices onto plates, conversation lagged into growing tension.

He'd leave soon, ending their unexpected seclusion. She had no claims on his friendship—no rights to his time—yet she wanted him to stay.

She nibbled her slice, then placed another log on the dying fire and returned to her chair.

Samuel cleared his throat. "I haven't properly thanked you for cleaning my home, washing clothes, and fixing meals."

"I loved doing it." So that was the reason for this visit. Rose forced the corners of her mouth up. Time to part ways. "If there's anything else I can do..."

～

*S*amuel heard the generous offer, wishing Rose could mean what he hoped. But she didn't understand the purpose for his visit.

He stared at the cozy fire's blaze. "After you left my house that day, I remembered our easy comradery. How we always laughed together. I remembered feeling comfortable with you. I didn't feel that way with the other girls—at least not until Ginny came along." A heavy sigh escaped. "Last evening reminded me of your calm, gentle friendship." He moved to the spindle-backed chair closer to Rose. "I need you."

Her eyes widened.

"I need help with the children. I don't know how to cook and"—he shrugged, palms up—"you saw the house."

"I'll do anything I can. I'll come next Saturday and clean."

He was making a mess of this proposal. "Please hear me out." Samuel sprang from his chair to pace in front of the fireplace. A nippy breeze from the open door rifled through his hair. "I buried Ginny six weeks ago. I'm not ready to marry again, but my children need someone to care for them." He stopped pacing and looked at her.

Rose stared at him with raised brows.

This wasn't going as he planned. Best begin again. "Mrs. Bradshaw paid me a visit. My minister's wife."

She twisted the locket at her throat.

"The church's women can't continue providing meals. She suggested making permanent arrangements." There. He'd said it. What a relief to get it out in the open.

"Permanent?" Rose's brow furrowed.

"She advised me to marry again." He paced again. Faster this time. "Soon, to bring stability back to my children's lives as well as care for them while I work the fields. Mrs. Bradshaw's arguments seemed wise. Then I thought of you." Sitting beside her, he sandwiched her cold hand in his grasp.

"Me?" Her hands covered her mouth. "Samuel, is this a proposal?"

He winced. "I won't make physical demands, so that will ease your mind. I'll build an attic bedroom for myself. Crops take priority."

Her eyes glazed.

Samuel clasped her hand to his chest. "Your teaching job shows you enjoy children. You're an excellent cook." He scanned the room. "Your home feels cozy, inviting. You'll have the benefit of a comfortable home. Life on a farm. A wonderful church with friendly folks."

Her expectant gaze clung to his, as if waiting for something.

"You'll quit teaching. Farm life's too busy for that. The biggest blessing will be living close to your brother's family."

~

*R*ose's heart shrank at his monotone. His feelings weren't engaged. Circumstances had forced his proposal. She withdrew her hand from his warm grasp. "I hardly know how to answer."

He rubbed his fingers through his thick hair. "Will you consider it?"

"I will." She stared at the orange flames. Would marrying the man of her dreams, even if he felt nothing more than friendship for her, be better than spinsterhood?

"I'll come for your answer next Saturday, but after that, spring planting will occupy every spare minute for at least a month. The following weeks won't be much better."

This had been her schoolgirl dream, yet there was no cause for elation. He didn't feel anything for her and certainly never would beyond their childhood friendship, because he'd married the woman of his dreams. Rose could never be like Ginny, and she could never replace her.

How could she tolerate the situation?

But this was Samuel, *her* Samuel, the man she'd loved almost as long as she could remember. He might not love her, but he needed her. His children needed her.

How could she refuse him?

"Rose? Will that be acceptable?"

"Next Saturday will suffice." She lowered her head. "I will give you my answer then."

His shoulders tensed. "I'll arrive before noon and return home the same day. Is that acceptable?"

"Of course." What if he traveled all day to hear a negative answer?

"Rose, I *am* sorry this isn't the romantic proposal you've no doubt dreamed of, but I can't give that to you. My children need a mother, a woman's touch around the home. Please pray about your decision. I'll pray, too."

His forlorn expression tugged at her emotions. She resisted the urge to brush a comforting hand across his cheek. Such a gesture wasn't part of this bargain.

"Reckon I'd better go." He stood.

She wrapped four biscuits and two chicken legs in a linen napkin while he hitched his team to the wagon. All too soon he disappeared down the dirt road.

Chaotic thoughts swirled as she cleared the table. Then she laughed. No wonder he'd had difficulty articulating the purpose of his visit. He'd put off the dreaded question until the last possible moment.

The dreaded question.

Her laughter died as quickly as it had come. Samuel didn't love her. Marriage was a sacrifice he would make for his children. If she married him, she must guard her heart against falling in love with him again.

Which was worse, marrying a man who didn't love her or growing old alone? Her last opportunity for a happy marriage reached out its hand. No, happiness was doubtful because he had lived a fairytale romance with Ginny.

And what about her job? She loved her students. Many had been with her from the beginning.

She carried the dishes to the kitchen, her heart in turmoil. It seemed she was trapped between two possibilities, neither of which would be her choice.

But having a man fall in love with her—for her—and living happily ever after? Seemed her heart's desire was not an option.

CHAPTER 5

On Monday afternoon, birds sang under overcast skies as Rose rushed home from school to welcome Celia and her family. She needed to talk over Samuel's proposal with her best friend.

An empty house greeted her, and her spirits sagged. She prepared vegetable soup and cornbread for supper. The soup was bubbling before Harriet rushed through the door.

"Roth! Roth! Gwa'ma!" She pointed to a yellow flower on her frock.

Rose hugged her. "Did your grandmother give you a pretty new dress?"

The little girl nodded, pulling the skirt wide.

"I love it. May I wear it sometime?"

Harriet giggled. "Too big."

"I believe I am too big." Rose laughed. "I missed you. What did you do?"

Her green eyes sparkled as she held up three fingers. "Gwa'ma make cake. I back on twain when I turn three."

Her tired parents straggled through the door. "Good afternoon. Or should I say, 'Good evening?'"

"Good evening." Fred dropped their bags beside the door. "Our train was sidetracked two hours while workers repaired a rail. I'll see to the horses." He stepped back outside.

"It was a tiring trip, but tell me about Samuel." Celia searched her friend's face. "You're blushing."

"It's the soup." A trail of steam wafted from the kettle. "We'll talk after Harriet goes to bed." Her stomach knotted. Talking with Celia might provide clarity.

"That's too far away. What happened?"

Rose finally had news not involving her students. "Later."

Celia groaned. Over supper, Celia and Fred took turns telling of their visit to Indianapolis.

Before long, Harriet leaned her head on her arm and closed her eyes. The adults laughed.

"I think our little one is ready for bed." Celia picked up her daughter. She tilted her head at Rose. "You and I will speak when I return."

Fred glanced at both women. "I'll be in the shop." He supplied shoes and boots to Mr. Keen's dry goods stores in the village. An increasing number of customers also brought shoes to Fred's shoe shop for repair. His hard-earned reputation for quality work had reached surrounding communities.

Celia hurried into the kitchen a few minutes later. "Tell me."

"We had a wonderful supper." Magical, in fact. No matter what followed, she had the memory of their one evening together. "Then Samuel invited me to a picnic on Saturday."

"Wasn't it rainy?" Celia stacked bowls in the cupboard.

Rose scrubbed a coffee stain on a porcelain cup. "We ate here instead."

"Supper was a thank-you for your help?"

"He asked me to marry him." Rose whispered.

Her eyebrows shot up. "He proposed?"

"Yes." Her spirits drooped at Celia's response. No joy. No squeals of delight that a good man wanted to marry her. It was almost as if she'd heard the unromantic proposal. "He needs help with his children. The pastor's wife told him to remarry."

"A marriage of convenience." Her brow furrowed. "*His* convenience."

Rose stiffened. "He buried his heart with Ginny."

"He said that?"

"Not in those words."

Celia stacked the last clean dish. "Are you considering it?"

Rose hung the wet dishcloth on a wall hook, uncertain how to explain her turmoil. The man of her dreams wanted to marry her, which should be a cause for joy…if only he returned her love.

"Why is this proposal different?" Celia untied her apron. "Those other widowers had children too."

"I know Samuel." Rose sank into her rocking chair near the fireplace and reached into a large round basket. Her latest quilting square still had the needle and thread where she stopped last night. "We used to be friends."

"He courted you?" Sitting beside her, Celia retrieved a blue calico dress for Harriet.

"No—not unless dinner Friday and lunch Saturday is a courtship. Once Ginny noticed him, he never looked at anyone else."

"Were you friends with her?"

"Not really." She stared into the fire, remembering her heartbreak to witness Samuel fall in love with Ginny. "I didn't like her at first. After they became engaged, she was more pleasant."

"I imagine they had a nice wedding."

"Probably. I didn't go. Papa was already sick." Though not ill enough to prevent her from attending. It would have been too painful to watch Samuel marry someone else. "That was the beginning of difficult days. Papa tried to keep blacksmithing. I worked as clerk at the dry goods store while looking for a teaching job. Papa was content to die once he thought I'd marry."

"You were engaged?"

She shook her head, already regretting her words.

"What happened?"

"Nothing, though it started out as something." Her one real courtship had begun with such promise. He'd ended up being more interested in the beautiful new girl...just like Samuel. Though her feelings for Reuben faded over time, the diminishing effect on her value as a potential wife stayed with her.

"Rose?"

"I met Reuben Bailey in the churchyard on a cold November Sunday. A gust of wind whipped off my blue hat, hatpin and all, and he chased it. I giggled at the sight of this young man in a somber suit pursuing my elusive hat. He introduced himself and walked me home. Papa invited him to dinner. Our relationship began that afternoon."

"He sounds nice." Celia put her elbow on the chair and leaned her chin against her palm.

"He'd been hired at the woolen factory and barely knew anyone."

"He courted you." Celia prompted gently.

"Yes. He spent Christmas Eve with Papa and me and then boarded the train to Cincinnati for a Christmas celebration with his family. Papa teased about hearing wedding bells.

"A new family moved into the old Masterson place. They had a pretty daughter. Becky's twin brother befriended Reuben. He stopped escorting me to church and sat with Becky's family during worship. Then I saw him and Becky driving in a buggy one evening."

"I'm sure you were disappointed."

"Looking back, I was more disappointed for Papa than myself. He thought highly of Reuben." Men she cared for always flocked to the prettier girls. "Papa was bedridden and didn't know Reuben's interest had waned. Papa's deepest desire was to see me settled before he died."

"Oh, Rose." Celia leaned forward. "You wanted him to believe—"

"I allowed Papa to believe I expected Reuben's proposal. He asked to talk with him since he'd not live to give me away." The old shame arose unbidden. Not only for lying to her father, but also for the pitying glances she'd received for weeks from fellow churchgoers. *So sad that her only suitor had a wandering eye,* she'd overhead someone say.

Celia covered her open mouth with both hands.

"I stopped Reuben after church the following Sunday. It was early April. Birds chirped. Flowers bloomed, and…Papa lay on his deathbed." A tear trickled down Rose's cheek. "He needed to believe I'd marry. Reuben agreed to meet him but refused to lie. Fortunately, Papa exhausted himself bragging about his fine daughter. I wanted to hide. Since he was so tired, he asked Reuben to return another day. He slipped into a coma the next morning."

Celia moved to kneel in front of her. She gave her a comforting hug.

"I promised my father I'd get married. The anniversary of his death is Saturday."

Her eyes widened. "The day Samuel returns for your answer."

"Yes." Rose blew her nose. "That seems significant, almost as if God is guiding me to accept. As for Reuben, he married Becky and moved to Kansas."

"Reuben wasn't the right man for you."

Was Rose the right woman for any man? Certainly not for Samuel. He'd made that clear. So often in the past two days, she had vacillated between joy at receiving his proposal and anguish that love didn't prompt his question. Now she felt emotionally drained.

"Samuel's proposal of a marriage of convenience differs from the others because you used to be friends." Her lips pursed as she returned to her sewing.

Ten years ago. Celia had a point—maybe it wasn't so different.

"Were you and Samuel close?"

"My closest friend. Boys didn't notice me because I was quiet." Averting her face, she placed another log on the fire. "Samuel did, probably because he was my brother's friend." No need to mention her dream of marrying Samuel before Ginny came along.

"Rose, this marriage may be harder than you can imagine—"

"Celia, I want a husband. Children. I'm lonely." She stood and crossed restlessly to the window. A lamplighter crossed the street, carrying a lantern and a long pole. "This may be my last opportunity. The only reason anyone proposes to me is to raise his children. I accept that." A candle flickered in a streetlamp. "At least I'd keep my promise to my father. But I'd lose a good job, students I love. I have friends in a town filled with folks who watch out for me. And I'd miss you, Harriet, and Fred. You're like a sister to me. You must know that."

Celia's eyes glistened. "We'd visit. Two hours by train."

Samuel had saved the train fare by riding his wagon there. "What shall I do?"

"Pray." Celia leaned across the space and gripped Rose's hand. "And I'll pray as well."

"That's what Samuel said."

"I like him better already."

Rose leaned her head against the cool windowpane. Fulfilling her girlhood dream required giving up her home, her job, everything familiar. Should she accept?

CHAPTER 6

*T*oo jittery to talk, Rose kept to her room after breakfast Saturday morning.

A week of soul-searching confirmed her decision. She wanted to marry a good Christian man. Samuel had requested she pray, and she had.

She peered out her bedroom at an empty room. That was good, for she longed for solitude. The aroma of baking ham piqued her appetite. She smiled in anticipation of learning Samuel's favorite foods in the coming months. Her mind raced with wedding plans as she rolled out crust for apple pie. School recessed for spring planting in a couple of weeks, the perfect opportunity for goodbyes.

It would break her heart to part with her students. How she'd miss their place of her life. They'd given her joy after Papa's death. She'd pray the village replaced her with a good, kind teacher.

Rose wanted to look her best on her wedding day. Her mother's dearest friend, Mrs. Theobold, was a seamstress. Rose ached for her mother, and inviting Mrs. Theobold to create a dress fancy enough for a wedding yet suitable for other special occasions might ease that sorrow.

Shafts of sunlight entered with the Robinsons.

"It's already noon?" Rose said. "My thoughts are so muddled I didn't notice the time."

"No matter." Celia put Harriet down, and she snatched up her doll. "We cleaned Fred's work area. A new customer commented on his wise organization of the space." A middle wall separated the shop from the barn.

"That was Papa's idea." Gone six years today, and Rose still missed him. Mustn't allow thoughts of him to make her melancholy.

Celia reached for an apron. "Need help?"

"Just your company." Rose added a generous dollop of butter to corn in a kettle.

Thirty minutes later, fragrant biscuits nestled inside a towel-lined basket, and the rest of the meal sat in the warming oven.

On the porch, they awaited Samuel's arrival. Yesterday's rain had refreshed the air. Harriet swung her legs as she sat between her parents on the white swing. Rose's rocking chair thumped as she peered toward Market Street, Samuel's likely route into the village.

The shoemaker shop separated them from their nearest neighbor. The young family waved and then strolled over and chatted with Celia and Fred.

Rose could hardly focus on the conversation. With one arm wrapped around a support pole, thoughts of Rose's future family brought her joy. Soon she'd have family stories to share.

Where was Samuel?

Perhaps he would ride up the main thoroughfare. She walked that direction and stopped at the corner.

No Samuel.

Footsteps approached behind her.

"I imagine he stopped to eat," Fred shoved his hands into his pockets.

"Perhaps."

"I rather doubt he wants you to wait dinner this long."

She shaded her eyes and stared up the street. "I'll keep some warm for him. He'll arrive before we finish our meal."

But he didn't. The women washed dishes while Celia carried on a one-sided conversation.

"He regrets his proposal." Rose couldn't keep her fears from spilling out.

"I doubt that." Celia led her outside. "He's a gentleman."

Rose scanned the road. "Something unfortunate has happened." The ladies sat on the swing. Harriet giggled as she played ball in the side yard with her father. "I expected him two hours ago."

"Perhaps some emergency with the children or the farm—"

"No." Rose leaped to her feet, her gaze on the parallel Market Street. "He's not coming."

"He'd have sent a letter."

"I didn't walk to the post office this week."

"I stopped in on Tuesday." Fred rested his right foot on the bottom porch step. "I'll walk over now. Harriet and I need exercise after that big meal, right, honey?"

"Thank you." Rose's voice shrank to a whisper.

Harriet put her tiny hand into Fred's big hand. "I walk."

"We'll wait here for Samuel," Celia said.

Rose berated herself for dreaming of a family. Even with all the difficulties inherent in a marriage of convenience, hadn't she learned anything from her past disappointments? Searching for the good in the situation, she thanked the Lord that only Celia and Fred knew of the proposal—and how important it had made her feel.

Samuel rode up ten minutes later, his shoulders sagging.

Rose rushed to his side. "Is everything all right?"

"Sorry to worry you." His blue eyes searched hers. "My horse threw a shoe halfway here. I waited an hour for the blacksmith."

She sighed. "It's a relief that it was nothing worse. Are you hungry?"

He shook his head. "I ate to pass the time." He gazed past Rose to Celia. "Good afternoon, Mrs. Robinson. I hope my late arrival hasn't upset plans."

"Not to worry, Mr. Walker." She joined them under the budding tree and spoke to Rose. "I'll meet Fred and Harriet in town." Celia disappeared down a side street.

Now that he was here, Rose's thoughts wobbled. Did she have the courage to agree to his proposal and turn her life upside down?

Samuel shifted his weight without glancing at Rose. "My horse needs a good rest."

"Stable him. I'll draw water while you brush him down."

The slump of Samuel's back rivaled that cold day in March when she visited his home. Rose squelched all hope. Best be sensible. No need to make the situation more difficult if he came to tell her he changed his mind.

In the barn, they talked of his frustrating morning. Then, Rose silently led the way to the porch. She gestured to the porch swing. He sat beside her, near enough that his leg brushed against hers. A shiver ran through her to be so close to him.

"Rose, did you—?"

"Samuel, I—"

They both stopped and looked at each other. Shared laughter eased the tension. He inclined his head.

"I understand if you've changed your mind." She stared at her clenched hands.

"I've been selfish." He sandwiched her hands within his and leaned close enough that she had to tilt her head back to look into his eyes. His nearness set her traitorous heart to thumping. "I've thought of little else since leaving you."

Just say it quickly and be gone before my control gives way to tears.

"You should marry the man of your dreams, a special man, one who can give you everything your heart desires. All I can give you is two grieving kids. I just want you to know that our friendship will be intact, no matter what. I'll understand if you refuse."

"You didn't change your mind?" Her voice squeaked.

"No." His thumb rubbed the back of her hand. "But I must be fair to you."

"I understand the situation." She took a deep breath. "My decision is made. I'll marry you."

His eyebrows lifted. "You're certain?"

This might be the closest she ever came to her dream of a happy marriage. Perhaps in time Samuel might love her. "I am."

Closing his eyes, he tapped a loose fist against his chest. "Thank you." A moment passed while he seemed to get his bearings. He had expected her to refuse. "How about we marry after spring planting?"

No hug.

No kiss on the cheek.

No elation on his face.

The joy she'd anticipated deflated like a balloon.

"Rose? Four weeks from today?"

"That may be enough time." Harriet skipped into her peripheral vision and Fred, laughing, caught her. Rose wished for another five minutes alone with her betrothed. But why? Their conversation wasn't private. "I'll speak with Mrs. Theobold, my mother's friend, about making my dress."

"I understand." He nodded. "Write when you discover how long that'll take. I'll make arrangements then."

Write? So she wouldn't see him again until the wedding?

The Robinsons climbed the porch steps, Harriet on her father's shoulders. "Roth, look!"

54

Rose stood beside her future husband. "Harriet, you're so tall up there."

When her father placed her on the porch floor, she raised her hands. "I tall."

Samuel grinned at Harriet, a real smile that reached his eyes.

Rose focused on her friends. "Samuel and I are to be married." Just saying the words brought joy, a sense of rightness. Even a sense of peace to calm the turmoil of being an unkissed fiancée. There'd been a time she'd been sure she'd never utter those words.

Celia hugged her. Fred shook Samuel's hand before kissing her cheek. Harriet jumped and clapped her hands.

The little girl didn't understand the importance of the news. She didn't know her 'Roth' planned to move miles away. That sadness would come later.

Today, Rose did her best to celebrate her life's new direction.

CHAPTER 7

Gray light peeked through a gap in the curtains as Rose
opened her eyes. Her wedding day had finally arrived.
By suppertime, she'd be Mrs. Samuel Walker. She
pinched her arm and smiled at the pain.

It wasn't a dream. Her life was taking on a new direction,
one she prayed led to Samuel learning to love her. Oh, not the
same fairytale romance he and Ginny had presented to the
world, perhaps, but a deep abiding love that would see them
through the years, nonetheless. The letters they shared to plan
the wedding had been friendly, leading her to hope for a
revival of their friendship, the first step to falling in love in her
mind.

She'd spent the last few nights at Richard's home. Samuel's
decision to have the wedding in familiar surroundings for his
children's sake had outweighed her desire to invite her friends
and students. Their sorrow wrenched at her heart. Giving up
teaching had been her greatest sacrifice.

Celia and her family had arrived yesterday. They'd
purchased Rose's childhood home, which compensated for
Rose's nostalgia at leaving it. She'd left them all her furniture

except a cedar trunk Papa had made for her sixteenth birthday, Mama's cherry armoire, and Papa's old rocking chair.

Rose's pale blue wedding dress, its soft silk decorated with delicate lace across the bodice and pearl buttons down the back, was draped across a chair in preparation for donning it in a few hours. It was the prettiest dress she'd ever possessed.

After throwing back the covers, she crossed the bedroom she shared with her still sleeping niece, Polly, to gaze into the small mirror above the three-drawer chest. Happiness hadn't improved her looks, though a pretty dress wouldn't hurt.

Donning a robe over her nightgown, she crept from the bedroom. She walked past the extra table set up for guests joining them later. A delicious aroma of cherries awakened her appetite. Hazel was preparing the meal to follow the ceremony.

She glanced up from her work and smiled. "Rosie, will you fix biscuits and gravy for breakfast? I planned to coddle you this morning, but I overslept." Hazel's curly brown hair frizzed up in the heat of the stove. "These pies must get in the oven. Only two fit at a time."

"Of course. Thanks for everything you've done for my wedding."

"Believe me, it's our pleasure. We never thought—" Cheeks bright red, Hazel glanced at her sister-in-law as if she'd been caught passing gossip.

"I know. Me, either." It stung that Hazel and Richard had believed she'd never marry.

"This is the last of the dried cherries from last summer." Hazel picked up the kettle containing the cooked cherries with a kitchen towel and stepped toward the prepared pie shells on the table. But she tripped on her skirt and fell, still clutching the heavy container. Cherries splashed out of the pot, which somehow remained upright as it struck the floor with a thud. Blistering liquid splashed both Hazel's hands and arms. She screamed.

Rose gasped, horrified at the terrible injury. Her school-teacher side took charge. She snatched the towel to brush the cherries off Hazel's skin. "Let's rinse your arms." She gently helped her sister-in-law to her feet and led her to the basin. Rose poured ladles of cold water over her arms.

Richard raced inside the house. "What happened?" He spied his wife and hurried to her side, wrapping an arm around her shoulder. "Sweetheart, are you all right?"

"She scalded herself on hot pie filling." Rose jerked her head toward the kettle on the floor.

"Bubbling," whispered Hazel, tears squeezing through her closed eyelids.

Rose poured water over the injured hands and wrists until Hazel motioned her to stop. Blisters had already formed on splotchy, scarlet patches.

"I'll fetch the doctor." Richard guided his wife to a chair. "Get word to Samuel. We may have to delay the wedding a couple of hours."

"The Robinsons are staying at his house. Celia will arrive after breakfast to fix my hair. Fred can inform Samuel." Rose read the concern in her brother's expression before he left. Hazel's burns were serious.

She wondered how to ease Hazel's pain until the doctor's arrival. Her eyes and lips were tightly closed. While Rose waited, Hazel opened her eyes. "I'm going to lie down to wait for the doctor."

"Of course." She helped Hazel recline on the already-made bed.

Four-year-old Polly, wearing her nightgown, shuffled into the bedroom holding a doll. "Mama, I'm hungry."

"Polly, Mama doesn't feel good," Hazel said. "Aunt Rosie will make breakfast."

"Sit with your mama while I cook." Rose kissed her cheek. "Call for me if she needs anything."

She nodded. "What's on your hands, Mama?"

Hazel's lips pressed together.

"She burned herself." Rose bent down to Polly's eye level. "The doctor will bandage her hands."

Polly looked from her aunt to her mother. Then, she dragged a chair from the corner to the side of the bed and sat, clutching her doll.

"Mama's fine. The doctor will make her better." Rose rushed back to the kitchen, hoping it was true. Those blisters worried her. The right hand had taken the brunt.

Most of the fruit filling remained in the pot. Rose cleaned the floor then filled the empty pie pans. Three pies, instead of four, must now stretch to feed guests. She rolled the remaining dough for a lattice top layer. While two baked, she prepared breakfast.

Only a few close friends and family were invited to the wedding meal. Trent and Catherine Hill and Charlie Ferguson were the only neighbors Samuel invited. The others were couples from church she didn't know. Samuel told her that Ginny's closest friends weren't even coming to the church. Ginny's parents, who lived a morning's train ride away in Columbus, rejected their invitation.

Rose's nerves stretched tighter with each roll of the pin over the biscuit dough as she wondered how Peter and Emma felt this morning. She whispered a prayer that she'd be a good wife and stepmother.

Seven-year-old Clay toted a pail inside, his uncombed brown hair falling into his eyes. Richard had enough property to keep two cows and a few chickens in this less populated area of Hamilton. "I finished the milking like Pa said before seeing Mama. Is it bad?" Milk sloshed as he placed the bucket on the table.

Rose placed an arm around his shoulder. "She hurts, but the doctor will arrive soon. Go on in. Polly's with her."

Both children remained with her until Rose called them to breakfast. While they ate, she carried a plate to Hazel, who refused the food. Her body shook as with fever. Rose gingerly covered everything but her arms with a quilt. Avoiding the blistered skin, Rose propped her injured arms with a feather pillow on either side.

Richard arrived, hat dripping, with the doctor.

Raindrops pounded against the roof in a comforting beat. Rose worried about splattering her dress on the wagon ride through muddy roads later. She pressed on her grumbling stomach to still its protests. No time to eat.

She couldn't cook in her wedding dress. The morning was half over and she still wore her nightgown.

~

"*D*oc says it's a bad burn." Richard filled his plate with gravy and biscuits. "Apparently, infection is the biggest danger. Pain medicine will keep her sleeping for hours. The doctor will change the dressing daily to monitor her progress."

Rose wiped a dripping plate and put it on the shelf. "Let's delay the ceremony."

"Might be best. You'll have to prepare the meal and dress Polly."

That left little time for her to fuss over her own dress. There was no help for it.

"Hazel anticipated this day for years. That's what upsets her most. You're her only sister. She wanted to spoil you today."

Tears filled Rose's eyes. "What a sweet wife you have."

"Don't I know it. I'll ask Mrs. Redmond, a neighbor, to sit with her while we're gone."

As soon as Celia and Fred arrived, Rose told them the news, and Fred left to inform Samuel and the minister to delay the ceremony one hour. Unfortunately, no one had time to ride to each guest's home.

Once she had Polly ready to go, Rose arranged her hair in a simple bun, her everyday style. She swallowed her disappointment at such an ordinary look. A sprig of orange blossoms—a gift from Richard and Hazel—woven through her hair by Celia was the only special decoration. Harriet pleaded to wear the remaining orange blossoms. Her mother relented and fashioned a little halo for her. Rose picked her up and waltzed her around the room until she giggled. How she'd miss this sweet girl.

Polly and Harriet played while Rose and Celia began preparing the wedding meal. While the ham baked, Rose donned her dress. Celia declared her to be the most beautiful bride she'd seen in years. The little girls fingered the lace reverently. Their sweet compliments were a balm to Rose's nerves. All too soon, Fred returned and took his family off to dress for the wedding.

The ham was in the warming oven, and it was time to leave for the church. Richard, wearing the same black coat and red and black striped vest as on his own wedding day, lifted Polly onto the wagon bed. The little girl touched her lacy pink dress with gentle fingers. Clay climbed up on his own. Richard helped Rose onto the wooden seat, being mindful of her dress. The rain stopped, but dark gray clouds remained, promising more afternoon showers. Seated beside Richard, Rose breathed deeply of fresh air to calm frazzled nerves.

About fifty people were supposed to attend the ceremony. Everyone waited inside the brick church located across from an impressive two-story courthouse, as Richard lifted Rose onto wet grass. She raised her skirt, stepping gingerly over large flat stones imbedded in the ground leading to the church steps.

"You there." Richard pointed to a newsboy holding a stack of papers on the street corner.

He ran over. "Buy a paper, suh?"

Richard tossed him a coin. "Earn that by taking my team and wagon over to the stable." He pointed down the street.

"Thank you, suh." The boy held the reins while Clay jumped from the back of the wagon directly into a puddle, splattering his black pants, and ran into the church.

Richard grimaced. "I'll be back." He carried Polly to the door, and they disappeared inside.

Her wedding day. A longing for her father to give her away, her mother to whisper words of advice pierced through her. She blinked back tears.

Richard joined her at the bottom of the worn steps.

He placed her hand on his arm. "Everyone knows about Hazel's accident." He kissed her cheek, something he rarely did. "Samuel will be a good husband, Rosie. Today is a good day."

His words swept her doubts away. Taking a deep breath, she clutched her tiny bouquet of orange blossoms.

He helped her up the stairs and pushed the door open. Next to the minister stood Samuel, looking more handsome than usual in a black suit, gray pinstriped vest, white shirt, and black string tie.

About thirty people filled the pews, but she barely saw them as Richard escorted her up the aisle. Her gaze was fixed on her betrothed.

When she reached him, Samuel searched her face. "Sorry about Hazel's accident. Are you all right?"

She nodded and smiled tremulously.

He clasped her cold hand in a warm grasp. Celia stood beside her in pale pink satin, radiating joy. The couple faced the gray-haired, soft-spoken Pastor Bradshaw. A sober Richard stood at Samuel's side.

Did their guests wonder, just as she wondered, why Samuel had chosen her?

She glanced at their family in the front row. Peter, dressed in a similar manner as his father minus the vest, stared at her. What would his reaction be to a new woman in the home? Emma sat beside him, her blond curls pulled back at the temple and tied with a blue ribbon to match her ruffled dress. Polly whispered in her ear.

Rose met Samuel's intense gaze.

Whatever Pastor Bradshaw said, it didn't penetrate her chaotic thoughts.

Did Samuel think of his first wedding day, his first bride? Her glance lowered to her bouquet as the unwelcome possibility slashed through her. *Please don't compare me to Ginny. No one can compete with her.*

Samuel slipped a plain silver ring on her finger. She stared at it in wonder. This was really happening.

"I now pronounce you husband and wife," the pastor said. "Samuel, you may kiss your bride."

He tilted her face. He met her gaze before lowering his lips to hers.

Their first kiss, brief as it was, flustered her and increased her longing for another. Many more, in fact, as her husband smiled at her.

He held her hand as the minister turned them to face the congregation.

Pastor Bradshaw placed a hand on each of their shoulders. "Ladies and Gentlemen, it is my privilege to introduce for the first time Mr. and Mrs. Samuel Walker."

Instead of walking down the aisle to the back of the church to greet guests on their way out, Samuel led her to his children. Emma stood and wrapped her arms around Rose's waist, who stroked her curls and returned her hug.

"Emma, you look so pretty today." She bent down to the child's eye level. "I love your blue dress."

"It's my favorite." Her chin quivered. "Ma bought it for me."

She'd already blundered. "Blue is my favorite color." Her

glance shifted to Peter. "And you are the image of your Pa today."

"Pa, why'd she steal Ma's name?" Peter glared at her.

Emma's brow puckered.

His angry tone stung as much as the words. It took a moment to realize Peter was reacting to Pastor Bradshaw's introduction of her as Mrs. Samuel Walker.

"She accepted my name, Peter, when she married me."

He crossed his arms over his chest.

Polly grabbed Emma's hand, and the giggling girls ran to the back of the church. Guests spilled out into the main aisle, filling the quiet church with chatter. Rose walked over to greet them while Samuel hunkered down to talk with Peter.

Celia touched Rose's arm, distracting her from her distress. "You're beautiful today. Every bride deserves to be the prettiest woman at her wedding, and you've achieved that and more. I'm happy for you." She hugged her.

"Roth." Harriet tugged on her sleeve.

Rose picked her up. "You look so pretty with your halo of flowers."

Smiling shyly, she touched the blossoms. "You do too."

"Why, thank you." Rose kissed her cheek. How she'd miss this precious girl, indeed the whole family.

Richard shook hands with his new brother-in-law before kissing Rose's cheek. "You're the prettiest bride I've seen since my own wedding, Rosie."

Samuel brought a short, gray-haired gentleman forward. "Rose, this is my neighbor, Charlie Ferguson. I mean, our neighbor." Crimson stained his face. "He lives across from my farm. We've passed pleasant evenings together on his front porch."

Mr. Ferguson smiled, a twinkle in his gray eyes as he clapped Samuel's shoulder. "That we have, Samuel, my boy. I'm pleased to make your acquaintance, Mrs. Walker."

Mrs. Walker. The name gave her a start. "It's a pleasure to meet you, Mr. Ferguson."

"Oh, no. We're gonna be neighbors." Kindness shone in his eyes. "Not just neighbors, but friends. And my friends, they call me Charlie."

Rose warmed to the grandfatherly gentleman. "Only if you will call me Rose. My father used to call me Rosie."

"The name suits you. Since I'm old enough to be your pa, how about I call you Rosie?"

Her smile broadened. What a treasure to find such an agreeable neighbor.

Samuel's eyes twinkled as he and Charlie moved to speak with Richard.

Catherine Hill introduced Rose to her husband, Trent. They were the same height, yet he appeared shorter. After she greeted him, Catherine said, "Marrying you was a right smart thing for Samuel to do."

Rose clasped her hand, glad to find another champion. "Thank you. Will you come to Richard's house for lunch?"

"No, we'll get on home to our youngins. We already waited through the delay on account of the accident. Rennie, my oldest, is twelve. She does a good job, but her brothers are a rambunctious lot. No, we'll get along, but thanks just the same."

After the couple left, Rose realized Catherine's husband Trent hadn't uttered a word. She giggled. His wife more than made up for his quiet nature.

She recognized faces from when she'd visited Richard and his family but remembered few names.

Samuel returned and introduced her to the next couple then walked outside with them. He seemed more concerned with his guests than his new wife. Rose sighed.

The last person in line was Mrs. Bradshaw. The pastor's wife, dressed in a yellow floral gingham, clasped Rose's hand. "Mrs. Walker, I'm certain you'll remember me." She waited until

Rose acknowledged the prior acquaintance with a nod. "I'm pleased Samuel chose sensibly."

Ah yes. There was nothing quite so romantic as being the *sensible* choice.

"You were a teacher in Harrison?"

She nodded warily.

"Just as I thought. I'm glad that, this time, Samuel chose a wife with more brains than hair."

"I beg your pardon?"

"The first time he married for love and beauty." Mrs. Bradshaw wagged her index finger. "You are a sensible choice."

Rose's face flamed. "I'm sure I thank you for your kind encouragement."

"Think nothing of it, my dear. And if you need anything at all, we live in the parsonage across the street. Not the courthouse, mind you. The red brick house on the right."

"Thank you. I must find Samuel. How lovely to see you again." She forced a smile before turning away. Her inadequacies must be apparent to everyone.

The sensible choice.

Perhaps Rose had been foolish to believe she'd marry for love.

CHAPTER 8

*R*ose had finally greeted all the guests. Somehow, she was a married woman but still found herself alone.

She shook off the maudlin thought. Samuel was here, just visiting with friends, same as she. Well, they weren't *her* friends yet, but someday, she hoped.

There he was, at the back corner. Maybe he sensed her presence, because he turned and caught her eye.

If she'd expected to see love there, or even contentment, she'd have been disappointed.

He hurried over, and she realized what she saw in his eyes was fear. "Have you seen Peter?" Samuel asked.

A sense of foreboding washed over Rose. "I last saw him staring out the window. Did you ask Clay?"

~

*"H*e hasn't seen him." Samuel rubbed a hand across his clammy forehead. "Where is he?" He peered out the window at the churchyard. All he saw was Clay digging in the grass. Why wasn't Peter with him?

"Did you check the church grounds?" Rose bent to peer under the pews.

Good idea. He bent to check the other set of pews. Nothing but a tiny halo of orange blossoms. "That's where I went first."

"Are there stairs to a bell tower? Maybe a cellar?" Rose's gaze circled the room.

"No." His heart nearly exploded in his chest. His son had been upset to hear Rose referred to as 'Mrs. Walker.' Samuel should have taken him aside and explained the situation more fully. Listened to his concerns and not put off the important conversation. What was more important than his children? "Maybe I should check our farmhouse."

"Wait a minute." Rose caught his arm as he started for the door. "Where is Ginny buried?"

"Greenwood Cemetery." His heart tumbled to his feet. A boy missing his mother—yes, that's where he went. But could Peter find the cemetery on his own? Samuel had taken the children to the large city cemetery twice from the church. "You're right. That's where he'll be. I'll take my wagon." Wait. Their guests. And he'd have the wagon so he couldn't drive Rose and Emma to the wedding meal at Richard's house. "Look, will you—"

"We'll take Emma to Richard's," she said. "I'll get started serving our meal. Follow with Peter whenever he's ready."

"Thank you." It wasn't what anyone wanted, but Peter came first. "I'm sorry about this. I thought he understood you'd live with us after the wedding."

"Perhaps the ceremony upset him." Her heart ached for his sorrow.

"No boy should go through…"

When he didn't finish, she squeezed his biceps. "Take your time."

A wedding meal without the groom. Not exactly the ideal way to start a marriage.

Her bouquet wilted in her left hand. "Please, go on."

He grasped her forearms as she struggled to smile. "We'll be there as soon as we can." Then, he let her go and turned away. Emma. He should tell her what was happening.

Samuel strode to the back where she playing with her cousin. "Emma." He crouched down. "You'll go with Rose and Polly to her house. I'll bring Peter in a few minutes."

"All right, Pa."

Her calm demeanor gave him one less worry. He kissed her cheek and then bolted. Within minutes, he was driving his team along the roads leading to the cemetery, his gaze bouncing in every direction.

Then he spotted a lone boy walking with his head down. Relief at finding his son lightened the fear that had gripped him since Peter went missing.

He pulled up beside him and locked the brakes before leaping from the wagon. He ran to him. "Peter?"

His son, standing on the side of the road, raised miserable eyes. "Pa, I don't remember how to get to Ma."

They'd have another talk about Heaven later. "I'll go with you." Squatting, Samuel opened his arms. Peter laid his head against his chest as Samuel held him close. "You shouldn't have gone off alone. Next time, talk to me first."

"I will. I brought this flower." Peter held up a bloom.

An orange blossom from his new wife's bouquet.

"I wanted Ma to have a pretty flower too."

Samuel's heart melted at his son's gift. Standing, he held out his hand. "Let's put it on her gravestone."

Peter tucked his hand inside his pa's strong one. They walked to the wagon in the gloom.

Grief bound them together. Always would. And maybe someday, the love they all felt for Ginny would rise above the pain of missing her.

~

*R*ose fumbled with the buttons on her wedding dress. Besides Celia's family, there'd be three guests—the Bradshaws and Charlie Ferguson—when Hazel had planned for a dozen.

In her heart, she knew that Samuel had found Peter or he'd be here requesting help. Still, the worry for the hurting boy wouldn't ease until she saw him. Wearing her nicest Sunday frock, Rose coaxed a smile to her stiff lips and left Polly's bedroom to greet Samuel's friends.

The meal remained in the warming oven until Richard spotted Samuel's wagon in the yard an hour later. Rose's anxiety eased somewhat when meeting Samuel's gaze. There was something comforting in his reassuring nod, the silent sharing of their worry and fear for Peter. A delicious meal soon lightened the mood between the subdued father and son.

Guests didn't linger after the meal. Celia hugged Rose and promised a weekend visit. Rose assured her best friend she was always welcome. Harriet clung to Rose, finally understanding she wasn't coming home with them. Fred coaxed her away, and her sobs ripped Rose's heart as she waved goodbye from the porch.

Her own heart broke as Samuel drove the Robinsons toward the train station.

By the time all the guests were gone, dark clouds hid the sun. Celia had brought extra clothes for Peter and Emma to don after the reception. Samuel and Rose had decided to allow the children to play outside before going home. Hazel's injuries added a new reason to linger, for Rose wasn't certain what assistance she required. The children changed out of their finery to play outside. Mud puddles and wet grass seemed to draw them like flies to honey.

Richard went in to check on Hazel.

Alone, Rose rubbed throbbing temples and then cleaned the dishes. Hazel's unfortunate accident could have been worse.

Unlike Peter's sadness. Rose remembered the dark days following her mother's death, the void that nothing filled, the overwhelming loss. She hadn't found an opportunity to ask Samuel about Peter, but the boy had perked up during the meal and was now running around the yard with Clay.

Her stepchildren had stolen her heart earlier that week, when she had been with them daily after moving from Harrison. She prayed she'd find a place in theirs.

Peter and Clay dangled their legs from the lower branches of a sturdy maple tree. Zeb's tail thumped against the grass beneath the thick foliage.

Rose crossed to the front window. The porch swing swayed with the giggling girls on it. She loved that sweet sound.

Richard, looking more comfortable in dark trousers and a blue shirt, emerged from his bedroom. "Hazel's complaining of pain. That's rare for her. I'll fetch Dr. Morrow. She can't have another pill until bedtime."

"Samuel will return soon from the depot. We'll stay as long as necessary."

"Please see to Hazel while I'm gone."

She agreed, and as soon as he left, she entered the master bedroom.

Hazel lay under a quilt with her bandaged arms resting on pillows on top of the blankets. "Oh, Rosie. I ruined your special day."

"Not at all. Everyone enjoyed the meal. We saved you a piece of pie. Please don't trouble yourself."

"I wanted it to be memorable."

"It *was* memorable." Heat infused her cheeks to recall her first kiss from Samuel. Worries over Peter had pushed it from her mind.

"I'm glad." Hazel readjusted her hand against the feather pillow and flinched.

"All the guests are gone. It's just family now. Are you hungry?"

"Famished. Unfortunately, I can't move my hands."

"I'll feed you." Rose jumped to her feet, jarring the mattress in her haste.

Hazel's mouth compressed.

"Forgive me." She berated herself for her clumsiness.

"Rosie?" Hazel's weak voice stopped her at the door. "How are the children?"

"Contented. Playing outside. It finally stopped raining."

"Good."

Samuel returned while Rose sliced ham into bite-sized pieces. He had stopped at home, which was only three miles from her brother's house in the city, and looked more comfortable in brown trousers and a brown-checked shirt. "Where are the boys?"

After the emotional afternoon she suspected he had, the nervous tone was natural. She pointed. "Climbing that maple tree. The girls were on the porch a few minutes ago."

"They're still there." He sauntered to the back window. "All I see are kicking feet from that old tree." He leaned against the basin facing her. "Sorry about Peter's disappearance. He's never done that before." He told her about finding him on the street, unable to locate the cemetery. "He had a flower—one of your orange blossoms—to put on Ginny's grave. It seemed to satisfy a need in him. We talked a few minutes and he was ready to leave."

"That dear boy. How he has suffered." Her heart went out to him. "When we moved my furniture over, both children seemed excited. It seemed as if Papa's old rocking chair was brand new." She paused in slicing a loaf of bread. "Today I guess he reacted to hearing me introduced as Mrs. Samuel Walker."

"May I have a piece?" asked Samuel, reaching for the bread.

"Of course." She gave him a fresh slice.

"Losing a mother at such a tender age is difficult." He stared outside as he munched. "I'll do a better job of protecting them. I promise."

She gestured towards the loaded plate. "That's not our only problem."

He quirked an eyebrow.

"Richard's gone after Dr. Morrow. Hazel's suffering, and her next pill isn't due for hours."

"We can take all the children with us this evening instead of them staying here as we planned." He studied the wood floor as if fascinated.

"That's fine." It was the right thing to do, but his tone seemed almost relieved to have the children with them on their wedding night. "I'm happy to do it, especially after Richard and Hazel fussed over us all week." A disappointment. Taking the children meant no private conversations with her new husband. "Will you help me prop Hazel up so I can feed her? We must be gentle."

After Hazel ate her fill, Richard returned with the doctor. Rose and Samuel left the bedroom and closed the door behind them.

Excited voices drew the newlyweds to the porch. A patch of sunshine pierced the late afternoon gloom, and gentle breezes blew loose tendrils back from Rose's face. She sank onto the white porch swing between the girls, grateful to relax. Samuel strode to the barn with the boys.

Polly and Emma stumbled over their words to tell her about a deer they saw, each tugging on Rose's sleeve. "One at a time, please." Laughter eased tension from her neck. This felt normal.

Richard followed the doctor outside. "Thanks for coming. Hazel's not one to complain."

"Happy to oblige." The silver-haired doctor shifted his black bag to his left hand to shake Richard's hand. "Remember the salve and my other instructions."

"I will. Need a ride?"

"Walking helps these old bones." The doctor set off on foot toward the center of town.

Samuel hurried over from the barn. "How's Hazel?"

"No worse." He indicated the adults should follow him inside. "I forgot to apply salve to red areas. She can't get her blistered skin wet. Her burns will be sensitive to heat for some time." He sighed. "She can't cook or wash clothes or dishes. Can't even bend her fingers because of the blisters. I'll need help. Rosie, it's good you live in Hamilton now."

Samuel cleared his throat. "We'll take the children with us."

Richard shook his new brother-in-law's hand. "I appreciate that, especially this being your wedding day and all."

"You'd do the same."

"We'll warm leftovers for supper." Rose reminded herself to be sensible. This evening wasn't special to Samuel anyway.

"Nice to have my little sister back." Richard hugged her.

She laughed. "I've received lots of hugs today. Maybe I should get married more often."

Richard grinned. "Soon, you'll receive more hugs than you can count."

Her gaze flew to Samuel's back. The man who had never hugged her once silently gripped the windowsill.

CHAPTER 9

o streetlamps lit the muddy country road leading to Samuel's home. The children dozed in the back of the wagon. Rose must be exhausted, for she'd been silent most of the way. Clouds hid the moon. No matter. He knew the way. He guided the wagon beside his barn.

Pigs oinked a welcome. He wondered if his new wife found their odor offensive. She sat, stiff as an overstarched shirt, beside him in the darkness. He could discern nothing beyond her silhouette, so there was no way to know if her nose wrinkled. He'd grown so accustomed to farm animals that he barely noticed noises and smells, but she was no farm girl. She'd have to adjust, though, come to think of it, Ginny had often complained about the pigs.

Zeb's barks added to the clamor of the children's excited chatter.

Samuel applied the brake and jumped down, the boys doing the same, Clay carrying a bag containing their clothes. They ran to the house with Zeb at their heels. Lantern light glowed from the windows seconds after the boys disappeared inside.

After lifting Emma and Polly from the back, Samuel made

his way around to Rose. Her hands rested on his shoulders as he lifted her from the seat. Though a few inches taller than Ginny, she felt surprisingly light. He admired her trim figure before averting his gaze. Finding her attractive wasn't part of their bargain, though maybe someday...

Darkness masked her expression as her hands slid from his shoulders.

"I'll carry these chairs inside after feeding the animals if you'll help with the table." He gestured his dining room furniture in the back that he'd taken over to Richard's as seating for guests at the reception—and only three of twenty invited guests came. "It's too wide and long for me to handle by myself." Loud bellows from the barn reminded him of the late hour. "I hoped the boys might stay and help with the horses. I'll milk the cows." Hens clucked and flapped their wings from inside the henhouse where they already roosted for the night.

"Clay milks their cow." She gathered her shawl tighter around her arms.

"I haven't taught Peter yet." Samuel wondered at her shivers. The breeze felt good against his skin.

"I'll send the boys out." She retrieved a bag from under the seat and headed to the house.

He watched her graceful progress toward the back porch, his heart aching at the day's unfortunate events. Nothing was simple these days.

He led the team into the barn. Clay and Peter bolted inside the barn. The horses neighed in protest. Betsy and Bertha joined the din, though their mooing stemmed from a different need.

Samuel unhitched the horses and led them to their stalls. They'd receive a good rubdown after the milking. He set Clay to work on Betsy while he claimed a stool next to Bertha.

Clay explained how to milk Betsy and laughed at Peter's clumsy efforts.

Pigs grunted from their pen. No doubt, they'd gobbled up

the food left in the trough hours before. The pigs could wait. "I hear you," Samuel called to the grunting animals. "I smelled you half mile away. It won't hurt you to wait a few minutes."

The boys' laughter stopped. Two heads appeared beside Bertha's ears, and the wide-eyed boys stared at him.

He struggled to maintain a straight face. "I meant the pigs, boys. Carry on."

They returned to Betsy's stall.

They'd all had a long day. It wasn't over yet.

~

*T*he door to Emma's room slammed as Samuel carried two buckets inside an hour later. The girls were still awake?

Peter and Clay brought in a chair.

"Thanks, boys. It's past your bedtime. I'll be in to hear your prayers."

Clay won a race to Peter's bedroom.

The morning's frenzied activity to get the children ready for the wedding had left the place a bit of a mess. It wasn't anymore. Rose had been busy.

A delicious aroma of freshly-ground coffee wafted from the kitchen. Rose brushed back wisps of hair before selecting two cups and saucers from the cupboard.

"I just asked the girls to change for bed." She cleared her throat. "It seemed best to allow them to release pent-up energy so they could sleep."

"No doubt you're right." Samuel understood, but it was past ten o'clock. "Normally bedtime is strictly enforced. We don't want anyone sleeping at church."

"I'll hurry them along." Crimson-cheeked, she stood.

Perhaps he had spoken too harshly. "Sorry if I sounded abrupt. They're usually asleep by sundown in the summer."

"Good to know." She hurried into Emma's room and closed the door behind her.

He appreciated her gentle reminder that she didn't yet know their routine, as he lifted a latch hook on the kitchen floor and carried the milk to the root cellar. Afterward, he dragged his aching body to Peter's room to settle the boys.

Rose was in the kitchen pouring a cup of coffee as Samuel shut Peter's door.

"Will you help carry the table inside?" She looked so tired that he hated to steal her away from what was likely her first relaxing moment since the accident. "I'd ask Charlie, but he goes to bed with the chickens."

"I'll get my wrap." She entered his bedroom—now hers alone —where a colorful quilt lay across the bed. She returned wearing a brown shawl over a plain brown dress. She must have changed to clean the house.

Her accommodating attitude soothed his frayed nerves. It had been a tough day for everyone.

Outside, trees swayed. He was glad to see clouds thickening with the promise of rain. His crops needed it.

Rose grimaced at the weight of the heavy table—a gift from Ginny's parents—and then carried her end without complaint.

"Thanks." He briefly clasped her shoulder. "Relax while I finish up." He made several trips for chairs and table leaves.

She sprang to her feet when he set the last chair in place. "Want a cup of coffee? I believe it's still hot."

Samuel glanced at the cup already on the table. "You believe it's hot? Aren't you drinking it?"

"Mine is lukewarm."

"Why not pour a fresh cup?"

"I don't waste food. My salary had to stretch through the months I didn't work."

She'd endured financial hardships, something they had in common.

"If you like," she said, "I'll drink another cup with you now."

"Thank you." Samuel chose the chair closest to her.

Rose placed a steaming cup in front of him and brought one for herself.

"What a day." He breathed in the beverage's aroma. "Nothing like my first wedding day."

Coffee spilled down the bodice of her brown dress. "Ouch!" A dark stain spread across her chest. Springing from her chair, she jerked the fabric away from her throat.

Samuel grabbed a cloth from the sink counter. He started to reach toward the high neckline, but stopped at her wide-eyed stare. "Here, uh, sorry. Use this."

Cheeks bright red, she snatched the towel and turned away.

"Shall I fetch the doctor?"

"No. It's trifling. Thanks for the towel." She averted her eyes. "I'll say goodnight. You'll see to the lanterns and the fire?"

"Certainly. Rose?" She paused at the door. "I'm sorry today didn't go as planned. You handled everything beautifully—even my foul mood this evening."

"I'm glad to hear you say so." Tension eased from her shoulders.

"Goodnight, Rose. Thanks for the coffee. For everything."

"Sleep well." The door closed on the shadowy bedroom.

He smacked his forehead with his palm. What a fool thing to do, speaking of his first wedding. There was no reason to make her feel she didn't compare to Ginny.

Loneliness descended full force. The day's activity had kept thoughts of Ginny at bay. Now they flooded back. He released a long breath, thankful that the difficult day had finally ended.

CHAPTER 10

*H*uddled in her father's rocking chair near the
bedroom's lone window, Rose stared at the pink
curtains, pretty and dainty like the woman who'd once slept
there. Today had been difficult for Samuel even without Hazel's
accident.

Rose, wearing a white cotton nightgown, stared at the bed
where she'd sleep alone. Her trunk, her mother's armoire, and
the Rose of Sharon quilt she'd completed last week were the
only familiar items in the room. Light from a single lantern
glowed atop a three-drawer chest beside a pitcher and bowl.

Her new husband chose an unfinished attic bedroom over
sleeping with her. No surprise. Relief warred with rejection,
and she didn't know which won.

When Samuel had been tending the horses, she'd climbed
the narrow attic stairs and explored the large room by candlelight. Two side ceilings sloped, meeting at a high point in the
center. A window spanned an area six inches from the floor and
ceiling on either side of the attic. The large windows allowed
scant light from a half-moon, creating shadows on the wall.

Three cedar chests had lined the back wall opposite the

staircase. A tall four-drawer chest with a lantern on top, a bedroll, and a few of Samuel's personal items lay in the far corner. Shirts and trousers hung on hooks. A draft from an undiscovered source had left her shivering. The big, lonely room was Samuel's, while she stole this comfortable space.

She longed for her own home. She wasn't wanted in Samuel's.

Had she expected him to find her beautiful in her wedding gown? Of course not. And he must not have, for he hadn't remarked on it.

Weariness descended onto her shoulders. Her disappointment was no one's fault but her own. Samuel had been honest with her.

She pushed herself to her feet. Time to put her dreams to sleep.

~

A muddy walk to church—Samuel had whispered that the extra exercise worked out some of the fidgets in advance of the service—in the early morning sunshine took thirty minutes. Witnessing the tension ease from Samuel's face as he talked with the children restored Rose's spirits. They'd soon learn to get along, especially with the children enlivening every moment.

Mud puddles tempted Clay, but her stern look stayed his lifted boot. Laughing, she smoothed down his hair, and he gave her an impish grin.

There was no sign of Richard in the brick church when they settled on a middle pew.

Rose considered the two frantic hours of feeding and dressing four children that preceded their arrival—she was accustomed to children already fed and dressed. Now, they sat between her and Samuel. Clay's trousers were still mud-splattered from yesterday. All she'd had time to do was brush at the dirt. Clay was too tall and husky to wear his cousin's clothes.

She winced as her cotton dress brushed against the red splotch on her chest. The injury had been worth the pain, having saved her from hearing about Samuel's first wedding.

Folks filed out after the final prayer. She urged the kids forward, then caught sight of Clay's bare feet. "Clay. What in heaven's…?"

Samuel stifled a laugh behind a fist and ushered the others out.

"Why did you remove your shoes in church?" She urged him back to their pew, then folded her arms while he donned his stockings.

"Don't be mad, Aunt Rosie." He glanced up. "My feet got hot."

"That's no excuse." Sympathy for the boy who loved the outdoors softened her tone.

"It's hard to sit inside when the sun's awake." He applied pressure to the heel, and the boot slid onto his foot. "I don't want to work in a factory like Pa when I'm grown. Farming suits me better."

"Save your money to buy a farm when you're older." The corners of her mouth lifted. "But you'll still have to wear shoes at church."

"Unless I don't got none." Grinning, he ran down the empty aisle.

"That's another matter entirely." Rose laughed at his irrepressible spirit. God had blessed the family when He'd given them Clay—and Polly was just as precious. She smiled to think she'd soon know Peter and Emma just as well.

She stepped into the bright sunlight and spotted Samuel with Richard beside his wagon.

The crowded yard reminded her of her church back home. Lively conversations, sedate greetings, and children playing tag filled the grassy area between the church building and the wide city lane. Everyone appeared to be in conversation. Even her brood scampered off to play with other children.

Smoothing her freshly-pressed pink calico, Rose stood near two friendly women who'd attended the wedding in hopes they'd greet her. Neither glanced in her direction.

Four fashionable women nodded at her. Perhaps Rose should have worn one of her two better church dresses.

Samuel motioned for her. She crossed the yard and greeted her brother. "How is Hazel?"

"Resting." Richard's brow wrinkled. "Doc's pills make her sleep. She's frustrated. Until the blisters recede or open, she can't do much."

Rose took a deep breath. "I put a big pot of soup on the stove this morning. I'll make biscuits, and we'll plan the next few days."

Samuel lifted his eyebrows. "Plan what?"

Didn't he understand Richard's hints? "Do you mind if we take soup over?"

"Not at all. I'll gather the children." He strode through the thinning crowd.

Not the gracious response she'd wanted. Rose pressed her fingers to her temples as she leaned against the rough wood of Richard's wagon—which used to be Papa's. Perhaps Samuel was being cautious about the chores they'd take on for Hazel's sake.

~

"Thanks for keeping the children on your wedding night." Hazel, sitting in a wooden chair, stared out the open window. "I'd understand your resentment."

"Not at all." Rose plopped another bowl into the soapy water. Even if her marriage had been normal, she and Samuel had the rest of their lives together. "Please don't distress yourself."

"What a beautiful spring day." She looked out the window. "The new cousins are enjoying the sunshine."

"I love to hear them laughing." Rose giggled as she watched the boys running toward a tree, Samuel in pursuit. Playing with the children had shaken any lingering doldrums from her husband's mood, for which she was thankful. She discarded water from a kettle with charred vegetables stuck on the bottom. "I wish the soup hadn't burned."

"I've heard all stoves are different. You'll discover the hottest areas and how much wood to use over time." Hazel's arms and hands rested on her lap.

"I imagine it embarrassed Samuel." Heat spread over her cheeks. The burning smell had struck her as soon as Samuel had opened the door of his home two hours before. He'd opened all four windows in the front room while she'd salvaged the soup.

"He seemed fine to me. And everyone gobbled up the biscuits." Hazel eyed her cup.

"Do you want a sip?" At Hazel's nod, Rose held the cup to her sister-in-law's lips. When Hazel had had her fill of water, Rose resumed scrubbing.

The men entered the back door. "Any coffee left?" Richard kissed his wife's cheek.

Rose tried not to notice Samuel didn't kiss her. "I'll make a fresh batch. I promise not to scorch it." Laughing, she poured water into the coffeepot.

Richard chuckled. "Sis, you haven't burned anything that badly since you learned to cook. Samuel, don't expect burnt offerings every day."

He sat on the opposite corner from Hazel, straddling his chair to face his wife. "I know you can cook, Rose. Please don't trouble yourself."

Knots in her stomach relaxed at his gracious reassurance.

Richard sat beside Hazel. "Let's discuss the children. Will

you keep Polly this week? Too bad Clay and Peter don't attend the same school."

Unwilling to blunder again, Rose ground coffee beans into the grinder mounted on the wall, breathing in its aroma as she awaited her husband's reply.

Samuel agreed and invited the family to supper the following night.

The two girls played well together. Rose was thrilled they'd have Polly with them for her first week.

They chatted until Hazel complained of pain. Richard unrolled her bandages and gently applied ointment.

Rose tugged at her collar. "May I use some of that?"

Samuel grimaced. "I'm sorry you got burned last night."

His concern felt good. "Merely a tiny patch of red. It only hurts when my dress rubs against it."

Richard slid the round tin across the table. "Help yourself, Sis. Use Polly's room."

The girls were waiting at the door when she came out. "Aunt Rosie, I need clothes to sleep at Emma's house."

Smiling at Emma's glowing face, she helped her niece pack. When they left the bedroom, Clay and Peter sat on the floor with their backs against the wall.

"Ma's sick. I don't need to go to school." Clay folded his arms.

"Son, you'll go to school. *You're* not sick." Richard's firm tone silenced Clay.

On the ride home, the girls made big plans for the week while Peter scowled.

Rose used Samuel's silence on the drive to plan a quick supper. A bountiful supply of milk and eggs didn't compensate for an appalling lack of provisions that she had no time to worry about at breakfast. Omelets seemed the best choice.

The girls unpacked Polly's bag while Rose spread a white tablecloth over glistening wood. She hadn't yet unpacked

Mama's dishes, so she set the table using Ginny's plates and utensils. Breakfast had been so hectic that this felt like their first family meal.

Within minutes, a platter of steaming omelets and toasted bread made an appetizing centerpiece. The children washed their hands at the inside pump. Samuel took his place at the head of the table. Peter sat on his left, the girls on his right. Rose faced her husband as he asked the blessing on the meal.

Peter tugged on his father's sleeve. Eyes on Rose, he whispered something that had Samuel's gaze darting to her as well.

Remembering Peter's rainy walk to the cemetery, her heartbeat quickened. What now?

CHAPTER 11

The whispers stopped. Rose tried to distract her worry about what was coming next by smoothing wrinkles from the napkin in her lap.

Samuel fingered the rim of his glass. "Rose, Peter asks a valid question."

The boy peeked at her from the corner of his eye.

"Oh?" She served the girls a portion of omelets to fill the silence.

"He doesn't know how to address you. Not 'Ma,' because that's what he called his mother. What's your preference?"

Baffled, she stared at him. It had never occurred to her they'd call her anything besides ma or mama.

Polly tilted her pretty face. "Her name is Aunt Rosie."

"I'm not their aunt, Polly. I'm their stepmother." Rose spoke in gentle tones.

Samuel glanced from his niece to his wife. "Polly calls you Rosie?"

His gentle tone soothed her. "Richard's family calls me that."

"Shall the children call you Mama Rosie?"

She searched her stepchildren's anxious eyes. "That's fine."

Polly's face puckered. "Me, too?"

Samuel joined Rose's laughter. "No, Polly. You'll still call her 'Aunt Rosie.'"

"Can I have some?" Peter held out his plate.

"Of course." Rose filled his plate, thankful that difficult discussion was behind them.

His face cleared when she smiled at him.

It was a start. Rose met Samuel's satisfied gaze, happy to have pleased him.

$\sim$

*R*emembering Samuel's frustration the night before, Rose allowed the girls to talk for ten minutes after listening to their bedtime prayers. Then she entered Emma's candlelit bedroom. "Time to sleep, girls." She kissed each girl's cheek. "You'll have all day tomorrow to play. Sweet dreams." She blew out the candle, pulled the door closed, and listened. A few muffled whispers, and then all was quiet.

This was her first chance to relax since she'd awakened that morning. She carried a lantern to the small table between the sofa and the armchair and retrieved her sewing basket from her bedroom. The choice between sewing and resting was an easy one. Sewing relaxed her.

Samuel's shoulders slumped as he emerged from Peter's room.

A longing to hold him in the comfort of her arms filled her.

He bent until his lips were close to her ear. "Walk with me?"

A stroll in the moonlight with her husband? Her pulse quickened. Sewing could wait. She stepped out with him.

Stars dotted an inky sky. Lightning bugs lit their path. Crickets sang as Rose and Samuel strolled toward the wide fertile field behind their home. Rose's heart beat a staccato rhythm. The balmy May evening was as romantic as her dreams.

Neighboring homes were over three hundred yards away on one side and twice as far on the other. A thick line of trees hid both houses from view, giving Rose a delicious sense of isolation.

He stopped at the muddy edge of the field, where tender shoots broke through the ground. "I never tire of watching things grow." Moonlight caressed his face. "A planted seed produces a cornstalk taller than the average man. Provides for families. It's a miracle, isn't it?"

Rose nodded. This reflective side reminded her of their schoolyard conversations.

"That dark line of trees is my apple orchard." He pointed toward the right. "I planted two acres of trees the year I married Ginny. Apples were her idea. I didn't want to waste farmland. Good thing she insisted. The next year I added two more acres. Those early trees now produce well. Wish I'd planted more at the start. Last year was our best harvest. I added two acres this spring."

The 'our' he referred to was him and Ginny. Despite his earlier assurances, Rose wondered when he would consider her part of the family. "You've done well. The home has beautiful furniture, not to mention the luxury of an ice box."

"Gifts from Ginny's parents." Bitterness tinged his tone. "Only the best for their daughter and grandchildren. Luxuries were beyond my means, so they bought them. Ginny loved shopping with her mother. I tried not to let the extravagance bother me. But that's a topic for another day. Let's sit." He gestured a hollow log under a sturdy maple.

Shadows darkened the area. She peered all around it. Satisfied that no critters lurked behind it, she perched on the damp wood beside him.

"I asked you out here because I don't want Peter to overhear our conversation."

"Oh." That explained this moonlit stroll. Not a desire to be with her.

"He thrives on a schedule. And nothing's been the same since Ginny died."

"Routine is good for children." Something she'd learned early in her teaching days. Even so, she hoped Samuel would be patient with her as she adjusted to the family's daily habits.

"I understand things will never be the same. Peter's holding onto as much of his mother as he can."

Her heart went out to the grief-stricken child. "How can we help him?"

"I was hoping you'd have an idea." He rubbed his chin. "I figured you'd know—with your experience with children."

"Minimal changes at first." She placed her hands on the log and leaned back. "A relaxed routine."

"Good start. I'll keep a watchful eye on my children."

The weeks following her mother's death remained blurred to this day. They needed gentle, loving care. "I will also."

"Peter seemed excited you were coming. I'm not certain what changed."

"I was introduced as Mrs. Samuel Walker." Darkness hid his expression. The intimate seclusion was the perfect spot to suggest she'd not mind another kiss—this time without the crowds. "He also saw you kiss me."

Samuel stood abruptly.

Was he rejecting her? Their first kiss had been brief as befitted the ceremony. Rose, heart shrinking, clutched the splintered wood at her sides.

"I hope you didn't mind."

"Oh, I didn't mind at all." Her voice squeaked.

"That was part of the ceremony." His boots shuffled against the grass.

Her spirits plummeted.

"I'll abide by the boundaries we set." He leaned one hand on a low, sturdy branch.

She looked away. "You've made your intentions clear." No more kisses.

Crickets chirped.

He cleared his throat. "Displays of affection bother the children. Another good reason to avoid them."

"Understood." She stood, her legs as shaky as her voice. "You're not beholden to me."

He huffed out a long breath. "I'm sorry. I've expressed myself badly. I owe you a great deal. You made sacrifices to help my family." Samuel lifted his arms as if to pull her close, then let them flop to his sides. "It's too soon for me to think of someone else. I thought you understood."

"I do." A plain, drab woman like Rose didn't appeal to him after the vivacious, beautiful Ginny.

Samuel grasped her cold fingers. "Peter wishes you were more like his mother. His attitude influences Emma."

"No doubt." Her hand fit perfectly inside his warm grasp. "Emma likes me because Polly loves me."

His thumb caressed the back of her hand. "You have a great relationship with Clay. That may influence my son."

Samuel's touch was making it difficult to think. No one compared to Ginny—that was all she needed to remember. "Clay's a treasure."

"The burden to help them adjust falls on me." Samuel released her. "I'm their anchor."

"Peter and Emma will grow accustomed to me gradually. I've overcome difficulties as a teacher."

"That made you an ideal choice." He stepped into the moonlight. "My focus right now is Peter and Emma and their grief. I can't take on more than that." He walked toward the barn. "I'll check the animals."

He married her for her teaching experience.

Letting the truth, the cold, heartless truth, of that fill her, Rose rested her hand on a low-lying branch and leaned her forehead against it. She wasn't Ginny. She wasn't the love of Samuel's life. She wasn't the beloved mother the children longed for.

She was a pale substitute and always would be.

Memories of her mother's death flooded back. Papa's housekeeper, Mrs. Wiley, had come four days a week after that. The childless widow had not been kind.

If Rose would never be more to the children than a nanny and housekeeper, then so be it. But she vowed to be different from Mrs. Wiley. She would treat the children with kindness, no matter what happened.

CHAPTER 12

*R*ose scrambled eggs for breakfast. The girls' chatter masked Peter's almost silent meal. She exchanged a glance with Samuel, who shook his head.

He stood. "Time to go, son. Tell Mama Rosie thank you for breakfast."

"Thanks for the eggs." Peter wiped his mouth with a napkin and stood. "Bye, Pa."

Samuel hugged him. "Do well in school."

He buried his face against his father's stomach.

"Zeb's waiting for you." Emma pointed to the dog waiting at the open front door.

"Zeb goes with you?" Rose asked. After one of her students brought a snake to school, she'd put a ban on all pets.

He picked up his lunch pail. "Yep. He waits for me all day under a tree."

"I put extra food in his pail for Zeb." Samuel quirked an eyebrow at her.

Rose guessed she'd have to remember Zeb's lunch too after this.

"I keep a bowl under his tree for water. There's a well at school. I get him more when I'm excused for the privy."

"How clever." She smiled at Peter's grin. "Have a good day."

Samuel, a sturdy hand on his son's shoulder, walked out with him. The girls had run back to Emma's room by the time he returned.

Rose was clearing the table.

"Good job."

She flushed under his approving smile.

"He has a real bond with Zeb. That's another way to win his heart."

"Good to know." *What about* your *heart?*

"I'll be in the field." He paused with his hand on the back doorknob. "You probably won't see me until mealtime when I work with the crops."

"Fair enough." From the window, she watched her husband stride away from her, tall and confident, fulfilling his life's dream by working the land. Lost in dreams of her own, she nearly dropped a plate when Polly called her name from the bedroom. "What is it?"

"Will you brush our hair?"

That was one task she hadn't often done for her students.

Rose settled on Emma's bed and listened to their chatter as she braided their hair. After she left them to dress, she started washing plates, thankful that only the breakfast dishes needed a wash—not the entire contents of the cupboard like the first day she'd cleaned that kitchen.

The cousins entered the kitchen while Rose scrubbed a kettle.

Polly tugged on her apron. "Aunt Rosie?"

"Yes, Polly?"

"Aunt Rosie?"

"Yes, Polly, what is it?" Both girls wore white cotton shifts. "Ah, you need help dressing."

Emma, staring at the wood floor, clutched her doll to her chest.

"I want to wear my play dress."

"That's fine." She scrubbed harder on an old scorch stain on the pot that was definitely not from breakfast.

Polly tugged the wet apron until Rose bent down. "Emma doesn't have a plain dress."

"I'm sorry, honey." She stared at Emma. "I didn't realize you were out of clean clothes. I'll launder a pile this morning."

Scarlet spread across Emma's cheeks.

"Aunt Rosie." Polly cupped her hands together and whispered in Rose's ear. "She doesn't have *any* play clothes 'cuz she isn't allowed to get dirty."

She straightened slowly. Lace or ruffles adorned everything Emma wore. Rose suddenly remembered her standing at the churchyard watching other children play. Had Ginny insisted on dressing her daughter in frills all the time? Why?

"Polly, did you bring an extra play dress?"

She nodded.

"May Emma wear it?"

Her face brightened. "She's bigger than me but so is the dress." Polly grabbed Emma's arm. "We'll make mud pies to feed our dolls." The girls ran into Emma's room.

Rose laughed. This might be the first time Emma played in the mud. She dared not spoil their fun.

Ideas took shape. She'd spend the morning washing clothes, then she'd shop, if Samuel agreed.

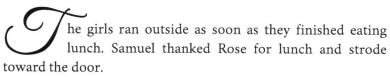

he girls ran outside as soon as they finished eating lunch. Samuel thanked Rose for lunch and strode toward the door.

Rose took a deep breath. "Do you have a moment?"

"Sure thing." Turning back, Samuel rolled up his sleeves. "Everything all right?"

"Just wondering… Why doesn't Emma own play clothes?" Rose carried a stack of dishes to the sink.

His lips slipped into a smirk. "Ginny dressed Emma in frilly clothes and admonished her not to stain them. I questioned it when I noticed that rule kept Emma from playing with friends. She told me I'd never been a little girl and didn't know the proper way to raise one."

"I see. Do you agree with Ginny's way of raising her? Because most girls get dirty when they're little, just like boys."

He looked out the window toward the girls running in the yard. "If you think it's all right for her to get dirty, then I don't mind."

"Then you have no objections to purchasing inexpensive calico for plain dresses?" She joined him at the window. The girls chased a butterfly across the green grass near the corral, where two horses grazed.

"Ginny hired seamstresses, but there are plenty of ready-made clothes in city shops."

"I enjoy sewing." Rose had often longed for children to sew for, as Celia did for Harriet. "I'll stitch the dresses to save money."

"No fooling?" He stared at her. "You'd shoulder that extra work?"

"Happily." Rose glowed at his smile. "Dresses for a little girl are a new challenge. May I buy fabric today?"

"Of course. That reminds me… Fred gave me half the money he owes for your home. He expects to pay the rest by Christmas. Does that suit you?"

"Yes, and I'm thrilled for they'll finally own their own home and shoemaker shop." Rose clasped her hands together. She'd helped her former boarders by making a gift of her furniture to furnish the home, but they'd given her a family to come home to every night. It seemed a fair trade.

"Do you mind using a portion to buy lumber for the attic room?" He folded his arms. "Not certain when I'll get around to building it. Farm chores come first. I'll build in my spare time, but there's no need to wait for harvest to order lumber if you're agreeable."

"We're married." Her cheeks flamed. He shouldn't have to build an attic room in the first place, though she preferred he fall in love with her before sharing her room. She sighed inwardly, for he was a long way from loving her. "My money is your money just as your home is my home. Please, do as you wish. Make the room comfortable."

"It won't require much cash because I'll do the work. I dabble with carpentry, but I've never built a room. Charlie explained how to do it. He may help."

"Two bedrooms will look nicer. Maybe add a storage room at the end of the hallway."

Samuel's eyes crinkled. "I didn't know I married an architect."

"You didn't." She laughed at his teasing. "Two rooms suit the large area." She dipped water from the heated stove reservoir into a pan to wash dishes.

"Reckon they do." He carried a stack of dishes over from the table. "That was my uncle's original plan. He proposed to a woman he courted after building the house. She rejected him. Married a lawyer instead. Uncle Roy remained a bachelor."

Rose felt a sudden affinity with Uncle Roy.

Samuel smiled tenderly. "He made many friends as a farmer and volunteer fireman. I doubt he felt lonely."

She knew all too well that a person might stay busy all day, every day, and still endure loneliness come evening.

She shaved slivers of lye soap into the hot water.

"I'll drive you and the girls to the grocery and dry goods

store this afternoon and order wood at the lumber mill while you shop. Do we need food for tonight?"

"Tonight?" Rose, soapy plate in hand, paused.

"Richard's family will be here for supper."

"I haven't thought about Hazel all day."

"Richard arranged for neighbors to check on her."

"Good." Soapsuds dripped onto her apron. "Very little food is left." It appeared that Samuel hadn't purchased groceries since Gin... Since February. "Let's restock supplies."

"I'll ask Charlie to watch for Peter in case we're delayed in town." Samuel strode out the open front door.

Rose raced through the dishes and then checked supplies. Many items were depleted or nonexistent. She made a mental list.

The back door creaked open as Rose finished. "Oh, girls, I meant to call you..." She turned and stopped midsentence at the mud smears on their clothing.

Emma's face turned ashen.

The child seemed frightened. Rose must handle this situation delicately. "It appears you've had fun today. Is that true?"

They exchanged a look.

"Emma never made a mud pie before." Polly lifted dirty palms. "I showed her how."

"I wish I had time to make a mud pie."

Polly giggled. "You can play with us next time." Polly looked at Emma, who nodded.

"Maybe I will." Rose laughed, touched by the invitation. "Because a little honest dirt never hurt anybody."

Emma held out the muddy skirt, eyes wide.

"That frock will be as good as new after I apply a scrub brush to it." She winked.

Emma's face brightened. "It will?"

"Certainly. Now, please change. Wash your face and hands first. Your Pa is taking us shopping."

They ran to the sink and took turns raising the pump handle. Water splashed on their faces, causing laughter that Rose joined.

She supplied clean towels when they finished. "It's time to change, girls. And if those dresses get dirty"—she wagged her finger—"remember, I know how to use a scrub brush."

Giggling, the girls raced to Emma's room.

Rose smiled at their happy chatter. One step at a time.

CHAPTER 13

*S*amuel tossed his daughter in the air until she giggled.

"Me, too." Polly chimed in.

Samuel laughed and set Emma in the back of the wagon. Then his niece squealed as he lifted her high and set her in the wagon.

"What fun." Rose emerged wearing the blue dress and hat she'd worn their first evening together.

Polly clapped. "Pick up Aunt Rosie, Uncle Samuel."

"Oh, my gracious." Her cheeks matched her name. "I'm too old for such frivolity, Polly."

Was that a wistful tone?

"You're not too old." He was tempted to swing her up onto the seat to prove it. Instead, he held out his hand.

Her eyes widened as she reached for him.

Samuel liked the feel of her hand in his. The size and fit felt just right. A familiar whiff of lavender suited her. Disturbed that he even noticed such details, he released her as soon as she was settled on the wagon seat.

"We need quite a few things." She made a fuss with arranging the reticule dangling from her wrist to rest on her lap.

"I'm certain of it." Restocking the shelves wasn't a problem, thanks to the sale of her house. He hadn't purchased anything beyond the barest necessities in months.

Spring sunshine felt gentle on his back now that he wasn't hard at work in the fields. A new shop, hotel, or manufacturer seemed to crop up every few months. The growing city crept ever closer to his home. Dread filled him for the day when buildings engulfed his farm. He'd already rejected one offer for his forty acres. He dreamed of expanding his orchard, not selling his land. Thankfully, cash from the sale of Rose's home ensured his farm's future. A welcome relief, indeed. Their marriage brought unexpected benefits.

He escorted his ladies inside the grocer and dry goods store and then drove to the lumberyard, where he told the owner what he needed. The man promised delivery in two days. Paying cash for the entire order brought unexpected joy. In recent years, Ginny's tendency to overspend had kept finances tight and an uneasy atmosphere between them.

Perhaps Rose was different.

The girls waved from a bench outside when he returned. Rose's contented face suggested a successful shopping expedition.

Dust clouds rose when he jumped from the wagon onto the dirt road in front of her. "Didn't you buy anything?"

Her brown eyes sparkled. "We did."

He blinked. Her pretty smile almost made him forget their errand.

Emma tugged his hand. "Mama Rosie will make me *three* dresses. I picked fabric and buttons, but I don't want ruffles, Pa."

"We selected our favorites." Rose's smile faded as she looked at Samuel. "Since she owns none."

"*Three* dresses, Rose?" He ground his teeth. At this rate, they'd spend all the money from the house in six months. "Isn't that extravagant?"

Stiffening, she glanced at his cowering daughter. "I apologize for not discussing the precise number of dresses with you." She gestured the open entrance. "Our supplies are with the proprietor."

Samuel strode inside the store. "Mr. Bunker, thank you for assisting my wife with her purchases."

The gray-haired man stepped from behind the counter. "I haven't seen you since the first Mrs. Walker died. The misses. and I regretted her passing." He shook Samuel's hand. "She had a way about her."

"Thank you." How many times must he hear those difficult words? "Our supplies are ready?"

"Your whole account is paid. That includes today's goods." He lifted a crate to the counter. "I'll put the rest beside the door."

More crates? Samuel rifled through dried lemons, lye soap, pickled cucumbers, crackers, soda, mustard, cocoa, honey, spices, catsup, horseradish, celery sauce, molasses, tea, loaf sugar, and vinegar. And there were more?

Three more crates, to be precise. Heat spread up the back of his neck as he silently loaded sacks of flour, rice, coffee beans, rye meal, and corn meal beside them.

Rose held a tied brown paper package.

"What's that?"

Raising her chin, she gave him a direct look. She obviously detected his frustration. "Fabric."

He lifted the girls into the wagon. No playful tosses or giggles this time. Rose climbed up unaided.

Samuel joined her on the seat.

"We were out of dried and canned vegetables." Rose stared straight ahead. "I guess vegetables from last fall's canning didn't stretch far enough. There's not much meat left in the root cellar or the smokehouse."

"Not surprising."

She averted her eyes.

He guided his team onto the road. "Ginny didn't can many vegetables. She hated the task, so she invited her friends over—made a big party of it. We sold most of our crops. I didn't realize we needed everything." It made sense, now that he thought about it. They'd been going without too long.

"I'll be frugal." Her frosty tone could have frozen the mud puddle on the side of the road. "I can't spare time to make butter, so I'll buy it. It won't be a regular purchase."

"No problem." Did he detect hurt somewhere in that anger?

"There's fabric for a new shirt for Peter. I didn't wish to neglect him."

Her thoughtful gesture surprised him.

"And bigger buttons." Her confession tumbled out. "They cost more, but Emma loved them. They're easier for little fingers to fasten."

"I'm sorry for my reaction. You obviously shopped wisely." Samuel placed his hand on Rose's tense arm. "Thank you."

She shifted her body away from him.

His hand returned to the reins.

The drive to the meat market passed silently. She selected bacon, ham, sausage, and beef without glancing at him.

He regretted showing his initial frustration at the expense. She hadn't wasted money.

She wasn't like Ginny at all.

~

*S*amuel opened the door to find Richard on the porch holding a peach pie that evening. "A neighbor brought two, so we'll share. Hazel's not up to company, but I promised to bring a plate home."

Samuel accepted the pie. "Please tell her she was missed."

"Papa!" Polly ran to her father, and Richard lifted her high. "Where's Mama?"

"Resting at home."

Polly pouted.

Clay skirted past him and ran through the house with Peter into the backyard.

"Maybe Aunt Rosie and Uncle Samuel will bring you to see her tomorrow." Richard looked at his brother-in-law.

Samuel raised his eyebrows at his wife, irritated that Richard didn't wait until they were alone to make the request. Rose gave a slight nod, and Samuel turned back to Richard. "Agreed."

Polly wiggled until Richard set her down. Both girls ran outside.

"Soup smells good." Richard crossed to the kitchen and lifted the lid. "I brought a few clothes over. We had so many wedding tasks that our laundry piled up. Remember Hazel can't put her hands in water."

Rose removed a pan of cornbread from the oven. "That's fine."

"I knew you'd do it." He patted her shoulder. "I told Hazel not to fret. She didn't want to send the clothes over without asking, but I reminded her that you're my sister. You don't mind."

Samuel, watching his wife's face, wondered if Rose *did* mind, after all. She had her hands full already with all the tasks left undone for the last few months, as well as her own family's laundry. Maybe Richard should have asked first.

"Will you bring the clean clothes over with you tomorrow night?"

"Tomorrow?" Rose exchanged a startled glance with Samuel. "How much is there?"

"I'll fetch it." Richard left the room.

"*Do* you mind?" Samuel crossed to Rose's side and sniffed the simmering vegetable soup appreciatively.

"I'm behind on everything, but Hazel did work with me all last week on wedding preparations." Her lips puckered. "I doubt

Richard knows how to launder clothes. Besides, he works long hours at the paper manufacturer."

"You work long hours too." Samuel had learned to wash clothes when need drove him to it, not that he'd done it often enough.

"It won't be easy, but I can't refuse because Hazel injured herself cooking our wedding dinner." She poked a potato inside the kettle with a long wooden spoon.

Before Samuel could respond, Richard carried in two bulging sacks. "This will relieve Hazel's worry."

Samuel took the sacks and toted them into his old bedroom, wondering why Richard just assumed Rose could drop everything for him. Samuel didn't want anyone to take advantage of his new wife.

Later, the men milked the cows as the sun sank toward the horizon.

Rose had the washtub out on the back porch, scrubbing a dress of Polly's, when they returned.

The children chased lightning bugs in the yard. Zeb leaped at a lightning bug three feet over his head, causing Peter to bend over laughing. The sound of his laughter healed what ailed Samuel faster than a doctor's elixir. Samuel marveled that their marriage had already brought positive changes. He leaned against a porch support pole that needed a fresh coat of white paint. Another task for the list.

"It's getting late, but I wanted to discuss something before we leave." Richard rubbed his hands together.

Samuel searched his face warily. "Coffee or lemonade first?"

"Neither." His eyes gleamed. "Rosie, did you get the money for Papa's house?"

Rose wrinkled her brow. "Part of it. Fred will pay the rest later. Why?"

"You know why." Richard drew back. "I've come for my share."

Emma's dress splashed into the water.

"What's this?" Samuel folded his arms. Mr. Walker had willed the house to his daughter.

"Everyone knows Papa left the house to Rose because she wasn't married," Richard said. "He probably expected her to die an old maid. I did."

Rose flinched.

"All that changed when she married you. Papa certainly would have wanted her to share the proceeds with his only son."

Color drained from Rose's face.

Samuel clenched his fists. "You inherited your father's blacksmithing tools. What happened to those?"

Richard scowled, staring across the yard at grunting pigs. "Sold 'em."

"They must have brought you a pretty penny."

"A buddy starting his own business bought everything." He shrugged. "Why keep them? I already had a good job at the paper plant."

"Did you share that money with your sister?"

Richard grimaced. "She had the house."

The back of Samuel's neck flamed. How dare Richard treat his sister so shabbily?

"Your father wrote a will?" Samuel looked at Rose.

"Yes." Her bewildered gaze fastened on him. "Richard inherited the blacksmithing equipment. Papa gave me the house so I'd always have a place to live. I paid on the mortgage for two years after he died. Then the house was mine."

"Papa provided a roof for his daughter." Richard swiped his palms over his trousers. "Rosie, you've forty acres now. I own two. You know he'd want you to share this inheritance."

Tears filled Rose's eyes. She bent over the washing. Her brother's laundry. Samuel widened his stance. "Richard, the boys have school tomorrow."

Richard scowled. "Hope I don't need to hire a lawyer."

Gasping, Rose stood and leaned against the railing, turning her back to both men.

"I don't know about that, but you might need a doctor if you stay another minute." Straightening his shoulders, Samuel glared at Richard. One...more...word.

Lifting her skirts, Rose rushed inside and returned with a kettle. "Please, Richard, let's speak another time. Here's Hazel's soup."

He accepted it.

"We'll bring Polly tomorrow." She swiped at her face with a handkerchief from her apron pocket.

"Didn't mean to upset you, Sis." His voice cracked. Before he said another word, the children burst onto the porch, filling the awkward moment. "Clay, your mama's probably starved. Thanks, Rosie, for the meal and the laundry."

Rose averted her eyes.

After he drove away, Samuel ushered everyone inside and shut the door. Dusk had fallen. "Children, change into your nightclothes. I'll be in to listen to your prayers."

When they were alone, Samuel massaged Rose's shoulders. "Why don't you leave the rest of the laundry for tomorrow? We'll talk after the children are in bed. Are you all right?"

Another tear trickled down her cheek. He wiped it away with his finger. Wet, dull eyes met his. He lifted his arms to hold her and then let them fall to his sides.

He turned away. Comforting hugs weren't part of their bargain.

CHAPTER 14

*W*et clothes dried on a line along her bedroom ceiling. Clay's muddy clothing soaked in a washtub. Standing for the first time in an hour, Rose stretched her lower back and then stumbled to the back porch swing, grateful for the darkness.

Restless shame that Samuel had witnessed her brother's outrageous demands drove her to her feet. She strolled past neighing horses in the corral and the pigpen, with its unfortunate odor, toward the field illuminated by pale moonlight. Last night she had talked with her husband in this spot. Tonight, she preferred to hide from him.

She was bewildered at her brother's behavior. He owned his house. Several men reported to him, so he must earn a decent wage.

Her brother hadn't cared for blacksmithing—that had been Papa's dream for his son—so he'd profited from Papa's old equipment while she'd nearly starved shouldering Papa's debts.

Footsteps approached, muted by the grass. She turned as Samuel halted a few feet away. "I regret losing my temper with your brother." He searched her expression in the dim light.

"I'm the one who's ashamed." She stared at the fields.

"Your father willed his home to you."

"True." Halting steps took her to the same log where they'd sat the night before. Darkness enveloped her underneath the spreading branches of the mature tree.

A dog barked in the distance. No answering barks. The mournful silence echoed her own loneliness.

"Help me understand." He sat beside her. "Did Richard make mortgage payments after your father passed?"

"No. I told him the amount Papa owed after the funeral. He never offered a penny toward the debt." He had merely patted her shoulder sympathetically. "I'd been paying the mortgage after Papa quit working anyway."

"Did Richard know that?" Still seated, he leaned back against the sturdy trunk.

"Papa didn't work for months." She cringed to speak ill of her brother, but Samuel deserved the truth. "He must know I supported us."

"What do you want to do?"

"The right thing. I just don't know what that is." Darkness masked Samuel's expression. "What's your opinion?"

He was silent a moment. "Richard sold his inheritance." His jaw clenched. "And he chose not to pay his father's debts. Your father must have weighed the fact that Richard already owned a home when distributing his possessions."

Yet Richard had threatened to contest the will. Everyone would lose. She covered her face with her hands. Such messy affairs destroyed relationships no matter who won.

"You disagree."

"No." She rubbed her temples at his dejected tone. "I agree, but is the inheritance worth this fight?"

He stared at her, his expression softening.

"Money can't divide our families. I spent too many years

away from Richard already. Our children *must* know each other."

"I need to pray." Samuel leaned forward, his head bowed, his hands clasped together. She put her hand on his and joined him in silent prayer. He twisted his hand so their hands entwined, his simple act comforting her as nothing else had. She added a prayer of thanks for her husband's strong faith.

"Let me mull over an idea"—he stirred, still clasping her hand—"and discuss it tomorrow."

"Richard won't let this rest."

"I know."

She leaned closer to her husband, wanting to lean on his shoulder, but he released her hand and stood.

Her face flamed. Of course, the comfort of resting in his arms was out of the question. "There's laundry to do." Any chance of finishing by tomorrow evening meant working past midnight.

～

*R*ose boiled clothes before dawn. Another batch went into fresh water immediately after breakfast. Samuel, dark shadows under his eyes, asked how much the monthly payments had been on Papa's house and how long she'd paid them before his death. Then he strode to the fields.

An iceman delivered a block of ice an hour later. A short, gray-haired man introduced himself as Mr. Douglas. He explained that Tuesday was his regular delivery day to this part of town. He emptied water from the tray and placed a block of ice inside the icebox.

Rose clucked her tongue at the luxury. She still used the cellar more than the icebox.

At noon, her red, chapped hands made her long for Hazel's salve to soothe the pain. Wet clothing hung on the outside lines.

Her lower back ached. All the ironing had yet to be done. Thankfully, the girls were playing well together and didn't require much from her.

Samuel washed the few remaining clothes after a meal of leftover ham and biscuits. She was grateful to begin ironing.

He recommended she subtract the amount she had paid from the sale price of the house before sharing with Richard, a significant number. Although she dreaded seeing her brother after his harsh words, she ironed all afternoon with a lighter heart. They had a solution.

When the whole family set off for Richard's home that afternoon, with piles of freshly laundered and folded clothes in sacks in the back of the wagon, Polly held onto the wagon seat in her excitement to see her mother. Somehow, her joy made the extra trouble Rose had endured worth the effort.

Richard wasn't in the house when they arrived. Hazel's face brightened when she kissed her daughter's cheek. She grimaced when Polly snuggled closer.

Polly must have noticed. "Mama, does it hurt?"

"Just a bit." Hazel brushed a wisp of hair from Polly's face with her bandaged left hand. "Don't worry. It'll be better soon."

Worry cleared from Polly's face. She talked with her a few minutes, and then the girls joined the boys in the backyard.

"How do you feel?" Rose sat on the cushioned chair beside Hazel's.

"Ointment helps." She stared at her bandaged hands.

Samuel carried in a basket of folded clothes. "I'll retrieve the other one." He strode out the open door.

"All the clothes are washed. Some shirts still need pressing." Rose gave a crisp nod toward the basket. "Where are your irons? I'll finish while we visit."

"In the cupboard by the stove." Hazel flushed. "Richard doesn't realize the work involved. I hope you know that I understand what a precious gift you've given me."

Her gratitude softened Rose's hurt feelings. "Glad to help." Exhaustion settled into her back.

Samuel carried in the last basket. By working continuously and keeping the irons hot, she'd finish in an hour. She placed three small, flat irons on the hot stove. The sight of dirty dishes in the basin threatened to sap the rest of her energy. No, that wasn't her job.

Her brother could wash them.

Richard entered the back door with a full milk pail. "Evening, folks." His words were chipper, but he avoided her eyes and Samuel's.

"Good evening." A weight descended on Rose's shoulders.

Samuel extended his hand. "Evening, Richard."

Richard hesitated before shaking Samuel's hand.

Rose held her breath as the two men took each other's measure.

"Let's walk outside." Samuel swept his hand toward the door.

Richard kissed Hazel's cheek before following him.

Hazel walked to the window. "I begged Richard not to ask for that money. It stirred up trouble between our husbands."

It stirred up hurt for Rose too. No one but Samuel seemed concerned about her feelings. Arms tight against her body, she joined Hazel at the window. Richard whittled a piece of wood with his pocketknife while leaning against the barn door. Samuel, hands on hips, faced him.

"We prayed together. Samuel found a way to satisfy my brother."

"I hope so. I prayed not to lose the only sister I'll ever have."

Tears pricked the back of Rose's eyes. "No chance of that. We've got years to catch up on."

"I'll hold you to that promise."

Silence settled over them as Rose resumed ironing. Hazel sat beside the window as dusk fell.

Finally, the men entered as Rose hung the last shirt on a hook in Clay's room.

Clasping her hand, Samuel gave her an encouraging smile.

Richard walked to where Rose stood in the center of the living room. "I didn't understand about the mortgage payments. Samuel explained everything. Money can't come between us. Why don't you keep this first installment, and you and I will split the rest? I didn't mean to hurt you." Richard glanced at his wife. "Hazel warned me, but I figured I knew you best. If you don't feel it's right to share the proceeds, we'll drop the matter."

A weight on her shoulders fell away. Her husband had worked a miracle. Her heart lightened. "We'll share the last payment." Since Richard felt it just, it seemed the best solution. Time to put this ugliness behind them.

A lamplighter lit a streetlamp as they plodded along on their way home that night. Gratitude for her husband's wisdom relaxed her. Too many tumultuous days in a row left her craving a long, restful sleep.

The lull of the horses' hooves, the warm breeze...

She awoke with her head resting against Samuel's warm shoulder.

He lifted her from the wagon seat, his strong hands lingering on her waist. He drew her close.

She snuggled against him, feeling like she was really home. "Go to bed." His whisper tickled her ear. "I'll care for the children."

His arms held the strength, the solace she craved more than sleep. She rested her face against his chest one precious moment and then bid the children goodnight. Peaceful sleep descended as soon as the sheet covered her exhausted body.

CHAPTER 15

*R*ichard dropped Clay off on Friday evening. "He asked to see Peter." He avoided Samuel's gaze. "I work tomorrow as usual. Hope you don't mind if he stays till Sunday."

Samuel remained silent to allow Rose to make this decision. After all, she was the one who'd done the lion's share of the work for her brother this week. Samuel shared some of the reserve he sensed in his brother-in-law, though he'd not tolerate a repeat of Richard's behavior toward his wife. They'd been friends for years, and Richard had never acted like that before. He'd convinced himself it was temporary lapse.

The boys stroked the horses' necks from the bottom rung of the corral fence.

"Peter likes to have him here." Rose put her arm around Clay. "Leave him with us. Clay's my favorite nephew, after all."

"Aw, I'm your only nephew," Clay said.

She mussed his hair. "That doesn't make you any less my favorite."

Samuel chuckled. He hoped she soon enjoyed a similar rapport with Peter. "Fine by us. How's Hazel?"

"A bit improved. I'd like to keep Polly here another week."

It wasn't a problem for Samuel, but he wasn't the one shouldering responsibility for her care. He quirked an eyebrow at Rose.

"I'd love that. She's no trouble." She glanced at the girls who sat on the top porch step while playing with their dolls. "The children entertain one another. I've been able to accomplish much this week."

Samuel couldn't argue with that—his wife had already worked wonders in his home. He'd given in to his urge to comfort her the other night—and hadn't wanted to let her go.

By Sunday services, Rose counted hosting Clay and Polly a blessing because their presence had allowed her stepchildren to grow accustomed to her gradually. The family sat with Richard, who seemed to feel uncomfortable around Samuel. Perhaps he was embarrassed.

She, for one, was glad to put it all behind her. One unexpected blessing from the ugliness was Samuel's protective attitude toward her. He asked for her opinions and seemed to consider her feelings more often in the last few days. He'd even embraced her. Things between them had definitely improved.

After church, Richard loaded up all the children to pick Hazel up for dinner at Rose's house.

After they watched them leave, Samuel placed Rose's hand on his arm. She basked in his attention amidst the crowded churchyard. Her lips froze in place when he stopped in front of a group of fashionably dressed women who hadn't attended the wedding. A cool nod had been their only greeting the previous week. Perhaps they didn't approve of Samuel's quick remarriage.

Rose's hand fell from his arm when he stepped forward.

"Mrs. Walton, how nice to see you," he said.

The dark-haired woman inclined her head.

"Thank you again for the wonderful meal you brought my

family." He turned back to Rose, drawing her into the circle that had closed when Samuel entered it. "Please allow me to introduce my wife. Rose, this is Mrs. Clara Walton, one of Ginny's friends." He smiled at each woman. "In fact, all these ladies were her particular friends. Mrs. Sophia Owens." He inclined his head at a woman wearing a flamboyant orange hat. Samuel gestured to the green-eyed beauty beside her. "Mrs. Lily Ann Black probably visited this spring as much as anyone, bringing cakes, pies, and bread." He sandwiched Mrs. Black's outstretched palm between his larger hands. "I hope you know how much my family appreciated those treats."

"Samuel, you know my love for baking." The stunning woman slanted her eyes up at him. An aquamarine dress emphasized light eyes against dark hair.

The ladies seemed to feel close friendship with Samuel.

"You look your old self today, Lily Ann. I'm happy to see your good spirits." Samuel patted her hand and then released it.

Lily Ann's smile dimmed.

Grief for Ginny? Or someone else?

Samuel swept an open palm toward a red-haired woman. "And this is Mrs. Augusta Carter. Richard works with her husband at Miami Paper Mills. Ladies, it's my pleasure to introduce my wife, Rose."

They chatted another five minutes, directing all comments to Samuel and sweeping glances at Rose's pink floral gingham.

"Oh, there's Charlie. If you ladies will excuse us?" Samuel offered his arm to Rose.

She took it, and they strolled toward the street where Charlie stood by himself.

Did everyone feel Samuel had married beneath himself? Her inexpensive frock didn't compare favorably to Ginny's stylish dresses. How Samuel agreed to such extravagance was a mystery when her purchase of cheap calico had so angered him.

"Those ladies began attending church two years ago and

flocked to Ginny immediately." Good memories took Samuel back to happier days. Ginny had felt a kinship with the women that made him like them all the more. "We dined at their homes on several occasions."

"Did Lily Ann grieve Ginny's death more than the others?"

"Possibly." His steps slowed. The two of them shared more than grief for Ginny. "Unfortunately, her husband passed last fall. Drowning accident. I admire her courage. Beautiful woman too. She won't have any trouble finding another husband when she's ready to remarry."

Rose's hand slid from his arm.

"Good morning, Charlie." They shook hands. His neighbor was almost like a father to him, and he was always happy to see him. "Care to have lunch with us?"

"Sure thing, and I thank you. Mornin', Rosie." Charlie sandwiched her hand in his work-roughened grasp. "That pink dress sure brings out the color in your cheeks. You look mighty pretty today."

"Agreed." Samuel studied her sweet expression. Why hadn't he noticed? "Very pretty."

"Thank you." She gave a playful curtsy.

"Charlie accepted my dinner invitation." Samuel nudged her arm.

"If it's agreeable with my new friend, Rosie." Charlie winked at her.

She laughed. "I'm delighted. My brother is bringing his family."

Charlie rubbed his hands together. "Spending time with the children will be a treat."

Samuel chuckled. "They're a lively bunch." And they all needed to put the week's unpleasantness behind them. They were family.

"Good. Maybe they can keep up with me."

"I hope *I* can." Samuel chuckled. Charlie was a lively

welcome addition to any gathering, in his opinion. The cheerful smile on Rose's face hinted at her agreement.

~

*T*he sight of Hazel laughing with the children dispelled Rose's guilt for the accident. Hazel's burn continued healing with manageable pain and no sign of infection. Rose was grateful to Charlie for sharing childhood memories with them over dinner, for it lightened the atmosphere between her husband and her brother.

That afternoon, the adults sat on the back porch to enjoy mild sunshine on the last Sunday in May.

Charlie tossed a ball with the boys. This led to a friendly baseball game with all the children that also included Samuel and Richard. The men ran bases with as much energy as the youngsters.

Rose couldn't keep her eyes from Samuel when he hit a ball into a row of foot-high cornstalks. He jogged the bases, giving the opposing team time to locate the baseball, and then laughed when his son tagged him out at home plate.

The lost look on Peter and Emma's faces disappeared under the camaraderie of the game. They needed these carefree moments.

Rose went inside to prepare cold drinks for everyone, leaving Hazel to enjoy the game.

The back door creaked open as she pumped cold water into a pitcher.

"Rosie?" Charlie said. "Can I come in?"

She wiped her hands on her apron. "Of course. Just preparing raspberry shrub. Everyone will soon be parched. I'll pour one for you."

"A cold drink is most welcome right about now." Charlie sank onto a wooden chair at the table. "Don't tell anyone, but

I'm not as young as I used to be." He placed a wide brimmed hat on the table in front of him. "I can't chase after these youngin's all day anymore."

Rose laughed. "I'll keep your secret." She filled two tumblers.

"I hope you don't mind me sticking my big nose into your business, but I saw your face during the conversation with them uppity women today."

She smiled, hoping her expression would mask her agitation.

"You looked like your feelings was hurt."

"A little." Rose gathered more glasses from the cupboard to avoid his eyes. "I feel inadequate. No one wants to allow a stranger in."

"You're no stranger to your husband." He mopped his brow with red print handkerchief.

She set a filled glass on the table in front of Charlie.

"From where I sit, Samuel made a wise choice."

Tears sprang to her eyes. She'd found a friend to champion her. "Thank you, Charlie."

He drank half the beverage in one long gulp. "Sweet and snappy, just like my Esther used to make, before the Good Lord took her home." He contemplated the scarlet liquid. "I never told you about her, did I?"

Rose shook her head, though she really wanted to discuss Ginny's friends.

"But that's a story for another day." The kind-hearted gentleman searched her eyes. "Ginny socialized with Lily Ann in particular. Women tend to watch out for their friends' families."

Rose carried a drink to the table and sat opposite of Charlie. It didn't seem likely she'd be close to Lily Ann or any woman at church except Hazel.

He held the glass between work-worn hands. "Maybe her friends don't like Samuel getting married so soon. I heard a few folks muttering about how he should have waited longer to marry."

"They'd be happier if I were like Ginny."

"Reckon so." Charlie grunted. "Samuel feels sorry for Lily Ann. The poor woman lost her husband and her friend within months. They suffered the same loss. That's bound to make him feel closer to her."

She tasted her sweet, tangy drink. Samuel's compassionate nature was one of the things she loved about him.

"Remember, Samuel chose *you*. Even when other women were available. There's a reason for that."

She looked out the open door to the yard beyond where her husband chased a ground ball back to the field while Richard ran to second base.

She knew the reason—to care for his children. Despite the rekindling of their former friendship, she'd best remember that fact.

CHAPTER 16

*S*amuel kept a watchful eye on Peter in the midst of changes in the next two weeks. The school session had ended and they had all four children most of the time. Clay's presence actually smoothed the transition for Peter with his new stepmother.

One hot afternoon, Samuel paused in weeding. He removed his hat to swipe his brow. How did weeds continue to thrive no matter the weather while good plants need nurturing?

He rested his chin on the long hoe handle and watched the children playing near the fenced cow pasture. Rose had taken them berry picking earlier, but it seemed they were finished with that. He'd been hard at it all day with barely a break at lunch and had only weeded four long rows.

"Pa." Peter ran between the rows with an empty bushel basket in his hands. "Do you want me and Clay to gather the weeds you dug up today?"

"That'd be a big help." Samuel grinned at the boys.

"Aunt Rosie's making blackberry cobbler for supper."

"Something to look forward to. We need rain. If this dry spell continues, I may ask you boys to help water the plants."

"I'll do it." Clay perked up. "I love working in the fields."

"You do?"

"Yep. I want to be a farmer like my new uncle."

"It's good, honest work." Samuel held out his dirt-covered palm. "You'll get calluses like these."

"Good. I want strong hands." Clay swiped his fingers over his uncle's palm. "Dusty, too."

"Yep." Samuel chuckled.

"It washes off." Peter brushed at dirt on his pa's sleeve.

Clay looked up with wide eyes. "Will you teach me how to be a farmer, Uncle Samuel?"

"Sure will." He liked the sound of that. If only Peter were as interested. "I'll teach you both. I'd appreciate the help." If this year's crop did well enough, he'd hire someone to work with him next year.

"Oh, boy." Clay grinned at Peter. "Let's get those weeds picked up."

Samuel laughed as the boys raced down the rows. What he wouldn't give for a smattering of their energy.

He surveyed what he'd accomplished in the past week. Small weeds grew again in the first few rows he'd finished. Better to nip them in the bud than start a new row.

Gray clouds on the horizon might hold rain. Samuel sure didn't want to have to tote water in June, when they usually had enough to make do. It was almost a sure thing in the dryer months of July and August.

Sighing, he whacked at another clump of weeds. Then he eyed his house.

Blackberry cobbler sounded mighty good right now.

~

"*S*amuel, are you done for the day?" Rose took a pan of cobbler from the oven and placed it on the work table. The sweet aroma was enough to make her hungry. Hopefully it would taste as delicious as it smelled.

"I'll work another two hours." He rubbed soap over his dusty hands and forearms. "I needed a cold drink. And I hoped for a bite of that cobbler."

"It's steaming under that crust."

"If you dip some up now, it will cool quickly." He rinsed his hands.

The request thrilled Rose. She liked pampering him.

"Eat with me." Grinning, Samuel selected two plates from the cupboard. "It will be our secret from the children."

"Don't you think they'll notice the missing slices?" Laughing, Rose dipped out the portions. "I'll make us some cold drinks."

"Blackberry shrub?" Peering at a Mason jar on the long table filled with purple liquid, he moved closer.

"It should be ready. I made it a week ago. Too much berry flavor?"

"Not for me. It's my favorite shrub."

Flustered at his nearness, she decided the next batch of berries wasn't bound for cobbler, jam, or jelly. No, blackberry shrub now topped her list.

～

"*I*finished this last night." Rose held up a yellow calico dress with white daisies as tall as her finger. "What do you think, Emma?"

The little girl's mouth opened but no words came. Morning sunlight shone on her blond hair as she reached for it.

Polly squealed. "Now you have your own play dress."

Emma hugged the garment to her chest.

"Wear it today." Polly grabbed her hand. The girls, still clad in their nightgowns, ran into Emma's room and closed the door.

That happy smile was thanks enough. Long nights of sewing had borne fruit.

Samuel was working in the fields with the boys, now a daily occurrence. The days had developed into a pattern. Rose could scarcely believe they'd been married almost a month.

Hazel's injuries continued to heal. Tonight, Richard planned to pick up the latest batch of clean clothes—and his children. As Rose slowly caught up on neglected tasks around her home, the extra work had ceased to burden her.

Her face heated to remember savoring blackberry cobbler alone with her husband the previous week. He'd acted like a boy stealing a cookie. Such a brief, precious time because quiet moments with him were rare with all the children running about. If he didn't work in the barn in the evenings, he erected a wall in the attic. Her lonely nights were spent sewing after the children went to bed. It didn't matter. There was plenty to occupy her hands.

Catherine brought her younger children over for a visit the following day.

Emma, wearing her new yellow calico, sat on the back porch with the women and watched three sisters, aged two, seven, and eight, squish mud pies. Peter climbed trees with the brothers. Zeb ran back and forth between both groups as if unwilling to miss any adventures.

"I'm happy summer finally got here." Catherine waved a fan in front of her face hard enough that Rose benefited from the breeze. "Though I ain't partial to real hot weather."

"Agreed." Rose's attention riveted to Emma. "Emma, don't you want to play?"

The girl looked over with miserable eyes.

"Go on over." When Emma didn't budge, Rose glanced at Catherine. "These children don't seem to know each other very well." She had witnessed too many schoolyard snubs not to sympathize.

"Me and Ginny didn't visit much. My boys know Peter from school, but Peter's younger than Zach by two years and older than Bart by the same amount. My two oldest boys went fishing with friends. Rennie's makin' blackberry pie instead of visitin'."

Emma clutched her doll as she stared at the redheaded sisters squatting beside a muddy patch. Rose, accustomed to Catherine's plain speaking, decided to be blunt. "Will you ask your daughters to include Emma? I believe she feels left out."

Catherine straightened. "Veronica." The oldest girl jerked her head toward the house. "Bring Candace and Bettina here." The girls ran over. "Ugh. Wash that mud off your hands first."

They rinsed their hands at the water pump and then returned. "Did you want something else, Mama?" Veronica flung droplets from her hands.

"Include Emma in your playing."

"She can't get dirty, remember?" Candace pointed to Emma's dress.

Rose raised her eyebrows. "Emma, you have permission to play."

Emma's face brightened.

"Come over here." Candace grabbed her hand, and they ran toward the barn. The girls climbed on the bottom row of the wooden fence surrounding the pigs.

Catherine laughed. "We ain't got no pigs. Candace thinks they're funny—wallowing around in the mud and grunting. We ain't farmers, but we have two cows and a few chickens." She glanced at Rose. "My husband, Trent, is a quiet one. Most folks wonder how we come to be married, but I'll tell you."

She looked at the children gathered at the pigpen, where

Emma chatted with Catherine's middle daughter. Rose couldn't keep their names straight yet.

"He was too bashful to ask me to wed so I did the asking." Catherine's voice dropped to a whisper. "I ain't never been the shy type."

Rose coughed to cover her laughter. "No, I don't expect so."

"I didn't see no sense in waitin'. He'd been comin' to my house for supper every Saturday evening for two years. Somebody had to speak up. He might still be eating my mama's suppers instead of mine if I hadn't taken the bull by the horns."

Rose burst into laughter. "I haven't seen you at church since our wedding. Want to walk with us tomorrow?"

"No, we attend a church that sits beside the river. That's another reason the children don't know each other too good. We been to your church for picnics and such." Late afternoon sun cast long shadows in the yard. Catherine stood. "I reckon I'd best gather my youngins and get home to cook supper."

"Please come back soon." Rose meant it. This was her first impromptu visit from a Hamilton neighbor. How pleasant to set chores aside for an hour.

Catherine nodded. "I will, now I know you ain't the uppity type. Bring your family over to see us too."

They disappeared behind the copse of trees that separated the two homes. Rose laughed again. One thing about her neighbor—she never left anyone in doubt of her opinions.

 ~

Samuel, standing alone in the shade of a maple tree in the crowded church yard, tapped on a letter in his pocket from Ginny's parents. It had been waiting at the post office for a few days when he stopped by after picking up Clay and Polly on Friday. It had been hectic ever since—at least that's the reason he tried to convince himself that he hadn't told Rose Mr. and Mrs. Sawyer were coming for a week's visit.

Right now, Rose was talking outside the church to Mrs. Bradshaw, the preacher's wife. It gave him a brief respite before breaking the bad news. The truth was, he dreaded seeing them. They hadn't come to the wedding to support his decision to marry. They were difficult to please, though their adored daughter never had any problems on that score.

Mr. Sawyer's letter stated that they wanted to see their precious grandchildren and meet Rose.

Samuel stifled a groan. Why hadn't the well-to-do couple given them all a little more time to adjust to one another before swooping down on them? This wouldn't be an easy week. He was certain of that.

His gaze swung to the children playing tag in the yard. Peter was always in the thick of things, and this time, Emma—who had insisted on wearing her new play dress—was too.

Rose, her cheeks flushed, looked his way. No putting off the bad news. He beckoned to her. He enjoyed the graceful way she skirted the few remaining small groups while strolling across the yard.

"Samuel, the most wonderful news."

"What is it?" He was glad for whatever put that happy spark in her eyes.

"Mrs. Bradford invited me to a quilting at her house this Thursday. I'm to bring a dish to share for lunch. Emma and Peter can come. They live there." She pointed to a red brick two-story home opposite the church and down the street. "The children play while we sew. I'll be home in plenty of time to cook supper."

"Ah, that's why your eyes are sparkling. The children will enjoy that, too, if they go." He rubbed his jaw. "I've put off telling you something."

"Yes?" She steeled herself.

He kicked a clump of dirt. "I've received a letter. Ginny's parents arrive tomorrow for a week's stay."

She gasped. "I wish you had told me. I need to clean, plan meals—"

"You're right. I'm sorry." The look in her eyes was akin to panic. "The letter came Friday and it's been hectic..." The excuse sounded ever more unacceptable when spoken.

"I imagine they want to meet me."

"Yes." He shoved his hands in his pockets. "You may as well know that they disapprove of our marrying so soon. They can be overbearing, but please be gracious for the children's sake." An unnecessary request. Rose was always gracious.

"Of course." Her hands twisted together.

"They usually sleep in the bedroom you occupy," he said. "I hope you won't mind giving up your bed for a few days." This was the real reason he'd hesitated, because they didn't often discuss their unusual sleeping arrangements.

She stilled. "Will I sleep in Emma's room?" She glanced at Emma, who talked with two little girls while Peter chased a frog.

"No." He swallowed, his Adam's apple bobbing. "Ginny and I slept in the attic room for their visits."

Rose caught her breath. "You mean..."

"The main dividing wall between rooms is finished." He maintained eye contact only for a moment. His ribs squeezed against his lungs. This mess was his fault. "There's not time to complete the wall to close off the rooms. I'll stay on one side of the wall and you'll stay on the other." His lips pressed together, waiting for a response. When she remained silent, he blew out a long breath. "I can bed down in the barn loft."

A becoming flush infused her cheeks. "What's your preference?"

"The attic." The Sawyers didn't miss anything. They'd discover the truth. While humiliating, it wouldn't change anything. He'd agreed to too many of their schemes over the years to appease Ginny. No more. "They won't make decisions for me, as they always tried to do for Ginny in our household."

Rose lifted her chin. "We'll make it work."

He nodded and strode across the yard to Emma.

A cloud hid the sun, giving him a sense of foreboding that this might be the hardest week of their short marriage.

CHAPTER 17

$\mathcal{A}$fter a restless night, Rose dragged herself up before dawn to launder her sheets and prepare the bedroom for the Sawyers' mid-afternoon train arrival.

She baked a pie while the children cleaned their rooms. Samuel worked in the fields until noon and then washed in the main bedroom. He emerged holding a brown coat to wear with matching trousers and a white shirt.

Rose hung her dresses on wall hooks in the room farthest from the staircase in the stifling attic. Good thing she'd only be up here to sleep. She leaned against the dividing wall and fanned her face.

The staircase creaked, and a moment later, Samuel stepped into the space. "It's only for a few days." He cranked the hall window to its widest opening.

Thank the Lord for that mercy. "We'll manage." A welcome breeze stirred wisps of hair.

"Wish I had time to build beds." His gaze swept over blankets on the floor. "Charlie must have a couple of cots to spare with all those grandchildren." Booted steps thudded toward the stairs.

"Samuel? Does Charlie know our...arrangement?" Her face flamed.

He halted. "No. Best it stays that way." He went downstairs without a backwards glance.

Rose flapped her hand over her face. This week promised to be awkward at best.

Disastrous at worst, considering who was visiting.

The house was ready by early afternoon. Samuel didn't have to meet the train since the Sawyers planned to rent a landau. He crossed and recrossed his legs while reading a newspaper—or trying to, anyway. He seemed as nervous as Rose.

Emma, unusually quiet, wore a frilly pink dress. Rose coaxed a few responses from her while braiding her hair. She tied matching ribbons to the ends. Even Peter changed his blue plaid shirt for a plain white cotton shirt and wet his hair into place.

The children weren't excited about their grandparents' visit —or, if they were, anxiety seemed uppermost. Why? Samuel hinted the couple were difficult to please. Did Peter and Emma feel the same?

Rose had best be on her guard. Everything must be perfect, which it wasn't. She studied dingy white ruffled curtains in the main room. She'd been too busy to wash them. Perhaps Mrs. Sawyer wouldn't notice.

The lingering aroma of baked apple pie mixed with the smell of freshly roasted coffee beans gave her an appetite. She took one last glance around the room as a landau stopped in front of their home. Everything was in its place.

Samuel raised his eyebrows at his children, whose straight backs resembled soldiers standing at attention, and then opened the door.

Mrs. Sawyer swept inside.

Rose met her hard gaze, and her heart sank. The stylish woman wore a high-waisted, full-skirted black dress. She was beautiful, even with gray streaks in her blond hair. What wasn't attractive was the distasteful glance she directed at Rose's blue gingham dress.

She smiled at the children. "My precious lambs, come kiss Grandmother."

Emma dropped her doll and kissed Mrs. Sawyer's cheek before bending to retrieve it. Peter gave her a peck on the cheek.

Mr. Sawyer, dressed in a black coat with an arm band to signify his mourning, stood in the doorway. He searched Rose's face without meeting her gaze. His lip curled. Then, the gray-haired gentleman greeted the children with a smile.

Mrs. Sawyer turned her face as Samuel bent to greet her. "Mother, how nice to see you again." He kissed her cheek.

"Samuel." Her gaze turned frosty. "I trust we find everyone in good health?"

"Very well, thank you." He shook Mr. Sawyer's hand. "I hope your trip was without mishap, sir."

"Tolerable." Tapping an ivory-handled cane, the tall man inclined his head. "I presume this is…Rose?"

She adjusted her skirt. Why must she be so unlike the flower she was named for?

Samuel drew her into the group. "You may remember Rose Hatfield."

Hatfield? Her shock must have shown in her expression, but Samuel hurried on.

"I meant Rose Walker. Hatfield is her maiden name." His face darkened at Mrs. Sawyer's glare. "My wife."

The atmosphere turned even chillier. Rose forced her lips into a smile. "You may not remember me. We met several years ago in Harrison."

"How do you do?" Mrs. Sawyer's pale blue eyes offered no acknowledgement of the prior acquaintance.

"Very well, thank you." Heat spread up the back of her neck. Baffled by their aloof behavior, she looked at her husband.

He gave a slight shake of his head. Apparently, this was no

surprise to him. He could have warned her they'd be so rude. "I'll fetch your bags." He gestured for the children to follow him and Mr. Sawyer outside.

You're leaving me? The steps creaked, taking her last support out the door. "May I serve you coffee? Or tea?" Rose wiped moisture from her forehead.

"I prefer tea. No sugar." Mrs. Sawyer sat at the table facing the front door, her back to the kitchen.

"Tea is also my preference." Rose filled the kettle and put it on the stove. The knots in her stomach gave her second thoughts about the beverage.

"So, you're the woman who couldn't wait to get her hands on Samuel."

Rose swiveled to Mrs. Sawyer's rigid back. "Pardon me?"

Mrs. Sawyer turned and gave her a scathing stare. "My daughter has scarcely been buried four months, but she's already been replaced. What am I to think?"

Rose clutched the edge of the stove. "You don't understand. Samuel—"

"Let's take these into the bedroom." Samuel stepped inside carrying a trunk on his shoulder. He quirked an eyebrow at Rose. "I'll see to the horses after that."

Mrs. Sawyer stood and followed them into the bedroom, leaving Rose at the stove feeling emotionally battered. What had just happened? Did the Sawyers really have such a low opinion of her?

The sound of paper ripping drew her to the open bedroom doorway.

Surrounded by remnants of brown packaging paper, Samuel held a painting in his hands.

"A fitting remembrance of your wedding day." Mr. Sawyer beamed. "We commissioned an artist to paint this portrait from a photograph. It was the happiest day of your life."

Rose stared at the two-foot by three-foot canvas. Ginny

radiated joy in her white wedding gown, the lacy bodice matching the veil shimmering against her perfect blond ringlets. Samuel stood with his arm around her, wearing a black formal suit and a proud smile.

He'd been filled with joy the day he married Ginny. The bride's face was just as blissful. They had loved each other.

There had been no photograph to commemorate *her* wedding, much less a portrait.

The children crowded beside him, and he lowered the canvas to their level.

Emma traced the curve of her mother's face with her tiny finger. "Ma."

"Yes, that's Ma." Samuel ripped the remaining brown paper from the bottom edge.

Peter grasped the ornate gold frame. "Ma's pretty."

Mrs. Sawyer put her hand on his shoulder. "No one has ever been more beautiful." Her eyes misted.

Rose was certain Samuel agreed. She turned from the door. With shaking hands, she somehow managed to fill a teacup.

The children's exclamations of wonder were only rivaled by Samuel's effusive thanks, which carried out the doorway to echo through the house.

A discussion ensued about the best place for it. Mrs. Sawyer insisted on hanging it on the wall as the focal point in the main room.

Samuel left to get his tools, and then the children watched him hang the portrait.

No one consulted Rose.

Perhaps this gift intended to bless the mourners, but Rose had no doubt it was also meant to hurt her, the woman who'd taken her daughter's place, as Mrs. Sawyer had so bluntly put it.

With such a start, what was coming next?

∼

*M*rs. Sawyer turned up her nose at supper's crispy fried chicken. She accepted a biscuit when Samuel passed the bread basket and helped herself to mashed potatoes but refused everything else. Neither she nor Mr. Sawyer complimented any dish.

This was her best meal, and it wasn't good enough. Never mind that, even if it hadn't tasted good—and it had—only the rudest guests would refuse to even try it.

Peter and Emma turned often in their seat to study the new painting, bringing smiles to their grandparents' faces.

Mrs. Sawyer spoke almost exclusively to the children, who fidgeted, perhaps unused to such devoted attention.

Mr. Sawyer engaged Samuel about the crop.

Neither guest addressed comments to Rose, and it seemed Samuel and the children had forgotten she was there.

After their one disastrous interaction that afternoon, Ginny's mother had ignored her completely. Rose didn't know how to correct the woman's mistaken assumption. Then again, what could she say when Samuel insisted on keeping the details of their marriage private?

She prepared another cup of tea for Mrs. Sawyer, who'd barely glanced her way as she'd slid the empty cup across the table after supper before joining Emma on the sofa.

Samuel and Peter changed into comfortable clothes while Mr. Sawyer smoked a pipe on the back porch. The two men and the boy left for the barn as soon as Samuel emerged from the attic.

Mrs. Sawyer told Emma all the fun activities she'd planned for the week.

Rose sipped her own tea at the table and waited for the older woman to include her in shopping plans. In vain. After a few minutes, she and her granddaughter entered the little girl's room.

Rose scraped the dishes rather harder than necessary. No one offered to help. She was being treated more like a house-keeper than a wife.

The last dish was stacked in the cupboard when Mrs. Sawyer stalked out of Emma's room with the yellow dress in her hands. "What is this garment?" She shook the dress.

Emma, a few steps behind, stuck her finger in her mouth.

Rose, puzzled by the child's distress, bit her lip. "Emma's new dress."

"Where did she obtain it?"

Emma flinched.

The child's misery stoked Rose's anger. There was no reason to upset Emma.

"Answer my question."

The little girl buried her face in her hands.

"From me." Lifting her chin, Rose met Mrs. Sawyer's eyes squarely. "I made her a play dress."

Before Mrs. Sawyer could respond, Samuel carried in a pail of milk. The others followed him into the kitchen.

Meeting his anxious gaze, Rose indicated Emma with a slight nod.

Samuel set the bucket on the table before picking up his cowering daughter. She nestled against his shoulder, her arms clinging to his neck. "Is everything all right here?" Samuel's glance darted between the women.

"Of course, son. We're discussing Emma's clothing." Her tone cooled. "I understand she requires a dress to play in. I'll happily take my grandchildren on a shopping expedition tomorrow."

"That won't be necessary, Mother. Rose graciously offered—"

"My dear, I'm sure she has, but we simply cannot inconvenience her." Her thin smile didn't brighten her eyes.

Rose said, "It's no trouble."

"You'd not deny me the pleasure of purchasing a few trinkets." Her voice broke. "I have so little left. My grandchildren are my only joy in life."

The truth silenced Rose, cooling her anger. She was no stranger to grief either.

"Thank you, Mother." Samuel rubbed Emma's back. "It's very generous."

Her eyes took on a feverish hue. "Now, children, we'll make a day of it tomorrow. Grandfather and I will treat you to dinner. You can order anything you want from the menu."

Peter's face brightened.

Emma released her grip on her father to stare at her grandmother.

"We shall have such fun together. It will almost be like our shopping expeditions with your moth—" She raised a lacy handkerchief to tear-filled eyes. The proud woman dissolved into broken-hearted sobs.

Rose's jaw slackened. No longer haughty, Mrs. Sawyer was simply a mother grieving the premature loss of her child. Rose moved to comfort her, but Mr. Sawyer reached her first. He enfolded his wife in his arms.

Emma sobbed against her father's shoulder.

Peter stared at the portrait of his parents.

Samuel drew Peter to his side with his free arm. He closed his eyes as he rested his head against Emma's. The grandmother's tragic tears had smashed the family's thin armor.

Rose was the outsider.

She stumbled out the back door.

CHAPTER 18

*S*amuel led his children into Emma's room. For the first time, he encouraged his children to talk about how they missed their mother. The painting evoked deep-seated sorrow and reminded everyone of the loss that lingered always just beneath the surface.

Emma's tears broke his heart as his little girl reminisced about Ginny and considered all the things that were different now that she was gone. Samuel rocked her back and forth with a hand on Peter's shoulder.

When her words were finally spent, Samuel helped his daughter into her nightgown and then held her hand until she fell asleep. Afterward, he sat at Peter's bedside and listened to his son pour out his sorrow.

Rose's presence hadn't helped as much as Samuel had hoped. He must take a greater role to ensure their healing. From now on, he'd insist they turn to him for everything. They must be free to express their feelings to someone who understood their pain. Rose could never fill that role.

Reflecting that his former in-law's visit had already reaped unexpected benefits, he left his son's room. He hadn't felt this close to his children since the funeral. Shared grief bound them together.

"How are my precious children?"

Olivia Sawyer's feeble tone of a broken woman aroused Samuel's deepest sympathy. She and her husband sat at the table with empty cups in front of them.

"Calmer. Emma's sleeping. Worn out from crying. Peter will soon be asleep." He searched the shadowy room. Why hadn't his wife lit the lamps? "Where's Rose?"

"She ran off while the children cried for their mother." Solomon Sawyer retrieved a pipe and tobacco pouch from his pocket.

That didn't sound like Rose. Samuel decided to ignore the derisive tone. He lit four lanterns and carried one upstairs. The attic was as black as midnight. He knocked on the inside wall partition. "Rose, are you awake?"

No answer. Flickering flames revealed an empty room.

She must be outside. He scanned the pale pink horizon from the window, remembering how she enjoyed strolling along the field in the evening.

He returned downstairs and headed for the back door. "I'll fetch her. Feel free to go to bed if I tarry too long."

Solomon frowned.

For once, Samuel ignored his disapproval. They could entertain themselves.

Rose wasn't in the barn. He headed toward the crops, hoping Zeb was with her.

A niggling of concern expanded into worry. He'd spent two hours with his children. Two hours was a long time to be absent.

An owl hooted while the crickets carried on a constant hum. He scanned rows of waist-high cornstalks as he strode along the field. Nothing. He picked up speed past the cow pasture, where he'd hoped to find her leaning against the fence, as she had last week when they'd strolled with the children at dusk.

In the apple orchard, lightning bugs illuminated the young saplings. Was that her dress?

Yes, a welcome patch of blue. Each footstep closer turned relief to anger. He had enough to do—like comforting his children and entertaining guests—without searching for her. She had no right to wrench his attention from Ginny's parents on their first evening there.

"Where have you been?" he hissed.

Rose sat with her back against a tree, shredding blades of grass. Zeb nestled against her, tail flopping on the ground. "Your family needed time alone."

"Solitude is one thing. Not knowing where you'd gone is quite another." He barked the words.

She didn't look up or defend herself or respond in any way.

Taking a deep breath, he set the lantern on the grass. "Didn't you notice the darkness?"

She rose slowly, her right hand pressed against the trunk. "I did."

"You should have entertained our guests while I calmed the children." Didn't she realize how difficult the older couple were to please?

Rose raised her palms. "They didn't want me there."

"They made their own coffee." He clenched his jaw. "Since you weren't there to do it."

"She prefers tea."

Clipped words fed his ire. "Then make tea." He crossed his arms. "Regardless of what she's drinking, she made it *herself*. Ginny never allowed them to lift a finger here. She even—"

"I'm not Ginny. I am not perfect." Rose tilted her chin. "I don't cook like her. I don't act like her. I don't look like her."

His fury boiled over. "Well, pardon me for missing my wife of almost nine years." How could she act so selfishly? "Pardon my children for grieving the loss of their *mother*. You know something about losing a mother, don't you?"

"How dare you." She stepped closer, her narrowed gaze capturing his.

"I'm sorry. That was uncalled for, but someone must awaken you to your obligations. The Sawyers altered their plans to meet you."

She folded her arms. "Did they? For a couple who convinced you they wanted to meet me, they've certainly hidden their interest well."

"Can't you understand?" He studied her mutinous expression. "Grief overwhelms them. They adored Ginny."

"That's abundantly clear."

"Please help me make this a pleasant visit. I'll work as little as possible, but neglecting my crops for a week isn't feasible. You must entertain them, be a gracious hostess."

"They don't wish to talk with me." She looked away. "Ginny's father hasn't said one word to me. And Mrs. Sawyer..." Her voice trailed off.

"No one understands better than me how thorny they are. Please show some compassion. They lost their daughter four months ago. Their only daughter."

She stared out over the crops in the growing darkness.

"They need sympathy, not criticism. If you'd been at the funeral"—images of them on their knees at the grave, weeping brokenheartedly in the cold—"you'd feel differently."

"Catherine mentioned their inconsolable grief." Rose brought a shaky hand to her forehead. "I'll keep that in mind."

"Thank you for your patience. I think it will make things run smoother." With any luck, the Sawyers had retired by now. He didn't want another emotional conversation that evening.

*T*he following afternoon, Samuel splashed cold water from the outdoor pump on his hands and arms at the end of a full day's work. The sound of wheels warned of the landau's approach. Brown-paper packages covered the seat beside Emma. His sweet daughter's wave was as welcome as her smile. He greeted them all and then watered the horses and gave them a good rubdown before entering the house, where the purchases were displayed on the table in front of his children and the Sawyers.

"Look, Pa." Emma tugged on his hand. "Grandmother bought me dresses to play in. They don't have any ruffles or lace."

"Very pretty." Samuel admired the pastel dresses, raising his eyebrows as he fingered the expensive fabric. The ready-made clothes might not have frills, but the Sawyers still paid for quality. He smiled at his daughter's glowing face. "Did you choose them?"

Emma nodded. "Grandmother and me picked them out—at three different shops. I got five dresses. Grandfather said I could have all I wanted."

"Look what Grandfather bought me." Peter held up a red drum about half the height of a milk bucket and twice the diameter. He plunked on it with two wooden sticks. "Clay will like it too."

Samuel examined the instrument. "A fine drum. Did you get clothes?"

Peter's gaze fell away. "On my bed. Grandmother picked them out."

"I'm certain you thanked them for their generosity." He gave his son a warning look.

He tried not to mind the amount of money Ginny's parents spent as Peter and Emma thanked their grandparents. Mr. Sawyer's job as a lawyer provided a more than adequate income. In Columbus, he'd built quite a reputation for his tough approach. Ginny had often laughingly remarked that her parents could afford to splurge.

"Pa, my new doll has red hair and brown eyes." Emma straightened a bow in the doll's hair, which matched the pale blue dress. "Isn't she pretty?"

"Very pretty." Samuel tugged Emma's braid.

"I named her Betsy. She needs to meet my other doll, Sarah." She ran into her bedroom with the doll, leaving the clothes behind.

Peter disappeared into his room. Drumbeats resumed.

Where was Rose? No tantalizing aromas emanated from the oven. No kettles of food simmered on the stove. It was time for supper. He hadn't seen her all day, choosing to munch a sandwich in the field. He'd avoided private conversations after last evening's silent walk back to the house. Thankfully, the Sawyers had already retired. He had mucked stalls to give Rose time alone. The lantern was out on her side of the attic an hour later when he climbed the stairs.

"Not here." Mr. Sawyer rubbed his mouth. "Emma wanted to show her the purchases while we waited for you. She searched upstairs."

"Your wife has a deplorable habit of disappearing." Mrs. Sawyer's lips thinned. "One hopes this behavior will not continue."

"Actually, until last evening, she'd never done that, and she explained that she left so we could have time together." Samuel ran a finger under his collar. Supper had always been on the stove when he came in from a full day's work. She didn't mention plans to walk to Hazel's and wasn't friendly enough with other women for an unplanned visit.

He was headed for the front door when Rose opened it and stepped in, her expressive eyes anxious. She closed the door and leaned against it. "I'm sorry supper isn't ready. I visited Catherine this afternoon."

"You were with Catherine all this time?"

"Well, no. Charlie was sitting on his front porch when I passed his house. I walked with him to his fields and listened to family stories." Her cheeks flushed. "I didn't notice the passing time."

"You were with another *man?*" Mrs. Sawyer's face blanched.

Crimson infused Rose's cheeks.

Before she could speak, Samuel said, "Charlie's our neighbor across the street. His wife died a few years after all their children married and left home. He's a good friend."

Mrs. Sawyer's brow furrowed as if unconvinced.

"I'll have supper ready shortly." Rose gathered the discarded dresses and carried them into Emma's room.

Mrs. Sawyer perched on the sofa.

Mr. Sawyer went into his bedroom and came out without his suit coat. He'd transferred his arm band to his shirt. The pattern on his fancy gray vest over a white shirt and string tie gave him an air of success and authority. He lounged on a cushioned armchair. "Peter talks about Clay as much as Emma does about Polly. The new cousins?"

"Yes." Samuel sank into the other armchair, flexing sore fingers. He had taken advantage of his guests' absence and weeded all day. "The children have grown closer since the wedding."

Mrs. Sawyer pursed her lips.

Rose emerged from Emma's room. "Anyone care for a glass of cold lemonade?"

"Yes, thank you, Rose," Samuel said. "Mother? Sir, how about a cold drink?"

Mrs. Sawyer nodded.

"I'm parched, my boy. I believe I will have a glass."

They sat at the table to enjoy the refreshing drink, which Rose had retrieved from the root cellar.

Mr. Sawyer rubbed his index finger idly over condensation on the glass. "I'd like to meet Richard and his family."

A brilliant idea. Why hadn't he thought of it? "I'll drive over this evening to extend a supper invitation for tomorrow evening."

Mr. Sawyer held up his hand, palm forward. "No need to put extra work on Rose. We don't want to tax her unduly. You will be our guests for a meal."

"Thank you, sir." He remembered many meals at local hotels and restaurants when Ginny was alive. In fact, the Sawyers generally took them out for supper every evening when in town. Cooking hadn't been Ginny's favorite activity, though she'd enjoyed baking. "We'd enjoy that very much, wouldn't we, Rose?"

"Sounds lovely." She removed a skillet from a wall peg. "I'm sure Richard and Hazel will accept."

"That's settled then." Mr. Sawyer drained his glass. "We'll ride to the Hatfield home after supper."

"In that case, I'll bring the cows in from pasture and milk them now." Samuel gulped down his drink.

"I'll stroll with you, son." Mr. Sawyer stood.

"I'll lie down. Shopping exhausted me." Mrs. Sawyer disappeared into the master bedroom and closed the door.

Samuel was thankful that the women would be separated. "Rose, we'll return shortly."

She nodded, tendrils of hair escaping the bun to frame her pretty face. "Dinner will be ready." She tossed kindling into the stove.

Her light brown print dress brought out the color of her eyes while enhancing the shine of her dark blond hair. It occurred to him that she wasn't merely pretty. Her beauty didn't hit him in the face like Ginny's had. It was subtler. He wondered how he had missed it.

"Ready, Samuel?" Mr. Sawyer asked.

He shook his head to clear it, and then realized that he just indicated a negative reply. "Right behind you."

He stole another glance at his beautiful wife from the open doorway. She didn't look up as she arranged sausage in a skillet.

CHAPTER 19

a t least Rose's guests sampled the food this time, even if they picked over it as if it might be poisoned.

"I must admit I've never eaten biscuits and gravy in the same meal as apple pie." Mrs. Sawyer's lips twitched.

Peter's head jerked up. "Me, neither."

Rose rolled her eyes heavenward. Must Mrs. Sawyer feed Peter's dissatisfaction with her?

"I enjoyed the meal." Samuel gave his son a stern look.

Rose stabbed her dessert. Why didn't her husband direct a silencing gaze at Mrs. Sawyer?

"I believe this recipe uses more cinnamon than my Ginny's pie." Olivia Sawyer placed a hand to her throat. "Hers knew no equal."

"I agree, Livie." Mr. Sawyer patted the corners of his mouth with a white napkin. "No one baked like our little girl."

"I'm certain your cooking will improve with practice, my dear." Mrs. Sawyer's thin lips curved upward.

Peter snorted. "This ain't as good as my Ma's."

"Peter, that's enough." Samuel stared at his son. "Rose, *everything* tastes delicious."

"Thank you." He'd actually championed her? She was more shocked than pleased, considering he didn't defend her to his former in-laws. She had returned from pleasant visits with Catherine and Charlie to her family so they could ridicule her cooking. It was difficult to respect poor manners. "More coffee, Mr. Sawyer?"

He shook his head, barely glancing her way, as if she'd interrupted him. "Samuel, recall that we planned to visit the Hatfields."

Samuel glanced at Rose. "I'll help you clean the dishes so you can join us."

Before Rose could respond, Mr. Samuel said, "It'd be rude to drop in unexpectedly too late in the evening."

"True." Rose agreed, but doubted the Sawyers truly worried about rude behavior. She stared at her empty plate. There'd be no family visit for her—and she could use their support right now.

Samuel pinched his lower lip. "The sun will set soon."

"It's fine." No, it wasn't, but she could be gracious even if their guests didn't reciprocate.

Playing the courteous hostess grew increasingly taxing. At least no one would complain about tomorrow's supper.

$\sim$

*R*ose watched her brother study the elegant restaurant selected by the Sawyers. Richard seemed as impressed as she by the stylish atmosphere, where the tables were decorated with white linen tablecloths and napkins, red brocade curtains decorated the windows, and a courteous waiter rushed to fulfill Mr. Sawyer's slightest wish.

Polly stared openmouthed at the fashionable dresses of other diners.

Clay's attention was caught by ornately designed arches and gleaming cherry furniture.

Hazel smiled at Rose across the spacious round table. They'd had no opportunity for private conversation, but Rose guessed that Hazel had picked up on her discomfort. Richard sat between Hazel and Mr. Sawyer, who expressed a keen interest in his job. Mrs. Sawyer monopolized Samuel's attention on his right.

Each course was leisurely served. Conversation flowed naturally. Rose figured no one noticed that the Sawyers hadn't spoken to her since meeting Richard's family outside the restaurant.

She enjoyed a respite from cooking and savored every bite of her roasted chicken. She entertained herself by trying to identify the unfamiliar blend of seasonings.

"Samuel, how lovely to see you here." Lily Ann Black, more fashionably dressed than was the woman's custom for church, stood at his side.

"Lily Ann." He stood with a smile. "An unexpected pleasure. Have you met Ginny's parents?"

The men stood for the introductions. The Sawyers seemed thrilled to learn of her friendship with their daughter.

"I'm devastated we're so far into our meal. I would have enjoyed your company at supper." Mr. Sawyer sandwiched Lily Ann's hand between his. "Any friend of my daughter's is a friend of mine."

Rose lifted her eyebrows. *She* had been a friend of Ginny's. They didn't like *her*.

Lily Ann gave a tinkling laugh. "I'm dining with my dear friend, Mrs. Augusta Carter, but I'd be delighted to become better acquainted."

"We won't leave for a few days. May we persuade you and your husband to join us for supper tomorrow night?"

Lily Ann's smile faltered. "Regrettably, Mr. Black passed last fall."

Samuel patted her hand. "Ginny and Lily Ann became inseparable after that."

Mrs. Sawyer stared at Samuel's hand until he released Lily Ann's. "Our condolences."

"Thank you," the younger woman said.

"It will be our pleasure to host you and Mrs. Carter." Mrs. Sawyer tilted her head.

Lily Ann cast a brilliant smile at Mr. Sawyer. "May I amend the invitation slightly?"

He held up his hands with a mystified expression.

"Please come to my home for supper tomorrow evening." Her glance swept the table. "All are welcome. I'm hosting a few friends who also knew Ginny."

"How delightful," Mrs. Sawyer said. "Samuel, do you know where Mrs. Black resides?"

"Yes, Mother, we dined there several times."

Lily Ann clasped his arm. "I also miss those occasions."

Rose stiffened. Samuel had referred to himself and Ginny.

Lily Ann turned back to the Sawyers. "You must all call me Lily Ann. I absolutely insist upon it."

"Thank you, my dear," Mr. Sawyer said. "You may address us as Solomon and Olivia."

Had Mr. Sawyer treated Rose with the same grace, their visit would have been a joy rather than a chore.

"Can we bring anything for the meal?" Rose received few meal invitations where she didn't provide a portion of the food.

Samuel placed a hand on her shoulder.

Rose enjoyed the gentle touch of his hand until she realized the adults gaped at her as if she'd offered to bring her pet pig.

Lily Ann's tinkling laughter mocked her. "No, my dear. How quaint you are. My cook will provide everything."

Heat infused Rose's neck. She should have guessed that the

woman could bear the expense. "Thank you for your kind invitation. My family is pleased to accept."

"I look forward to seeing everyone there." She set arrival times and then rejoined Augusta Carter at their table on the other side of the room.

The Sawyers praised the delightful Lily Ann and peppered Samuel with questions about her.

Rose fought the depression descending over her. It seemed her husband had belonged in restaurants such as this one. He and Ginny had dined often with wealthy friends. As for Rose, she felt uncomfortable in such elegant surroundings. She tried to focus on the advantages of the invitation, for it shifted the responsibility of entertaining the Sawyers to Lily Ann's shoulders—a very good thing.

That night, as she lay in her makeshift bed awaiting Samuel's footsteps on the stairs, she tried to forgive the Sawyers' attempts to belittle her. She reminded herself of their suffering.

However, it was difficult to respect them as guests when they treated her like a servant.

A stair creaked. A beacon of light appeared around the corner of the wall, casting shadows on the attic wall. A boot struck the floor. Clothing rustled. Then the light extinguished.

All was silent except the crickets.

Sharing the attic with Samuel made her long for a closer relationship. A look in his eyes sometimes expressed appreciation for her efforts. She'd encountered his thoughtful stares this week. Maybe someday, he'd fall in love with her.

His even breathing told her he'd fallen to sleep already. Anxiety over Lily Ann's party kept Rose awake. She feared embarrassing her husband at her first fancy dinner party. She hoped her one elegant dress would enable her to hold her head high.

She finally fell into a troubled sleep, filled with disturbing dreams.

CHAPTER 20

*G*inny, breathtaking in Rose's blue wedding gown, floated *from guest to guest, each one more elegantly dressed than the last. The charming hostess's tinkling laughter lifted the spirits of everyone in the room, with one exception.*

Rose, in her green calico print, cowered from censorious eyes in the corner. Hiding wasn't difficult. Fleeting glances evaluated the cost of her dress and quickly dismissed her.

Ginny's home had been transformed into an opulent mansion where Rose didn't belong. Tears caked her throat when Samuel crossed the room to grasp Ginny's outstretched hand. He kissed her cheek and smiled into her eyes before greeting their next guest.

"Rose, wake up."

She opened her eyes to see Samuel kneeling at her side.

Sunlight poured into the room. Her dream faded slowly, but the memories haunted her—Samuel so loving and affectionate to Ginny.

Reality returned with a bang of a drum. Sitting abruptly, she smacked her forehead against his face. "I'm sorry." She caressed his cheek. "Did I hurt you?"

He backed up and gazed at her, and her heart thundered at

the intensity of it. She cupped his cleanly-shaven face, his mouth inches from hers.

His gaze fell to her lips. Shamelessly she leaned closer, inviting his embrace.

"No." He stood but continued to gaze at her. "I'm not hurt."

Her breath hitched at the longing in his eyes. The atmosphere charged.

"Sorry I had to barge in on you." His husky tone held an emotion she couldn't identify. "It's late. I've already cared for the animals, thinking you were preparing breakfast. Mother made coffee. Are you feeling poorly?"

The tempting aroma of freshly roasted coffee wafted upstairs. And how had she slept through that pounding drum? "Sorry. I barely slept." She pushed back the blanket. Her floor-length white nightgown shifted above her knees, exposing bare legs. Cheeks flaming, she snatched the blanket to her chest. "I'll be down."

Samuel's face turned the color of beets. Lips clamped shut, he strode from the room.

Rose had finally captured her husband's attention. For a moment, she'd thought maybe she saw something in his eyes, something akin to love. She'd felt it so strongly, she'd leaned in.

And he rejected her. Hurt battled disappointment—and won. It was too soon.

As her husband, he had the right to kiss her. Apparently, he only lacked the slightest inclination to do so.

Her cheeks flamed at his rejection. She tucked her love away...again

～

The Sawyers left with their grandchildren after breakfast. Grateful for the empty house, Rose prepared a peach cobbler to bake in Mrs. Bradshaw's oven.

Hurrying to the fields, she stepped between thriving rows of green beans toward Samuel. "Mrs. Bradshaw's quilting is today. The children are shopping with their grandparents."

"Again? What else can they buy?" Samuel hacked at a weed with the long-handled hoe.

Sun blazed into her face. Rose squinted in the light and tugged at her bonnet. "A party dress for Emma."

His laugh sounded hollow. "Like she needs another one." Pushing back his hat, he wiped his brow with a handkerchief.

"There's a ham sandwich for your lunch in the icebox. I'll return by mid-afternoon."

"Enjoy yourself." Samuel chopped another weed.

Friendly laughter from inside the Bradshaw home soon welcomed her.

"No need to knock." Beyond the open door, Mrs. Bradshaw beckoned her inside from a table that dominated the front room. Five women sat around a colorful quilt covering the table with her. "We almost gave up on you."

"I apologize." Setting her basket on the table, she pulled out the pan on top. "Is your oven heated to bake this cobbler?"

"Yes." Mrs. Bradshaw waved her hand toward the back of the home. "Millicent's roasted pork is in the warming oven. Hurry back and I'll introduce everyone."

Rose carried her sewing basket to the table within moments.

"Now, my dear, you must call me Pauline." Mrs. Bradshaw stuck her needle in a patch of fabric. "On my right is Millicent Hedrick."

The gray-haired woman peered at Rose over her spectacles.

"She's lived in Hamilton since childhood. And next to her is Helen Rhineheimer."

Helen's loose clothing didn't mask her protruding stomach. The dark-haired woman smiled warmly.

"She expects a blessed event in August. With six sons already, we're hoping for a girl this time. And Jane is our youngest member." Pauline indicated a sedately-dressed blonde. "How old are you, Rose?"

Well-acquainted with Pauline's blunt manner, she didn't mind the question. "Twenty-six." Rose threaded her needle with sweaty palms.

Pauline shook her head. "Jane's still youngest at twenty-one. Married last fall. And Mary is our oldest member."

The old woman chuckled. "I'm certain she could tell that, Pauline." Her white-haired bun brushed against the collar of her faded dress. "Pleasure to meet you."

Rose liked the twinkle in Mary's eyes.

"And sitting beside you is Cassandra Bauer."

Rose envied the peaches-and-cream complexion of the auburn-haired woman on her right. "No children. She's been married better than five years."

Cassandra forced a smile before jabbing a needle into a brown quilt square.

"I'm pleased to make your acquaintances. Thanks for the invitation." She spoke quickly, hoping to ease Cassandra's frustration.

"What are you working on?" Mary peered at the pink fabric in Rose's hands.

"A play dress for Emma." She stitched a side seam.

"Where are your children?" Millicent gave Rose's handiwork a critical glance.

"With their grandparents, who are here for a week's visit."

"Ah." Pauline tilted her head. "Ginny's parents."

Rose gave a crisp nod.

"Ginny was a beautiful woman." Mary held her cloth up to the sunlight pouring through the open window and studied the seams. "Everyone loved her."

"I hated what happened to her. In the prime of life, too." Millicent shook her head.

Helen stared out the window. "She made you feel special, like you were her closest friend."

"I still can't believe she's gone." Jane shook her head sadly.

"You're not like her, are you?" Millicent studied Rose over the top of her spectacles.

"Not at all." Rose did her best to keep hurt out of her voice. These women, even on an initial meeting, noticed her failings.

"Remember canning apples at her house, Jane?" Helen smiled as she drew blue thread through a quilting square.

"It felt like a party." Jane laughed.

"How kind of you to help." Apparently, Ginny had a way of making work enjoyable.

"It was fun." Cassandra's humiliated flush had finally receded. "We went every Saturday in August one year."

"If we miss her," Mary sighed, "imagine how those poor children feel."

And Samuel. Rose bent over her sewing. How did one compete with a woman so deeply loved?

❧

*B*right sunlight beat down on Samuel that afternoon. He had taken a quick break to eat lunch and now weeded, a relentless job.

Though he didn't enjoy fancy dinners overmuch, he was glad Lily Ann had invited the whole family to one this evening, shifting the burden of entertaining Ginny's parents off him and Rose.

And it *was* a burden. He could admit it to himself if he'd never voice the words. Ginny's absence while they were here only brought her death to the forefront of everyone's minds.

Rose had fallen into the routine of the home, and that somehow eased the oppressive atmosphere that had entered after Ginny died.

The Sawyers had noticed how Rose added to the home's comfort and they didn't like it. Had told him so. They took every opportunity to remind him and the children of all they'd lost, comments that were difficult to battle without causing more turmoil. The strain was beginning to show in Peter especially. He'd begun finding fault with Rose for no reason.

Just like the Sawyers.

Out of respect for Ginny's memory and their grief, Samuel had tolerated most of their barbs with only a mild protest. That's how Ginny, who spoiled her parents on every visit, would have wanted it.

However, he should have explained all of this to Rose the other night in the orchard. Who knew when they'd have another opportunity to talk before the Sawyers left on Sunday?

According to his pocket watch, it was time to wash up. He put his tools away and brought the cows in from the pasture for Charlie to milk later. He sauntered from the barn, grateful for good neighbors—and grateful for Rose. He'd have to tell her.

Mrs. Sawyer had changed into a different black dress when Samuel entered his home. Solomon was relaxed on the sofa with a newspaper, apparently ready for the party.

Rose and Emma exited his bedroom...his *old* bedroom.

"Emma, where did you get that pretty pink frock?"

"Grandmother bought it." Blushing, Emma held up one side. "Do you like it?"

"Three rows of ribbon above the hem are just the right amount, aren't they, Samuel?" Rose raised her eyebrows.

"Hmm." He pretended to consider the matter. "Yes, just right."

Emma beamed. "That's what Mama Rosie said."

"Did she now?" he said. "Well, she knows better than me."

"*I* chose the dress, Samuel." Olivia shot Rose a hard look. "It had nothing to do with Rose."

Whoa. What had happened while he worked? "Emma, you've had your bath?"

"She did," Rose said. "Could you help Peter?"

"I will." Then he'd get his bath and be dressed for the party.

He dumped the water in the yard when he finished. Rose was still wearing her gingham dress and apron while she braided Emma's hair. Why wasn't she dressed? He went to hitch the team to the Sawyers' rented landau as he considered it.

This evening was for his in-laws. He'd rather stay home and eat Rose's cooking, but he didn't regret having their entertainment planned by a capable hostess like Lily Ann.

Back inside, Rose was nowhere in sight. She'd probably gone upstairs to get ready. Ginny used to take hours to dress.

Olivia read a book on the sofa, her lips set in a thin line. The children played checkers on the table in a listless manner. Perhaps the oppressive heat affected them too.

Samuel poured everyone a glass of lemonade while waiting for Rose. They must leave in a quarter hour to be on time.

Mr. Sawyer checked his pocket watch for the third time in five minutes.

Samuel paced, looking toward the stairs with every turn. What kept her?

❧

*J*f everyone hadn't insisted on bathing first, Rose would have been ready an hour ago. Her hair wasn't completely dry when she pinned it up. Once she donned her blue silk wedding dress, she was finally ready.

Everyone waited by the door when, pinning on her best hat decorated with white silk flowers, she hastened down the stairs.

Mr. Sawyer consulted his pocket watch.

The man just had to make certain she recognized his disapproval. She lifted her chin.

"Rose." Samuel's smile looked a little strained. "You look lovely."

"Thank you." No man had ever described her that way. Perhaps he realized Rose needed the boost to her confidence. "Emma, that pink dress looks pretty on you."

Her stepdaughter touched the fabric and gave her a shy smile.

"Peter, you are very handsome in your new brown suit." It was only a matter of time before his carefully combed hair fell across his forehead. "Shall we go?" Without waiting for an answer, she stepped onto the porch. Samuel had already hitched the horses to the four-wheeled open vehicle, so they were soon on their way.

Her stomach fluttered when they stopped in front of an ornate, two-story brick home with a lovely view of the river. She admired the beauty of the black and iron fence and curved stone stairs leading to a spacious porch.

Inside, several guests chatted in a luxurious parlor. Lily Ann greeted Rose and motioned toward the next room for the children, then drew Samuel and the Sawyers into the parlor.

Rose took Peter and Emma by the hand. "Shall we look for Clay and Polly?"

Emma held her new doll close to her chest as if terrified someone might steal it.

Rose shared her trepidation and hoped Lily Ann had planned for her youngest guests. Thankfully, the next room held three tables with games. Polly and Clay sat at a table with scattered puzzle pieces.

"My name is Rhoda, Ma'am." A pretty maid curtsied. "I'll stay with the children. They'll eat here."

Relieved, Rose thanked the young woman and joined the adults. The crowded parlor hid Samuel from view, but Hazel stood in a corner by herself.

Just like Rose's dream. She joined her sister-in-law. "I'm happy to see you."

Hazel twisted her sleeve. "I feel out of place in such fancy surroundings."

"Me too. But I've discovered money doesn't make anyone more special than anyone else." Expensive furniture provided elegant comfort. A couple conversed on a divan. Two men smoked cigars on dark blue side chairs, which complimented pale blue floral wallpaper. Samuel was talking with other men beside a gleaming pianoforte.

"You've had a difficult week." Hazel sighed. "Richard was flattered by Mr. Sawyer's attention."

Before Rose could respond, Lily Ann descended upon them.

"Ladies, you must join us." She drew them by the arm to a circle of silent women that included Olivia Sawyer.

Hazel winced as Lily Ann's fingers brushed against her injury.

"Do you know everyone?"

Hazel nodded with a smile.

"Not everyone." Rose felt her cheeks flame. She wasn't accustomed to being the center of attention. "Although I recognize Mrs. Owens, Mrs. Carter, and Mrs. Walton. How lovely to see you all again."

Lily Ann performed introductions. Mrs. Walton asked about Rose's job in Harrison, and the conversation turned to children. Mrs. Sawyer mentioned her daughter, and the women almost interrupted each other to share personal remembrances of Ginny.

A dark-suited older man cleared his throat.

Lily Ann turned from the ladies. "Yes, Collins?"

The butler murmured that supper was ready and everyone had arrived.

Samuel, smiling, crossed the room to Rose's side. "I saw you talking with the other ladies. Are you having a nice time?"

Now that you're by my side. She tilted her head and looked up at him, handsome in his suit—that he'd worn to their wedding. As she was wearing her same dress.

"You really do look beautiful."

As if she didn't own a mirror, Rose drank in the whispered words.

Lily Ann ushered her guests toward the dining room.

Samuel placed Rose's gloved hand on his arm and covered it with his callused one. His smile melted her anxiety over her first fancy party.

She almost floated to the opulent dining room and found herself seated between her husband and her brother, with Hazel on Richard's other side. Lily Ann, at the head of the long table, sat between Samuel and Mr. Sawyer.

Mr. Black had left his widow in an enviable financial position. Rose fingered the fine white linen tablecloth covering a wide table that comfortably seated all twenty adults. She breathed deeply of a sweetly fragrant centerpiece of freshly cut pink roses in a glass epergne, flanked by molded jellies. A chandelier of twenty-four lit candles created a cozy atmosphere.

Samuel divided his attention among Rose, the Hatfields, Lily Ann, and the Sawyers. Richard amused them with stories about his workdays. Hearing Hazel laugh after the rough month she'd endured was a balm to Rose's spirit.

A maid placed a bowl of oyster stew in front of her. Somehow, the dish didn't appeal.

The other guests dove in.

"Delicious." Hazel ate a second spoonful.

It didn't smell right to her. She glanced around the table to find that even the excessively thin Mrs. Carter ate with apparent enjoyment.

Rose stirred the creamy soup before taking a tiny bite. Pleasant taste. She relaxed and ate half the stew.

Her head started throbbing halfway through the main

course. Nausea stole her appetite. She was even grateful to Lily Ann for monopolizing Samuel.

A maid placed a dish of pickled peaches in front of her. The pungent vinegar smell wafted up, and she leaped to her feet. Her chair crashed backwards.

All conversation halted.

Ignoring astonished stares, she ran from the room and down the hallway. A wide-eyed maid gestured wildly toward the water closet.

CHAPTER 21

*R*ose leaned against Samuel's arm in front of the mansion while her family gathered nearby. Her stomach still felt queasy. This was worse than her nightmare, for she'd surely embarrassed her husband with her appalling illness.

Richard and the maid arranged quilts in the bed of her brother's wagon. Samuel lifted Rose inside, and she sank against the bedding.

Emma burst into tears and launched herself into her father's arms. Samuel picked up his daughter and placed an arm around his son's shoulder. Peering over the side of the wagon, Peter rubbed his eyes.

Rose fought nausea as she stared at the weeping children. Her illness seemed to scare them. An idea struck. Ginny had probably been carried home in a wagon after her tragic accident. They might imagine—

"Please, let them come to me." She reached out her arms.

Samuel placed Emma on her lap. Then he lifted Peter beside her.

"I'm fine." Rose wrapped an arm around each child and

hugged them close to her side. "A little rest and I'll be as good as new. You'll spend a night with your cousins. Won't that be fun?"

Polly hoisted herself onto the wagon. "You can wear one of my dresses tomorrow. And take turns playing with my doll."

But Emma didn't respond to Polly. Instead, she stared at Rose, her little eyes filling with tears. "You won't stay sick? You promise?"

Rose's heart melted. How these children had suffered. "I promise."

Emma snuggled against her.

Rose's stomach protested. She feared she might disgrace herself. Again.

Perhaps seeing her distress, Samuel lifted the children out. Rose lay back, every movement torturous.

"Don't fret about anything." Hazel's voice. "We'll bring your guests home in the landau and pick up our wagon."

"Thank you." She only wanted her bed. Something that didn't move.

She endured the bumpy ride by closing her eyes and praying for relief.

Moments later, Samuel's arm slid under her shoulder.

"We're home. I'll carry you."

She'd waited so long to be held against the warmth of his chest. If only her stomach didn't protest the motion. Still, it *was* wonderful to nestle against him and listen to his thudding heart. All too soon, he laid her on her bed.

"Will your guests mind losing their room?"

"They'll sleep in Peter's room." He sat on the edge. "Need help putting on a nightgown?"

Her cheeks burned. "If you will unbutton my dress…"

"Of course." His fingers were gentle on her back. "I see what you mean. Small buttons are tricky."

"Yes." Was her dizziness attributed to her illness or his caress? "Can I trouble you for a bucket when you're done?"

"I'm finished." He left and returned in seconds. "It's beside the bed. I'll brush down the horses while you change."

She held her bodice tight against her. "Thanks."

He crossed to the door.

"Samuel?"

He turned back.

"Sorry to cause all this trouble."

"No trouble. I'm happy to do anything I can to make you feel better." He smiled. "I'll be back in to check on you."

$\sim$

*R*ose woke to the sound of raised voices. She rubbed throbbing temples, though her queasy stomach rebelled at the movement.

Flickering candlelight lit the space, reminding her she was back in her old bed. The Sawyers had been tight-lipped at the party after her mad rush to the water closet.

A heated flush infused her face. Good manners dictated illnesses not even be discussed during mealtime. Her offense had been far worse.

Lily Ann had graciously refused Rose's apology, which seemed to endear the widow to Samuel.

The argument in the front room escalated. Mr. Sawyer's voice penetrated the thin wall.

$\sim$

"*T*hat woman is all wrong for you and all wrong for my grandchildren." Solomon's face darkened.

Samuel stepped toward him. "If you could keep your voices—"

"Disgraceful." Olivia's lip curled. "Sleeps late when children are hungry. Takes off as she pleases. Returns only as the family awaits their supper."

She was as agitated as Samuel had ever seen her. "She explained everything. And anyone can oversleep."

"Son, you've chosen unwisely." He grasped Samuel's shoulders. "Admit it."

"No." He shook off Solomon's hands. "There's been no mistake."

"We can fix this. Dissolve the marriage. I've gotten annulments—"

"What are you saying?" Samuel stared at the pair. They'd stirred Ginny's dissatisfaction with his income. They'd shamed him time and again by buying things for his wife that they didn't need but she asked. They'd been unkind repeatedly to Rose. All of that, he'd forgiven.

This time, they'd gone too far.

"Everyone makes mistakes." Olivia twisted a handkerchief in her hands until it was a rumpled mess. "We don't blame you. You thought only of the children. A schoolmarm might have been a wise choice. But not her."

"She's done everything in her power to make you comfortable. Cooked meals with no thanks or gratitude from you. Even gave up her room. She's been wonderful." Samuel stepped away, unable to bear the contempt he heard directed at his wife. To think he had brushed off Rose's complaints, believing *she* lacked compassion. "I understand you're having a hard time with the fact I've remarried, but—"

"No." Olivia turned toward the wedding portrait. "That woman would test the patience of a pastor. She's nothing like my daughter."

A heaviness grew in the pit of his stomach. He'd imagined all they required was time to accept Rose.

"I will handle the legalities and pay—"

"No." Samuel's neck stiffened. "She's my wife. She loves my children. They are growing to love her."

"What if you're wrong?" Solomon asked. "We dined tonight with a woman who would be a fine choice."

Not only did they want him to betray a woman he'd vowed to love and honor until death, but they also presumed to choose whom he should marry next? He ground his teeth.

"Why didn't you choose one of Ginny's lovely friends?" Olivia's voice and breathing had returned to normal.

"Because Rose is kind and beautiful and gentle and generous, and she doesn't look down on my land or my profession." He widened his stance. "I stand by my decision."

"Our grandchildren are unhappy." Solomon puffed his pipe, and sweet-smelling tobacco smoke wafted through the room. "We asked them. Peter confessed that he doesn't like Rose."

"Stop stirring up trouble between my wife and my children." Samuel cranked the windows open wider to dissipate the smoke. Unfortunately, the oppressive atmosphere didn't banish so easily. "This discussion is over."

Olivia's lips set in a straight line. "Perhaps our presence isn't welcome."

Grim-faced, Solomon searched her expression. "We'll leave in the morning."

"That would be best." Not trusting himself to speak further, Samuel stalked into the darkness, leaving behind smoke, cruel words, and bitterness.

Long strides took him to the apple orchard. He sank onto the cool grass, wishing he had allowed Rose to speak freely when she sat under this tree. She'd bitten her tongue all week to please him and acted the gracious hostess with little thanks, even from her husband. He'd blamed their displeasure on her lack of compassion. It wasn't *her* compassion that was lacking.

Crickets chirped their familiar tune. The repetitious song soothed his frayed nerves.

He and Rose weren't a loving couple sharing newlywed bliss. They hadn't fooled Ginny's parents.

He bore the blame for this disastrous visit. Ginny had kept her difficult parents happy by spoiling them—and they acted as if they still expected to be treated as royalty.

The Sawyers had treated his wife like an unwanted guest in her own home. And Samuel had allowed it. What a mess he'd made of things.

Even worse—they'd asked his children if they liked Rose. He raked his hand through his hair. The Sawyers' disapproval was bound to color Peter and Emma's view of their stepmother.

He punched an anthill, glad only a hooting owl witnessed his frustration.

Did his in-laws think he had forgotten Ginny? Not so. But his new wife deserved their respect.

∼

The nasty conversation ended when the back door banged. The Sawyers whispered for several minutes. Then Peter's door closed.

All was quiet.

Even Rose, who'd heard it all, didn't make a sound as she wiped her wet cheeks with the sheet.

Samuel's defense of her had made her proud. The Sawyers' hints about Lily Ann sent cold chills through her body. The widow wasn't right for Samuel. Even the Sawyers agreed that a schoolteacher made a decent choice. Just not Rose.

Apparently, Peter didn't like her either. Little Emma followed her brother's lead. Difficult days lay ahead. A pity, for she'd thought that they'd laid a good foundation for the future in the first month. All that was undone now.

She buried her face in the pillow.

~

To avoid another confrontation, Samuel piddled in the barn until the lights were extinguished in Peter's room.

He tapped on his old bedroom door. When he got no response, he peeked inside.

Flickering candlelight showed Rose lying uncovered halfway across the bed with her feet dangling over the side. The urge to hold his sleeping wife proved too strong to resist.

He sat beside her and brushed wet hair away from her face. Was she sweating? He touched her cool forehead. Good, no fever. His fingers slid to her cheeks. They were wet with tears. Had she cried in her sleep? She must be hurting pretty badly.

He cradled her in his arms for one precious minute before gently shifting her to a comfortable position. She moaned but didn't awaken as he gently arranged the sheet over her.

He kissed the trail of tears on her cheek. He shouldn't take liberties, though. Married or not, it was wrong of him to touch her without her permission.

The memory of her innocent reactions when he'd awakened her that morning haunted him. She'd never know how close she came to being kissed. He'd run from her unforgettable temptation.

A sigh came all the way from his soul. She'd agreed to marry him with no promise from him that there'd ever be physical intimacy. Love. Children. Maybe in time she'd love him.

He wasn't ready for her. Memories of Ginny plagued him. The new painting reminded him of his and Ginny's joy at beginning their lives together. Certainly, Solomon and Olivia had spent many hours during their visit talking about her best qualities.

As if Samuel would ever forget her. Except for arguments about finances, theirs had been a happy marriage. Mostly.

Though sometimes, Ginny had been jealous of his time, sometimes even resented the hours he spent working their farm.

Rose showed no such resentment. She supported him, no matter what.

Precious minutes alone with his new wife often stirred deeper feelings, which made his chest tighten. He was being disloyal to Ginny.

But Ginny was gone.

He'd loved her, he had. But he had to move on. The children had to move on.

But he must conquer his guilt before pursuing a true marriage with Rose.

His lovely wife deserved a real husband in a real marriage. He needed time to make that happen.

CHAPTER 22

*R*ose didn't get the opportunity to say goodbye to the Sawyers, who left before she awakened the next morning. Samuel stepped into her room and conveyed their apologies for their early departure and their appreciation for the hospitality.

She doubted they'd actually uttered those gracious words, but she appreciated Samuel's sentiment. His in-laws were a part of her life now. Knowing what they were like, she'd be better prepared for their next visit.

Because she still felt ill, Samuel fetched the doctor later that morning.

Dr. Morrow pressed on her stomach and asked several questions. "My dear, I believe your body has reacted to something you ate."

She shifted higher in the bed, using the sheet to cover herself, and spoke to both the doctor and her husband, who hovered in the doorway. "I don't understand. Twenty people ate the same thing."

"Perhaps you are allergic to something that was served."

She recalled her reluctance to eat the oysters. "I became ill when I was a child after eating fried oysters. Mama never cooked them again."

"I believe you've found the culprit."

"Dr. Morrow, I've eaten my last oyster."

"I'll remind you if you forget." Samuel grinned.

She laughed. She liked both his teasing tone and his reminder of their future together.

Rose slept most of Friday. Every time she awakened, her husband was near.

Samuel brought her the hot tea and crackers her shaky stomach craved for supper. After her assurances that she'd be fine for an hour on her own, he drove the wagon to fetch the children. He returned without them. They'd stay with Hazel until Sunday services.

Her weakness continued on Saturday. Catherine brought over some cornmeal gruel that settled her stomach. After resting in bed all day, she dressed and sat on the front porch as the sun sank beyond the horizon, painting a pink and yellow sky. The fresh air restored her. Horses neighed from the corral as Samuel poured a bucket of water into their water trough.

"Evenin', Rosie." Charlie stood on the street beside the fence.

"Good evening, Charlie." She smiled without getting up from her chair. "Please join me. Samuel will come when he finishes with the animals."

"Just back from an evening stroll." He placed his cane against the railing and sat on a high-backed chair beside her. "I hear you fell ill at Widow Black's party. Hope you're improving."

"Much better, thank you. I'll attend church tomorrow. How will I face Lily Ann?"

"Why worry about her?" Charlie extracted a knife and a piece of wood from his shirt pocket and started whittling.

"I ruined her supper party."

"Pshaw. You ruined nothing."

Samuel strode onto the porch. "Couldn't have stated it better myself." Arms crossed, he lounged against the wooden pole support at the top of the steps.

She folded her hands in her lap. "I ruined your meal. Everyone's meal."

He chuckled. "I couldn't eat another bite by the time you ran from the room."

"Really?" The heat in her face receded.

"I barely ate breakfast yesterday." Grinning, he patted his stomach. "Richard mentioned the pastry course, but I knew I'd never be able to partake in it."

Rose clutched her sore stomach as they all laughed. Charlie left shortly after, and Samuel sat beside her.

"Lily Ann has endured much." He stared at the sunset. "Losing her husband and a very dear friend within a few months is difficult."

"Tragic."

"Rose, I'm sorry about this week. I didn't give you time to prepare properly for the visit. The Sawyers can be prickly and demanding, but I've never seen them act that way. To anyone." He sandwiched her hand between his. "I'm sorry for not putting a stop to it sooner."

"Why didn't you?" His weak defense had hurt.

"I thought it would be less upsetting for the children if I kept my peace." His thumb caressed her hand. "That meant you shouldered it alone. I regret that. I promise you—they won't treat you the same again."

His tender care during her illness had gone a long way to lay groundwork for forgiveness. The rest of her hurt melted under his heartfelt apology. "I'll hold you to it."

Samuel kissed her hand. "You've been wonderful these past weeks. Caring for four children when you expected only two, learning the responsibilities of farm life, putting up with difficult guests—you've handled it all with grace."

Her heart drank in his praise as if parched for it. "Thank

you." She wished she had the right to rest her head on his shoulder.

Instead, she turned to watch the sun slip behind the trees, content that her hand stayed tucked inside his strong one.

$\sim$

*L*ily Ann had little to say when Rose approached her the next day. The two women were alone in the back of the church after the congregation filed out.

Rose clasped her hands together. "I deeply regret ruining your party. Please forgive me."

"These things happen." Lily Ann didn't look up though her words were gracious. "One wonders why it only happened to you."

"We assume an allergy to oysters. Please accept my apologies for disrupting your guests' meal."

"It was unavoidable—though regrettable that Samuel was unable to finish his supper. I trust your health has improved?" She adjusted her white glove.

"Oh, yes. Thank you."

"Delighted to hear it. Good day." She flounced away.

Rose bit her lip and followed Lily Ann to greet Pastor Bradshaw, though in truth she'd known they didn't have enough in common to be friends.

$\sim$

*C*atherine brought her children over the next day. Gray clouds blocked the sun. A cool breeze promised welcome relief from rain later. The ladies took advantage of cooler temperatures to observe their children at play from the back porch.

Catherine rocked Bettina, her sleeping two-year-old. "I saw Ginny's parents last week."

"Yes." Rose leaned her head against the rocker.

"I met them before the funeral." She watched as her sons played with a snake near the barn. "Emma don't like being chased with a snake, does she?"

Rose blinked. "Who does?"

"Thought so." She straightened. "Zach, Bart, put that snake down. It might be poisonous."

"He won't bite, Mama. He's friendly." Nine-year-old Zach held up the three-foot snake.

"Put him back where you found him." They traipsed in the direction of the pasture with Peter. "Them boys sometimes chase their sisters with snakes. My girls got used to it, but I didn't know about Emma."

Rose put her hand over her mouth to smother a grin, recalling students like them. "I'm certain Emma won't care for the experience."

"Most folks don't." She leaned forward and called, "Veronica, don't climb inside the pigpen. I don't need you girls getting all muddy. Candace—that means you, too." The toddler in her arms stirred, but did not awaken.

Emma stood on the lowest fence rung. Horses neighed for attention from the corral.

"Now, where was I?" Catherine asked. "Oh, yes, the Sawyers. Did you enjoy the visit?"

Impossible to answer honestly. "I had met them years ago in Harrison. They gave Samuel a gift. An artist painted his and Ginny's wedding portrait."

Catherine asked to see it, so Rose took her inside to admire it.

Once they were reseated on the porch, Catherine broke the silence. "They don't want no one forgetting her."

"Not that anybody would. She seemed pretty unforgettable."

Catherine's bright eyes surveyed her friend. "I wouldn't want my youngins forgettin' me."

"I don't want Emma and Peter to forget their mother either. I want to help them find joy in life again."

She tilted her head with a smile. "I'm right glad you're my neighbor."

"Me, too." Life would never be boring with the Hill family stopping in for neighborly visits. And three of her children stayed home today.

~

$\mathcal{T}$wo days later, Rose toted an empty basket to her house and rubbed her back. This was the third batch of clothes hanging on the line today. A full kettle of clothing bubbled on the stove with one more to go.

She halted at the back door. Emma sat on the floor with her face tilted toward the new painting. The little girl sniffed and rubbed her eyes with her little fists.

Rose plopped on the wood floor beside her and gathered her close.

Sobbing, the child nestled against Rose's shoulder.

"There, there." She rocked her back and forth as the storm of grief gathered strength. Her throat swelled, stealing the power of speech. Tears streaked down her cheeks at all Emma and Peter and Samuel had lost.

Running footsteps pounded on the floor, then froze. "Emma?" Peter dropped to his knees beside them. "Did you fall?"

Rose tried twice before she could speak. "She misses your mother."

He squatted and touched his sister's heaving shoulders. "I'll get Pa." He ran out the open back door.

Good idea. Rose figured Samuel would want to comfort

Emma too. She cradled her weeping stepdaughter in her arms. No words would lessen the sorrow.

Heavier footsteps strode into the room. Samuel took the child from Rose's arms. "Emma?" He carried her to the rocker. The chair creaked as he rocked. "How long has she been crying?"

"A quarter hour." Rose pushed herself to her feet.

"Thanks for comforting her. Next time, call for me immediately." He laid his face on top of Emma's head. "I'm her father. It's my place to comfort my children."

She shrank against the wall. He didn't want her comforting *his* children.

"We share the same loss." He reached to draw the teary-eyed Peter against his side.

As if that made up for the reprimand that not only stung, but also pushed her away. Worse, he had humiliated her in front of the children.

One more wedge between them when she'd hoped to build a bridge.

~

*N*ursing her hurt, Rose avoided private conversations with Samuel the next few days. His reaction over her comforting Emma had lowered her esteem in the family. The children shied away from her. The situation improved when Richard left Clay and Polly with them for the week after Sunday dinner. Rose was happy to have them. Unfortunately, it rained until Monday evening. Samuel was the only one happy about the weather.

By Tuesday morning, the children were snapping at one another. Rose feared they'd soon argue over nothing. She wanted to take them to Lane Free Library in the city, but suggested it to Samuel first. Otherwise, if she suggested it in front of the children and he disapproved, he'd say so regardless who heard.

She'd not seek that humiliation again.

Fortunately, he liked the idea. "A long walk might work out their fidgets."

"Agreed. We'll leave after lunch and stay as long as they like. Will you mind sandwiches for supper?"

"Not at all." He called them in from the backyard and told them the news.

The outing was *her* treat. She scowled at his back. Why must everything come from him? His announcing it made it *his* surprise.

The children's smiling chatter reminded her to focus on making this an adventure.

When Samuel smiled at her, she turned away. He wanted to control every aspect of his children's lives—fine.

He couldn't control her emotions.

~

Instead of taking a direct route up Cincinnati Street to Third Street where the library was located, Rose turned left onto South Avenue toward the river. The beauty of the mansions and large estates on Front Street took her breath away. They strolled along Chestnut Street to the Free Bridge. The girls crossed the bridge with Rose to the other side of Hamilton. The boys stayed on the side and skipped stones on the river.

After a pleasant half hour at the river's edge, she led the children back to Front Street. The boys wanted to tarry on the railroad tracks at Sycamore and received a lecture in her best teacher's tone about the dangers of moving trains.

They turned right onto the road where their church was located, Basin Street. A prisoner called out to them from the jail on the right. She admonished the children to pay no attention and hurried them across the street to walk in front of the courthouse, an impressive building which, along with two side buildings, encompassed a whole city square.

Rose planned to stop at the post office opposite the courthouse on High Street on the return trip to see if there were any letters from Celia.

Once their meanderings around the city worked out the "children's fidgets," as Samuel had described them, Rose led them to the octagonal Lane Free Library.

A smiling librarian of perhaps forty introduced herself as Miss Laura Skinner. She led them to shelves filled with books appealing to younger readers. She engaged the boys with a new novel, *The Adventures of Tom Sawyer*.

Familiar with Mark Twain's book, Rose approved the selection and turned her attention to the girls not yet in school. After finding a quiet corner to observe the boys, she began reading a story from *Grimm's Fairy Tales* to Polly and Emma.

On the way home, Rose drew the children off the street at galloping hoofbeats behind them. A stagecoach stopped at its office at Hamilton House. Rose indulged the children's fascination and followed them down High Street to watch the activity. The coach door swung open, and two boys jumped down followed by a sedate woman they resembled. Two businessmen alighted next.

The travelers disappeared inside the hotel.

"Where did they go?" Polly frowned.

"Into Hamilton House." Rose enjoyed her curiosity, reminding her why she loved teaching. How she missed her students. "That's a hotel that serves meals to stagecoach passengers. While they eat, a fresh team of horses are hitched for the next leg of the journey."

"Can we watch?" Peter's gaze fastened on the red coach.

"Of course." He'd talked to her more that afternoon than he

had since his grandparents' departure, which filled her with a mixture of joy and relief. "Let's cross the street for a better view. Mind you, wait for that wagon to pass."

They waved away clouds of dust from a barrel-hauling wagon as they crossed to face the three-story white building with big black letters reading 'Hamilton House.' Rose sat on a bench on the sidewalk. Her companions perched on a step and watched two teenagers change a four-horse-team in record time. Grinning, the driver tipped his hat at the children and drove away slower than he'd approached.

The boys whispered together, then Clay said, "Aunt Rosie, we want to go back the river way."

She smiled at both boys. "Exactly what I was thinking."

They whooped and scampered toward the Great Miami River, the girls on their heels.

She trailed them, reflecting that the afternoon had gone better than she'd hoped. They'd do this again. Her stepchildren, when away from Samuel's watchful eye, accepted her presence and respected her guidance.

Why didn't her husband do the same?

CHAPTER 23

$\mathcal{R}$ose brushed away a wisp of hair with the back of her hand. Steam from gently bubbling green beans drifted to her face. Freshly washed jars lined the counter in readiness for another batch of vegetables.

In the three weeks since the Sawyers had made their angry exit, the harvest had begun. Samuel, his face lined with exhaustion, spoke little at meals and spent every free moment with Peter and Emma. He went to bed shortly after the children.

Working in the hot July sun was enough to drain anyone's energy. Still, Rose's heart ached at the rift between them, for things hadn't been the same between them since Emma's outpouring of grief. She'd talk to him about it if she thought it would change anything.

Lily Ann avoided her at church for two weeks before leaving for an extended stay with her sister in Boston. Rose's lingering humiliation finally dissipated.

Celia's most recent letter brought the happy news that she was expecting another child in mid-winter. Unfortunately, the busy harvest prevented Rose from traveling to see her to celebrate the wonderful news. How she missed them. And not only them, but also her job and her students. She'd belonged there. Had been respected and cared for by townspeople who watched out for her.

How long before she belonged here?

~

Someone tapped on the open front door as Samuel and the boys came in the back after a hard day's work. He glanced at Rose, bending over a steaming skillet in the kitchen, and crossed to the door.

"Charlie, come in." Samuel wiped his hand, wet from a good scrubbing at the pump, on his pants before extending it. "We just finished for the day."

The shorter man entered with a big smile. "Where are the girls?"

"Staying at Richard's this week." Not that Samuel was happy about that. This schedule helped Hazel as her burns healed, but he sure missed Emma. He'd prefer to keep all four children at his house. Rose agreed for she had voiced the same desire to Richard a couple of weeks ago.

"Looks like you've been working hard." He focused on Peter and Clay. "I'll wager you're plumb proud of these boys."

"More than I can say." He ruffled Peter's hair. "They helped water the crop."

"A hard day's work."

Peter rubbed his arm, which was probably already sore.

"Makes you thirsty." Clay swiped his sweaty brow with his sleeve.

"Charlie, I'm happy you're here." Rose wiped her hands on a dishcloth.

"Pleasure's all mine, Rosie. Home-cooked meals are too good to pass up." He sniffed. "Fried steak."

"Smells delicious." Samuel peeked at the skillet. Steaks browned with a crispy flour crust.

Charlie patted his stomach. "My belly's ready for something tastier than my cooking."

Rose glanced at Samuel before saying, "You're welcome anytime, Charlie."

A twinkle lit his gray eyes. "How about next Wednesday?"

They laughed.

"Next Wednesday it is." Samuel grinned.

Rose shifted the steak into a platter. "Almost ready. Boys, wash up."

"They already did. Let's sit." Samuel gestured to the chair on his left. They chatted about crops while Rose set the table. Conversation flowed throughout the satisfying meal.

After eating, the tanned boys scurried outside.

"Mighty fine meal, Rosie." Charlie leaned back in his chair, his hand resting on his glass of strawberry shrub. "Much obliged."

"My pleasure." Rose pushed her plate to the side. "Do you see your daughters often?"

It pleased Samuel that Rose resisted her practice to clear the table immediately. He sensed their guest might view that as a hint to leave.

"I see the two that live in the city 'most every week. My boys and my other daughter all moved from Hamilton years ago."

"I imagine it gets lonesome."

Samuel's gaze darted to Rose. He'd never considered his neighbor a lonely man.

"Even small farms demand a full day's work. Wes and Tom, my grandsons, will spend the month of August with me again this year to help with harvesting." His eyes twinkled. "Those boys sure did earn their red hair."

Samuel laughed. "I remember them being a lively pair. Is Wes fourteen?"

Charlie rubbed his stubbly chin. "Yeah, I figure that's about right. Tom's two years younger. Sure appreciated their hard work last year."

Samuel traced the rim of his glance with his finger. "It's good to have help."

"Sure is." He sipped his crimson beverage. "My days stay busy. No, it's the evenings that get long. I miss Esther. And the kids."

Rose's eyes softened. "Please dine with us more often. I always cook plenty."

Charlie fidgeted. "Don't wish to impose on friends."

Samuel shook his head. "You're always welcome, Charlie."

"It's true I feel more welcome these days." His brow furrowed but smoothed before Samuel could pinpoint the emotion there. "How about I plan on Wednesdays, unless you all are busy?"

Rose smiled. "Consider it a standing invitation."

"I get tired of searching my icebox for yesterday's leftovers." His face brightened.

Samuel stood. "My cows are mooing. Care to join me?"

Charlie laughed. "I ain't milked a cow in ten years. Ain't sure I remember how."

Samuel quirked an eyebrow. "Didn't you milk my cows when I was gone this spring?"

The old man snapped his fingers, his gray eyes twinkling. "I reckon you caught me on that one."

Chuckling, Samuel clapped his friend on the back and stepped outside. When he turned back, Rose leaned against the door frame with a sweet smile. His heart skittered. What a beautiful woman he'd married.

Compassionate, too. Her supper invitation to their neighbor had been a welcome surprise.

Charlie had filled a bit of the void left by Samuel's father's passing. He'd taught Samuel to let the land lie fallow. He'd been the one with suggestions about building the attic rooms. He cared for the animals in his absence.

Maybe they'd bless him too.

~

*R*ose missed Celia sorely, and sweet little Harriet must have nearly forgotten her. A letter received from her the last Thursday in July brought news that she'd not be able to travel until her continuously queasy stomach settled. Rose missed their conversations, their friendship. She tucked the letter in a drawer with a sigh. Maybe they could go to Harrison for a visit after the harvest.

Clay and Peter burst through the back door that day before she had lunch on the table.

"I'm hungry, Aunt Rosie."

"Well, I'm starving," Peter said.

The boys argued over who was hungrier.

She laughed and held up her hand. "You're both famished. Wash up."

They ran into Samuel at the back door. "Hey, boys, slow down. You'll trip over your own feet."

"They're hungry." She retrieved a platter of sandwiches from the icebox.

"Boys are always starving." Chuckling, Samuel scrubbed his hands at the sink pump. "I'm proud of their hard work the last two weeks. Clay's interest in farming has been a blessing. That's why Richard wants to leave him instead of Polly. It's good to have him here, but I sure miss Emma."

"I do, too." She carried a steaming bowl of fresh green beans to the table. "I think they feel guilty leaving all four children with us. I truly don't mind."

"Same here. I'll have enough beans, corn, and cucumbers to

sell at the market tomorrow," he said. "The first trip of the year is almost as much fun as the last one."

"The market on Second Street?" She placed a glass of cold lemonade beside each plate.

He downed one of the cold drinks. "I hope there's more of that. That sun's a scorcher."

Rose refilled his glass.

"No, I'll travel to a Cincinnati market. Charlie offered to care for the animals, so I'll take the boys along."

I'm here. Ask me to come. An opportunity to spend a few hours in the big city would be welcome, especially with her husband.

Samuel crossed to the back door. "They're splashing more water on themselves than their hands." He chuckled as he stepped out. "Makes me wish I'd thought of it first."

She stepped onto the back porch in time to see Samuel duck his head under the water flowing from the pump. The boys splashed Samuel and each other as Zeb barked and ran out of range.

She giggled, her hurt at not being invited to accompany him easing at their joy.

Peter laughed with a young boy's abandon. What a welcome sound. Time spent with his father had begun the healing process.

She leaned against the porch support pole, sending up a prayer that it continued.

~

*L*ater that hot afternoon, Samuel removed his hat to wipe his face with a red handkerchief. He'd broken his pocket watch, a gift from Ginny, that morning. Another tie to her gone. He pushed the grief aside. There was work to do. Just one more hour, and he'd call it quits for the day.

He toted a heaping basket of green beans to the wagon for tonight's ride to Cincinnati. The boys could slumber on the way, but he'd lose a night's sleep. The benefits were worth it. He fully expected to sell everything at the busy market.

"Pa?"

He turned at Peter's hesitant tone. "Yes, son?"

The boy kicked up hay.

Samuel hunkered down to Peter's eye level, ruffling his blond hair. "What is it?"

Peter pulled on a loose wagon splinter. "Ma's birthday is next week."

Samuel straightened, overcome by a sudden onslaught of grief. He adjusted a couple of baskets to recover his composure. August second was just a week away? They'd always celebrated Ginny's birthday with a picnic. "How about a picnic on the river?"

Peter shook his head. "I want to be close to Ma."

Samuel's throat constricted. He clasped his son to his chest. "Let's make a day of it. Decorate the grave with pretty flowers. And how about some fishing?"

"Yeah, that would be good. Thanks, Pa."

"I'll ask Rose to pack a meal." He picked up an empty basket for that last row of beans.

"Pa?" Peter tugged on his arm. "Just you and me and Emma can go."

Frowning, Samuel searched his worried face. Perhaps it was best to allow the children to speak of their memories without Rose. "All right. Just the three of us."

∾

*A*ll the vegetables sold within three hours on Saturday. Samuel celebrated with servings of Graeter's French Pot Ice Cream for himself and the boys.

When he arrived back at home, Rose had jars of catsup to show for her busy day, something Ginny had never attempted. In fact, all but three cupboard shelves held mason jars filled with various vegetables. His praise for her efforts brought a becoming flush to her face. He was proud of all she'd accomplished and made certain she recognized it. He'd made too many mistakes during the Sawyers' visit and wanted to make amends.

Samuel spent his next free evening building shelves in the cellar. Their combined hard work fulfilled rather than exhausted him. He didn't mind selling fewer bushels. It amazed him how quickly his wife had adapted to farming life.

After Wednesday evening's supper with Charlie, Rose brought her sewing to the porch and they talked with Charlie in the cool of the evening. With Charlie puffing on his old pipe and the children playing in the yard with Zeb, they felt like a family.

Ginny, who'd possessed a jealous streak, wouldn't like that. Guilt over his growing feelings for Rose was difficult to combat.

His jaw tightened. He and Peter and Emma would spend time at the cemetery the following day—just what the three of them needed. He hadn't told Rose yet. Since he wouldn't be working, she also deserved to rest.

He'd tell her tonight after Charlie left. Preparing a picnic shouldn't take her long. He'd cook whatever fish they caught for supper, freeing her until sunset. She'd be happy for the break.

CHAPTER 24

*R*ose collapsed into her rocking chair after the children went to bed. She'd peeled too many tomatoes that day.

Even the wooden headrest felt like a feather pillow after three weeks of canning vegetables. Samuel checked the cupboard every night, seeming satisfied—maybe even proud—at the growing number of filled shelves.

Being the cause of his smile was worth all her efforts. They were becoming partners, each with their own specialty. Her days held purpose, meaning. She loved farming life, the children, and…Samuel. Some days, her dreams of winning his love seemed closer. Other days, he seemed to be waging an inner battle. On the occasions when he seemed to shutter himself away from her, she prayed for him the hardest.

She watched Samuel leave Peter's room and close the door. "Want me to pour you a blackberry shrub?"

"No, thank you." He patted his flat stomach. "I'm still full from supper." He sat on the chair nearest hers.

She retrieved her sewing. The lantern on the table beside her illuminated the fabric. Curtains were drawn against the darkness. Open windows invited refreshing breezes, and glowing candles created a cozy atmosphere.

"I'm taking the children for a picnic tomorrow." Samuel leaned back, his clasped hands behind his head.

Where did he get his energy? "A picnic?"

"Yes." He stared at the painting that made up the centerpiece of their home, as he did so often. "Ginny's birthday is tomorrow."

"I see." That was news.

"Peter asked to picnic at Greenwood Cemetery, just the three of us."

"You and Peter and Emma," she clarified. Even as she recognized they needed time together to grieve, her isolation hurt.

"Yes." His gaze shifted to the floral rug.

More bricks for the barrier between them. She stabbed the needle into the fabric. "I'll prepare a basket."

He nodded. "I'd appreciate that."

Silence stretched too long.

"Don't work tomorrow. Visit Hazel. Shop in town. Sew—whatever you want. You've worked hard. Relax."

Minutes ago, a day of rest was what she most desired. Now the idea was abhorrent. "Will you be home for supper?"

"No, we'll fish in the river. I'll fry whatever we catch and be home before dark. Will you milk the cows and feed the animals if I'm late? I'll keep them in from the pasture tomorrow."

"Of course." She dropped her fabric in the basket at her feet. "How fortunate the boys taught me. Good night." She walked away, and the bedroom door closed between them.

Rose pushed open the curtains in the dark room. An owl hooted. A horse neighed. Her heart responded to the lonely night sounds.

Peter didn't want her company. Apparently Samuel and Emma didn't either. It was Samuel's fault because he allowed it.

The family rarely left the farm and when they did, he didn't want her.

Maybe he should pack his own picnic.

~

While Rose set the sandwiches in the basket, Emma hummed from her seat at the table.

Peter asked Rose for gingerbread in their lunch, and she added a few pieces. That the boy liked her cooking was some comfort. Of course she was packing their lunch. Samuel hadn't seemed to notice her rebellion anyway. Why would he? Her feelings didn't matter.

Samuel entered from the back door. "Who's ready for a picnic?"

"I am!"

"Me!"

Samuel laughed. "The horses are hitched." He lifted a square of linen off the prepared basket. "Sandwiches, cheese, crackers, gingerbread, and pie. Delicious. Thank you, Rose." He gave her an approving nod.

"Have fun today." She looked at the children.

Peter ran to the wagon. Emma skipped out the door behind her father. Rose trailed them as far as the porch.

Samuel hoisted a barking Zeb into the wagon bed with the children. With a wave, he guided his team onto the road.

What was she supposed to do? Rose surveyed the empty front room. Peter's unfinished shirt nestled among her needles and thread. Too much trouble.

A pile of neglected laundry littered her bedroom floor. Definitely not today.

It was too hot to walk to Hazel's. Samuel might have offered to drive her there, but no, he didn't bother with her comfort at all. Though, contrarily, she didn't ask for a ride because she didn't want to visit anyone. She was too despondent to be good company.

She trudged to the back porch steps and leaned against a pole. A buzzing bee chased her inside the house.

Wandering listlessly from room to room, the painting of the happy couple drew her like a magnet.

Samuel and the children needed to grieve her. Needed to remember her. Without a doubt they'd feel freer to talk about events of their lives with Ginny when Rose wasn't there. They'd speak of memories she knew nothing about—and no one would feel the need to explain them.

Her mind traveled back to the loss of her own mother. If Mrs. Wiley, her father's housekeeper, had asked to join a picnic specifically planned in memory of Rose's mother, she wouldn't want her to come.

When thinking of it in those terms, she understood Peter's request. Her resentment eased.

This would be a difficult day for all of them—herself included. For didn't she hurt when they hurt?

She did. Better for all of them if she prayed for the healing such remembrances might bring. The knowledge that Ginny would never be forgotten.

Her eyes fell on the wedding portrait again. She remembered Ginny just that way. Young. Happily in love. Gone too soon.

Rose spotted Samuel's blue shirt at the top of the laundry pile. It was similar to one he'd worn to escort Ginny to a fundraising picnic for their high school, the day their courtship began.

Picking it up, she sank into the rocking chair.

So many memories. For her, too. Some of them weren't the best. Like watching Samuel fall in love with Ginny.

There was enough hurt to go around.

She must remind herself that grief had its own timetable when Samuel seemed to shutter himself away from her.

Her own losses had taught her that truth.

She needed to pray for her family. And today they'd need her prayers as much as ever.

Lord, help this hurting family in their grief. Bring them healing. And give me wisdom to know how to help them.

～

R ose stared at the crumpled shirt in her hands. The last thing she remembered was praying for Samuel, Peter, and Emma. She must have fallen asleep.

The cows were lowing from the barn. Gracious, had she slept the afternoon away? Apparently so. She stood gingerly, and then rubbed her lower back. Wooden rocking chairs weren't the most comfortable place to take an extended nap, but she had needed it.

Too many long, full days without sufficient rest had taken a toll on her.

She felt refreshed. Samuel had been right about her need for a day of rest and relaxation.

The cows mooed at her again. She stretched, and then dropped Samuel's shirt on top of the laundry pile before heading to the barn.

It felt good to be needed, and this family usually needed her.

Just not today.

CHAPTER 25

"Will you plan a birthday party for Emma?" Samuel had waited until Charlie left and the children were asleep before bringing up the matter.

The home felt cozy and inviting with the lanterns lit along the wall and on the table beside his wife. She hadn't talked much since they got back from their picnic last week. He regretted that their picnic excluded her. The children had cried for their mother, convincing Samuel to keep his focus on them. Rose kept herself busy with drying and canning vegetables and such anyway. There'd be time to focus on his marriage later.

"A party?"

"I hate to put a new task on you." He'd mulled over the idea for two days before mentioning it. But his daughter needed the celebration. He studied his wife's lovely face, a becoming shade of pink in the soft light. "Ginny planned a big party on her fifth birthday. So much has changed." He forced himself to breathe evenly. "Which makes this birthday all the more important."

"Agreed. Let's celebrate on Saturday." She guided a needle through the sleeve of Peter's new green shirt. "More people can come, and that's her actual birthday."

"Nothing elaborate." He wagged his finger. No one knew better than he how easily expenses became unmanageable. "We'll invite Richard's family. She'll want her new cousins there."

"And Catherine's eight children. They're a lively bunch. I don't know how she does it."

He raised his eyebrows. "Didn't you have twenty students?"

"Twenty-one." She giggled. "But they went home each day."

He chuckled. "Charlie and his grandsons will enjoy the party as well."

"Definitely." So far, so good. "Wes and Tom have earned a fun afternoon. Charlie's already made one trip to the Hamilton market."

"Let's see, that's twenty-one altogether." She rubbed her forehead. "In three days?"

"Is it too much?" Another burden for her busy day. Why had he brought it up?

"No." She folded the shirt and placed it in her sewing basket. "I just remembered two bushels of green beans waiting for me to can."

"Leave them for me to sell at the market." His conscience smote him for adding a party to her overfilled days. This one he could alleviate.

"I'll need to shop tomorrow."

"No problem. I'll hitch up the wagon after breakfast." He'd tell Emma about her party in the morning. He was determined to make her birthday as happy as possible.

～

Samuel was relieved that Saturday's rain had stopped by the time the guests arrived. He worried about the outside games planned for the party's entertainment, but surely Rose would ask for his help if she needed it.

Adults smiled indulgently at the children's excited chatter when they sat down for lunch. The table only seated ten, even with two extra leaves. Six adults sat at the table with an empty place for Richard, who'd come after work. Rose had set up two colorful quilts on the sitting room floor, one for the girls and the other for the boys.

Samuel ate perfectly roasted beef as the children's laughter eased the burden on his heart. He wanted Emma to have good memories on her first birthday without her mother, and her giggles proved they'd given her that.

Charlie told several stories from his mischievous childhood that soon had the adults laughing. Samuel reflected that his neighbor's playful twinkle had been earned.

Rose led the children in parlor games while sunshine dried the grass. They played Blindman's Wand, Deerstalker, and twenty questions.

Catherine asked to join the game when Rose pulled out a cup and winks for Tiddly Winks. "That's my favorite game."

Rose laughed. "Join us."

Charlie rubbed his hands together. "Well, now, if adults are invited…"

"Of course, Charlie. Anyone else?"

Trent leaped to his feet. "I'll play."

Hazel couldn't shoot with her injured hands, so Samuel declined also. Richard arrived after the game started.

The Hill family obviously played this game often. Zach and Veronica rarely missed when flipping the small disks into the cup.

Samuel marveled at the way his wife included all ages. Wes, Charlie's fourteen-year-old grandson, was just as engaged as two-year-old Bettina, who played with assistance from her sisters.

Tom, Charlie's younger grandson, gave Catherine's oldest

daughter, Rennie, sidelong glances. At twelve, they were young to be interested in each other.

Rennie glared at Tom, raising her fist when she caught him staring. Samuel smothered a laugh. That girl had inherited her mama's spunk.

After Zach won the game, everyone headed outdoors. Adults sipped lemonade on the back porch while the children played tag, hide and seek, and tug-of-war. Finally, everyone entered the house for cake.

Emma's eyes sparkled when she opened Rose's gift—a hand-stitched doll dress to match one of her new frocks. His daughter's joy expanded room in Samuel's heart for Rose, who had worked miracles all day. It was all he could do to refrain from grabbing her and kissing her, right there in front of their guests. His heart nearly burst with gratitude and love. Wait...love? Wasn't it too soon to delve into his feelings for his new wife? Of course, it was. He pushed the thought aside, but the feelings lingered.

Catherine gathered up her children at suppertime. "My youngins ain't had this much fun packed into one day in a long time."

"We're happy you all came." Samuel shook Trent's hand. "Emma, thank our neighbors."

His daughter crept over, a finger in her mouth. "Thank you for the spinning top."

Samuel barely heard her. He took her finger out of her mouth. "Now, say it again."

Catherine bent to listen as she repeated it. "Why, you're ever so welcome, Emma. Thank you kindly for inviting us."

As the lively bunch sauntered away, Samuel wondered if Trent had uttered more than ten words the whole afternoon. His boisterous family made up for his quietness.

Richard's family gathered in the main room near Charlie.

"Wes and Tom had a fine time today." Charlie, standing

between his grandsons, sandwiched Rose's hand in his. "You made a lot of little ones happy today, Rosie. Thanks for including us." He gripped Samuel's hand. "You're a lucky man. God blessed you with great youngins and a fine wife."

Words lodged in his throat at the words. Ginny would hate Charlie's comment. Guilt tightened his chest. He turned from Rose's searching eyes and looked at the wedding portrait, where Ginny radiated joy.

Beside him, Rose stiffened. "Emma and Peter *are* fine children, Charlie. Thank you for the hair ribbons. All the colors match her dresses."

Rose's gracious words penetrated the tightness in Samuel's chest.

"I ain't good with frilly things." Charlie shook his head. "If we pleased the birthday girl, that's enough for me."

"I picked them out." The tall, red-haired Wes tapped his chest. "I chose ribbons like my sister's."

"Hey, now." Tom's face flushed almost as red as his hair. "I picked the blue ones."

Wes spun to face his brother. "You didn't want to pick out no girl stuff—"

"Boys." Charlie laid a calming hand on each boy's shoulder. "Emma liked our gift. That's what matters." He reached around Wes to shake Richard's hand. "Richard, Hazel, it's always a pleasure."

Rose smiled. "Don't forget supper on Wednesday."

"Never happen." He winked at Samuel. "I fast all day so my stomach will hold more."

Laughter eased lingering tension as the door closed behind them. The cousins ran out the back door.

"Rose, you managed to keep the children happy all afternoon." Hazel gave her an incredulous stare. "You must have been a wonderful teacher."

She laughed. "I don't know about *that.* The important thing is that the children enjoyed themselves." Her smile dimmed as she glanced at Samuel.

"It was a wonderful party." He turned his back on the painting. Rose had been a marvel today. She put it all together at short notice too. What an amazing woman. "Thank you."

She turned away and picked up dirty cups from the table. "I enjoyed it."

"That pretty doll dress." Hazel walked with Rose to the kitchen. "What a lovely gift."

The men followed. Samuel, who wanted to be near Rose, leaned against the stove. She had succeeded in giving his daughter an even better party than the one Ginny had thrown the year before. Rose had made Emma happy today. Peter had also enjoyed the celebration. His wife wasn't merely a capable woman with a knack for adjusting to a new way of life and talented at entertaining. No, even more importantly, she was loving. Kind. Compassionate. Thoughts of her had begun to captivate a fair amount of his waking hours. And a few of his dreams too.

So why had he reacted so strongly to Charlie's description of her as a fine wife? Because Ginny still had a hold on him. He shouldn't have enjoyed the day so much without her.

"Her happy face was worth the lost sleep." Water droplets splashed as Rose pumped water into a bucket. "Samuel, will you build a fire to heat water for the dishes?"

"Of course." Thankful for something to distract his thoughts away from his guilt over enjoying the day's festivities without Ginny, he selected kindling from the wood box.

Hazel scraped food from plates and stacked them. "Please help me plan Clay's party."

"His birthday is in November." Richard leaned his chair back on two legs.

"I can plan ahead, can't I?" Hazel gave her husband an impish grin.

"I'd love to help." Rose tied on an apron.

"Can we eat supper here?"

"Sure. Leftovers are in the icebox." Rose put her hands on her hips. "If you want roasted beef sandwiches, you're welcome to stay. That's all I'm up to making."

"I didn't eat dinner." Richard winked. "I'm staying."

Samuel enjoyed the relaxing family evening that followed, but he couldn't shake his guilt over finding pleasure in his daughter's party. Without Ginny. He hadn't expected to enjoy the day.

How would Ginny feel, if she knew?

CHAPTER 26

*H*ot, dry weeks followed, which were perfect for drying vegetables. Rose marveled that Emma made a game of stringing beans and shucking corn. Samuel kept the boys busy with harvesting crops.

Emma's party had been a huge success—with everyone but Samuel. Rose's self-esteem plummeted at the pain in his eyes when Charlie had suggested that he'd been blessed with a fine wife. Rather than agreeing, Samuel had stared at the painting of his first wife.

Rose still suffered the humiliation. Charlie had merely meant to invite compliments for Rose's hard work. That her husband couldn't force himself to be gracious, even in front of his closest friends, slashed her heart and degraded her confidence.

Hazel had advised her to give him time. And Rose had seen improvements. Since then, he'd thanked her often for the growing number of filled mason jars and other tasks she regularly did—even cleaning the stove, which had surprised her. She didn't think he noticed.

After supper, he always spent time with the children. They

accompanied him to bring the cows in from pasture and other chores. His time with them often included playing tag or catching fireflies.

Rose hadn't been invited to join in. Her heart ached to be close to the children. She'd never find a home in their hearts if something didn't change.

September brought the start of school. Rose accompanied the children on the first day, holding Emma's trembling hand. "Are you nervous, Emma?"

The little girl's hand tightened around hers.

"It'll be fine." Peter kicked at a pebble.

Rose patted Emma's hand. "You'll sit with other boys and girls your age."

"Yep, you're in the little kids' room." Peter chased after the pebble. "Miss Ames is really nice."

"She is?" Emma's blue eyes were huge.

"She teaches you to write your name."

"And we'll practice at home." Rose squeezed her hand, happy to share the children's first day with them.

Children, some chatting excitedly and others dragging their feet, approached a brick building from every direction. Emma hid her face against Rose's arm.

"Other little girls are just as nervous as you are." Rose pulled her close for a hug. "If you play with them at recess, you'll help them feel better."

"I don't want anyone to feel bad."

"Of course not." Rose brushed back a wisp of Emma's hair. "You're kind and sweet. You'll make friends quickly."

Zeb, loping along beside Emma, licked the back of her hand, and she giggled.

Rose laughed. "See, even Zeb wants you to have a good day."

"He waits by that tree all day." Peter pointed to a tall hickory.

"I packed food for him. Don't forget to draw water for him

when you're out on recess." Samuel had warned her the dog couldn't be coaxed away.

"Are you sure I'll be all right?" Emma halted outside the building.

Bending down to her eye level, Rose placed her hands on Emma's shoulders. "Positive. Peter said that Miss Ames is very nice. I used to teach." She caught herself. She'd always played games the first day to make the students comfortable with her and each other. This teacher might have other ideas. "I loved my students."

"You did?"

"Truly." Rose smiled. "Shall I return and walk you home?"

"Nah," Peter said before Emma could answer. "I know the way." He addressed the dog. "Zeb, wait for us by that tree." The dog lumbered to the shade. Peter grabbed his sister's hand. "Come on. I'll show you your room."

"Tell me all about it tonight. Enjoy your day." Joy bubbled up as they ran toward the school. Once they were inside, nostalgia hit her hard. She missed teaching. She missed her students. Mostly, she missed feeling confident and appreciated, two things she rarely experienced in her new role as a wife and mother.

Left a job she loved to become barely a wife. Barely a mother.

She dragged herself back to the farmhouse that still didn't feel like home.

Emma's joyous face that afternoon heightened her longing to be teaching again. The sweet girl had made a new friend, Clara, and Miss Ames had played games with them.

Rose read with the children that evening from her McGuffey Readers. She limited the lesson to a half hour. It was such fun for all three that it became a nightly ritual. She rejoiced to see progress in Peter's reading and Emma's writing.

Best of all, Samuel didn't interfere.

He did eat lunch with her nearly every day. She treasured their solitude as a gift. Not teaching held some unexpected benefits.

*S*amuel cleaned his hands at the pump at noon on the second Friday of September while she sliced ham for sandwiches.

Rose peered out the window as he ducked his head under the gushing water. When he brushed his hair back from his red face, streams of water ran down his chest. His drenched shirt molded against his upper body, showing that the weight he'd lost last winter was back. In all the right places, for his stomach was flat. She wouldn't mind laying her head against his strong chest, listening to his heart beat, even when he was drenched. No, she wouldn't mind getting wet while locked in a passionate embrace.

She fanned her face. Gracious, what was she thinking? Those were dreams for days ahead. Still, she couldn't take her eyes off her husband.

After rolling his sleeves up over muscular arms, he doused his face and arms and headed to the house. It reminded her of that day he came to her schoolhouse.

She met him near the back door. "No dripping all over my clean floor, young man." Hands on hips, her face tilted up.

His gaze fell to the puddle forming beneath his feet. "This floor's seen worse." Then, he lifted his gaze to hers and held there as if he was surprised by what he saw.

Her breath caught at the awareness in his eyes. Did he have an idea what she'd been thinking while watching him wash up?

She was sure he'd step back or move away. He always did when anything more than distant regard passed between them. But he didn't.

Instead, his gaze intensified.

Suddenly afraid of her own feelings, she placed a hand on the side of her neck. "W-want a sandwich?"

"Perfect. Shall we eat outside?" He tossed his head at the sunny yard.

Outside, as if he wanted to linger? He usually scurried back to work quickly after lunch. "Sounds lovely."

They ate in the shade of the maple tree. Samuel relaxed on the grass with his back against a hollow log. "Profitable crop this year. And the apples are ripening faster than I can pick them."

"Better than last year?"

"It is." He peered toward lowing cows in the pasture. "My three varieties give me a harvest beginning late August until mid-October. I'm thinking about using harvest money to buy two or three acres of apple seedlings."

Her thoughts flew to all the jelly, canned apples, and pies she'd made recently. Apples hung on strings on the back porch to dry in the sun. "Next year will be even busier."

"Not from the new seedlings." His eyes were on the horizon. "Takes a while for new trees to produce. I'm building for the future."

Just like she was with her marriage. "I like the sound of that."

"Me, too." He looked at her, and there was something new in his eyes, almost like a promise.

Rose's heart skipped a beat. "Guess I'll make more cider and vinegar the next few weeks." She bit into her sandwich.

"No argument from me." He laughed, a teasing light in his eyes.

"Do you need help in the orchard?"

"Thanks for the offer, but I'm not putting anything else on your shoulders. The children can help on Saturdays."

"But—"

He touched her lips with his fingers. When she gasped, he jerked his hand away.

She stared at her sandwich, too scared at what she wouldn't see in his eyes to look up.

"I'm sorry," he said after a charged pause. "You've been busy all summer. Filled shelves. Sacks of dried vegetables. We've never been more prepared for winter."

All her hard work had been worth it. This praise proved he appreciated her.

"Thanks for everything you've done, Rose." He stood and reached for her hand to help her to her feet.

"My pleasure, Samuel." She gave his hand a little squeeze.

His expression stilled. He dropped her hand.

Rose didn't move as he strode toward the field. Had his thoughts turned to Ginny, again?

~

*L*unch became Rose's favorite meal. She and Samuel ate on the back porch or under the shady tree in pleasant autumn weather. Sometimes, when he erected a barrier between them, her husband ate in near silence. More often, lively conversations made the minutes fly, fueling her dreams of a deepening relationship.

Temperatures cooled. Leaves changed color. The vegetable harvest waned. Craving friendships with other women, Rose returned to the sewing group in late September that the harvest had prevented her from attending.

A new woman had joined the group. Twenty-one-year-old petite Selena Harris was beautiful with raven hair and blue eyes. Rose attributed the lively atmosphere to the vivacious single woman.

"Aunt Alice wants me live here. I'm tempted." Selena pulled a needle through a red cotton patch. "I've made good friends."

Rose had lived there for months and still didn't feel accepted.

"Please make Hamilton your permanent home." The normally sedate Jane pushed aside her sewing.

Selena laughed. "To do that, I must find employment. Does anyone know of available jobs?"

A yearning for her old teaching position surprised Rose in its intensity. She sighed as she continued sewing. No going back. It was worth the sacrifice if Samuel was falling in love with her.

"I'll speak to my husband." Pauline shrugged. "Pastors often hear news in the course of their daily business."

The group had warmed to Selena, who was as sweet as she was pretty. Perhaps she reminded them of Ginny. Was there no escaping her influence?

❧

A week later, the delicious aroma of cooked apples emanated from the open door as Samuel washed mud from his hands at the end of the day. His stomach rumbled.

He stepped inside the kitchen to chaos. "Smells delicious." He stuck his finger in a bowl of apple butter. "Tastes good, too."

"That's for canning." Rose tapped his wrist with a spoon. "You'll thank me in January."

He grinned. "I thank you now." Apple peels and cores filled bowls in a haphazard mess on the side table. Dirty kettles and dishes cluttered the stove. "You've been busy."

"You might say so. Supper's not ready." She shooed him from the kitchen. "Give me an hour."

"I can take a hint." The children were playing at the Hills', so Samuel headed to the cow pasture alone. Friendship with Catherine was another blessing Rose had brought them, for it bound the neighbors closer.

Samuel whistled as he fed the horses. He was in the middle

of his best apple harvest. He was growing closer to Rose, and the children seemed more settled at school and at home.

After dinner that night, Rose cleared the table. "Emma, please get your slate. Peter, you know where the book is."

This was the first evening Samuel had been free to observe nightly lessons. He peeked over Rose's shoulder as she demonstrated a few letters on the slate's left side for Emma. The little girl's brow furrowed as she copied the letters.

Meanwhile, Peter read aloud from a McGuffey Reader.

While he turned a page, she leaned over the slate. "Very good, Emma. Getting the 'E' straight comes with practice. You're much improved from last week."

Her eyes glowed. "I want to write my 'M's' next."

"Good." Rose smoothed back the child's hair.

Ignoring their conversation, Peter continued reading. Rose nodded along patiently.

Samuel watched, amazed. Her ability to listen to Peter read while correcting Emma's mistakes surely must be a skill honed in the classroom. His admiration for her multiplied. After observing one session, he knew he could teach them. It was his responsibility as their father. He'd stop work early tomorrow to take over the lessons. This was one burden he could take off her shoulders. She'd appreciate it.

∾

Samuel rubbed his hands together, eager to share his surprise with Rose. She'd be able to sew or catch up on laundry when he took over the lessons. Besides, Peter and Emma would enjoy teaching sessions more with their father.

Everyone ate fried steak with healthy appetites. Rose smiled at his compliments. "Thank you. It's been a busy day."

"I saw a new shelf filled with vinegar and cider in the cellar after lunch. You've really taken to being a farmer's wife."

She looked down, but not fast enough to hide her smile and a pretty blush.

Ginny hadn't done nearly so well. The comparison would have angered his late wife, but that wouldn't make it any less true.

"Children, we're getting a late start," Rose said. "Let's do our lessons as soon as the kitchen is clean." She scraped food from one plate to another.

"I'll take over now that it's dark after supper." He smiled at her widened eyes. "Relax after the dishes are finished."

Her eyes lost their luster. "You're not happy with my teaching?"

"Of course I am, but I'm their father." He rubbed Peter's head. "It's my job."

She turned away. Overwhelmed at his offer on her busy day, no doubt.

His children gathered their slates and books while Rose cleared the table. Plates knocked together loudly.

"Did those break?" She didn't look as happy with his surprise as he'd hoped.

"No." She wiped the table, shoving his elbow off one end with her arm.

He blinked but kept his arms off the table while she finished. Perhaps she was overly tired. He started Emma writing. He then listened to Peter read.

"Is this right, Pa?" Emma pointed to her slate.

It took a moment to reshift his focus from Peter's story about a dog. "Let's practice those B's again." He returned to the story.

"Like this, Pa?"

Dishes clanked together in the kitchen.

"Hmm. It's closer." Her letters were still shaky. "Do it again." He motioned for Peter to read again.

"When she has trouble," Rose said as she scrubbed a dish, "it's best to demonstrate."

Peter stumbled over a word, and Samuel corrected it as he snatched Emma's slate.

He wrote the letter. "Do you see now?"

Emma pouted.

What was wrong now?

"What's this word, Pa?" Peter asked

Sweat beaded on his forehead. He looked at the reader and read, "It says *something*."

"Yeah, but what?"

"No, the word is *something*." This teaching thing wasn't as easy as it looked.

"Can we stop now?" Lower lip protruding, Emma laid down her pencil.

"Of course. It's been a long day. Put your school supplies away."

They ran from the room as if they'd just received a reprieve from execution.

Rose glared at him as she wiped a cup.

He'd do better tomorrow. It was another way to spend time with his children. Why did it have to be so much work?

~

*E*mboldened by the strengthening friendship between her and Samuel, the next day at lunch, Rose explained that she really enjoyed teaching the children. If he really wanted to continue nightly lessons, perhaps they could do it together. He seemed happy to relinquish the task. She was just as thrilled to take it back.

As he caught up with the apple harvest, Rose cooked applesauce and apple butter. She canned apples and dried apples. Several gallons of cider were set aside to make vinegar. The family ate apple pie or cobbler every night.

The rest of the fruit would be sold. A final run to a Cincinnati market was planned.

According to Samuel, his crops had brought in nearly as much money as last year, even with her canning. He planned to slaughter pigs in November, smoke the meat, and then sell it to a butcher. That money should carry them through a whole year without scrimping. He'd do carpentry work for a downtown shop during winter, as usual, and save that income.

Days shortened. Vibrant orange, rust, and gold leaves enlivened the landscape. Mornings and evenings held a cool snap in the first two weeks of October before Indian Summer brought a refreshing return of hot summer days.

Rose cranked open windows, and the curtains flapped in the cross-breeze on a beautiful Wednesday evening in mid-October. The home smelled of cooked apples. The rest of the family was out gleaning the last fruit from the orchard. Samuel planned to travel to the Cincinnati market that night.

Dreams filled her heart because of her conversation with Samuel at their midday picnic.

"Owning an apple orchard satisfies something in me." His feet had crunched against the leafy blanket under the maple tree. "Doesn't make much sense."

"It does." She'd placed her hand on his arm. "It's like we're working with God to tend His land."

He caught a yellow leaf floating toward the ground. "That's it exactly. He doesn't always send rain when I ask. He has His own timing about these things." He looked at her. "About a lot of things, don't you think?" He clasped her hand.

Her heart thudded.

He pulled her to her feet, and his fingers caressed her cheek.

The atmosphere changed. Her breath caught in her throat as he drew her closer. All of the sudden, she wasn't ready for his kiss. Panicking, she tugged on her hand.

He immediately released her and stepped back. "Better get

back to those apples." He took a few steps toward the field before half turning back. "Please send the children to the orchard after school."

"Of course." She shoved the dishes into the basket so roughly that a plate chipped. She might have had her first real kiss from her husband if she hadn't pulled away.

Now, as the golden sun approached the horizon, she vowed not to pull away next time.

～

That evening, the children, exhausted from helping their father in the orchard after school, practically mumbled their bedtime prayers and were asleep by the time Rose closed their doors.

Samuel was asleep in an armchair. He deserved as much rest as he could get, for he'd not sleep again until tomorrow night.

Rose quietly packed a basket with beef sandwiches, hard-boiled eggs, an apple turnover, cheese, crackers, and bottles of water. Then she blew out the kitchen candles and hung up her apron.

The day's work was done.

A cheerful fire blazed. One wall lantern dimly lit the room, allowing her husband to nap before a long night of travel with a full moon to light his way. She tiptoed to the cushioned armchair beside him and sat. Leaning her head against the cushion, she shivered at a chilly breeze. It required too much effort to close the windows.

She studied Samuel's strong features, his straight nose, his firm jaw and sensitive mouth. His wavy hair fell over his forehead. She longed to brush it back with her fingers.

All of a sudden, his eyes opened.

Her breathing stopped.

He stood and looked down at her. Still holding her gaze, he

extended his hands. She placed hers in his, and he urged her to her feet.

He didn't move her closer to himself, as he had done earlier that day. He waited for her.

Don't pull away this time. Quivering, she stepped closer.

He let go of her hands and wrapped his arms around her, pulling her into the warmth of his embrace. Slowly, ever so slowly, he bent and kissed her.

Her heart stuttered, then thumped a rapid rhythm. He ended the kiss and drew back slightly to search her expression.

She wasn't sure what he saw there, but it must have been what he'd hoped to see, for his arms tightened and he lowered his lips to hers in a lingering kiss that she wanted to last forever.

Emotions surged that she'd never experienced as she molded herself against his strong chest, his firm stomach. Samuel loved her. She thrilled at strong arms that knew just how to hold her, feeling cherished in a way that would see them through the years. She clung to him, pouring all her love into the embrace.

He drew back mere inches and smiled at her. His fingertips caressed her face as he looked at her with so much love that she wanted to pinch herself to make certain it wasn't a dream.

As he leaned to kiss her again, her fingertips halted his lips. "Samuel, do you love me?"

His expression changed. Was that guilt darkening his eyes?

His gaze shifted to the painting that hung in the shadows, Ginny's white dress barely discernable in the dim light.

Sudden clarity slowed Rose's heartbeat to normal rhythm. He didn't love her. Of course not. Foolish dreamer. Memories of Ginny always overshadowed Rose. All the love in this relationship was in her own heart. She should have known. She shivered within his arms as if an arctic wind had swept through the home.

"Pa, what are you doing?" Peter stood at his bedroom doorway.

Her arms fell to her side. She stepped away from the lantern's light.

Samuel strode to his son.

"She ain't Ma." His body shook with confusion or maybe rage.

How much had he witnessed?

Rose covered her mouth. Had their embrace caused him more pain?

"No." Samuel bent down and wrapped his arms around him. "She's not like your ma."

True enough. Rose's body shuddered.

Samuel said something else, but it didn't register past her own agony. He guided his son back into the bedroom and closed the door.

CHAPTER 27

*R*ose didn't know how long she stood in the shadows before a log snapped, sending burning cinders up the chimney. One attached itself to the hearth until the ember died.

Just like her hopes of a happy home.

Their marriage had been a terrible mistake. She knew that now. She wouldn't be able to love him enough to heal his grief. It seemed that kissing her had only reminded him of all he'd lost.

She'd made a dreadful mess of everything when she'd only wanted to love them all through the pain. How had things gone so horribly wrong?

Violent trembling overtook her. Samuel might want to talk with her when he left Peter's room, but she couldn't bear witnessing again the shame that embracing her had caused.

Wobbly knees threatened to buckle, but dread of facing Samuel strengthened her feeble legs.

She made it to her bedroom and closed the door, seeking the sanctuary of her dark room.

After dragging Papa's rocking chair closer to the open window, she slumped onto it.

Her cheeks burned at the shameful way she'd invited his kisses, so tender yet passionate. At the first mention of love, his thoughts had flown to Ginny.

This family needed someone to cook and clean. That was all Samuel required of her. He'd stripped her of any standing with her stepchildren while pushing her to the background in her own home. She'd worked hard, believing herself part of this family and the farm's success.

All this in hopes of easing her family's pain. *Her* family? What a fool. She'd never been more than a live-in housekeeper. The truth pierced her heart. Only in her dreams had she belonged there.

The curtain flapped wildly, slapping her across the cheek. Cold breezes chilled her, but what did her comfort matter? What did anything matter now?

Nothing held her in Hamilton. Peter kept her at arm's length. Emma followed his example. Samuel didn't need *her* specifically. He simply needed someone to clean.

Ginny had been everything Rose wasn't. Rose laughed at her dreams of Samuel falling in love with her. The bitter sound mocked her. He'd explained that love wouldn't enter their bargain. Her heart hadn't listened. Now she paid the price.

Poor Peter had been beside himself tonight. The children paid the price, too.

Since her continued presence would do nothing but cause more pain, she must leave.

Within an hour, Samuel's wagon would exit the barn, lantern lights on either side illuminating his face for one final glimpse.

The Sawyers had been correct after all—she wasn't the right woman for Samuel. Deep down, she'd always known the truth. Samuel knew, better than anyone, that she wasn't like Ginny. Hadn't he admitted as much to Peter?

Celia had warned of hardships inherent in marriages of convenience. Why hadn't she listened?

Booted steps approached. A tap on her door. She grasped the arms of her chair. The darkened room might fool him into believing she was asleep. Hearing his regrets for kissing her or a reiteration of their original bargain was more than she could bear.

A moment later, his footsteps crossed to the kitchen. Window cranks squeaked.

Rose savored the muffled steps on the rug, the wobble in a loose floorboard as Samuel moved about the main room. All too soon, she watched through the window as he carried a lantern and the packed basket to the barn. The horses neighed as she imagined him hitching the team to the wagon.

Then the wagon seat creaked, followed by wooden wheels striking a rut. The horses hovered near her window for a moment. She sank into the darkness. Unfortunately, Samuel's wide brimmed hat denied her a final glimpse of his face.

The wagon paused for a minute at the road. The black night blocked out everything except the dim glow of the lanterns. Then, clopping hooves grew fainter.

He was gone.

A teardrop fell on the hand that gripped the arm of the rocking chair. She brushed it away. This was no time for weakness.

The abundant crop had provided sufficient funds for Samuel to hire a part-time housekeeper. Selena Harris from the sewing group was searching for a job. Perhaps he'd hire her. If Samuel had waited a few months to marry, he might have proposed to someone like Selena. After all, her personality was similar to Ginny's.

Rose's heart shied away from contemplating his future with another woman.

She had asked God to guide her decision in the spring. Why

had He steered her down a path filled with such pain? Sudden realization pierced her muddled thoughts.

Because she hadn't waited for His answer. She'd been so certain God was fulfilling her girlhood dreams at last that she'd followed her own desires, her heart. What if she had waited for His answer? Would God have guided her to wait a few months? Or to decline the proposal?

There was no sense dwelling on that question. Now was the time to be practical. Evidently, she couldn't inspire a man's love. Had she learned nothing from watching Samuel fall in love with Ginny all those years ago? From her courtship with Reuben Bailey?

Apparently not, but this experience had taught her well and good to never hope for a man's love. It wasn't to be—not for her.

She paced in the darkness. She had to leave, but where was she to go?

Not to Richard. Her brother would demand that she resolve her problems with her husband and send her home.

Celia and Fred had transformed her old bedroom into a room for their daughter. They'd welcome her, but Rose refused to burden her best friend, who was suffering through a difficult pregnancy. Besides, boarding with *her* former boarders created an awkward situation.

She still wasn't sure where she'd end up as she lit the candle. Wherever she landed, the first step would be the hardest.

There was much to do.

~

*S*amuel tugged on the collar of his coat upward to keep a cold breeze off his neck, grateful that moonlight illuminated the dirt road to Cincinnati. His thoughts weren't on his team.

He'd finally held Rose in his arms tonight. Those kisses were a long time coming. Her response had been everything he hoped. He would have confessed his love if not for that fateful question, *Samuel, do you love me?*

Ginny had asked the same question a thousand times. The beautiful woman had required daily reassurance of his love. She'd always been a little jealous of his previous friendship with Rose, though he cut all ties with her after realizing it.

This evening, Rose's response to his kisses had revealed her deep feelings. Maybe she even loved him as he loved her. He hoped so because he had recognized he was losing his heart to her when Emma unwrapped her new doll dress and Rose's beautiful face lit up. It was all he could do to refrain from kissing her. Tonight, he'd followed his heart and kissed her.

Rose's shattered look haunted him.

What have I done?

He'd been unfaithful to Ginny, that's what.

Peter's anger had poured oil on the fire of Samuel's shame. His son had awakened from a nightmare in which his mother needed help, only to find Rose in his father's arms.

Samuel had assured him that his mother was happy in heaven and that someday he'd see her again. Peter demanded his promise never to hug Rose again.

Samuel made no promises, but he hesitated to pursue the physical side of his relationship with his wife while his son resented her presence.

Sticking with his original plan for the foreseeable future seemed best for everyone.

~

*T*he rooster crowed the next morning as Rose stared at her note to Samuel. It was the best she could do.

Each moment now bittersweet, she milked the cows for the last time.

Perhaps due to Samuel's absence, both children were quieter than normal at breakfast. Rose focused on wrapping a couple of apple turnovers in a linen cloth, trying to hold onto tenuous control of her emotions.

She loved these children. She'd miss them so much.

Peter headed out the door with his lunch pail without saying goodbye. Emma followed. They were down the steps before Rose reached the porch.

"Peter. Emma."

They stopped at the gate.

"I expect your pa before school ends. If he isn't back, visit Charlie until he gets here."

Emma's eyes widened. "Where will you be?"

"I must go into the city later." The train depot was in the city so it was truthful…yet misleading. Her conscience smote her, but Samuel undoubtedly would prefer to explain her absence. He'd never trusted her instincts with his children. "Now, I need hugs."

Emma complied, her little arms snaking around Rose's neck.

"You be a good girl." Rose fought to keep emotion out of her voice. She released Emma and turned to Peter. "Your turn."

Peter half-turned toward her. She gave him a brief embrace, hurt when she realized he was merely submitting to her request, not hugging her back. Likely a response to witnessing her embrace with Samuel.

"Have a good day." She waved to their retreating backs. "I love you," she whispered. Tears refused their prison. They chased each other down her face.

Whimpering, Zeb pressed against her.

"You're the only one who knows I'm leaving, aren't you, boy?" She bent to stroke the protective dog's head. "Watch over Peter and Emma."

The dog licked her hand.

"I know you will. Go on now. Follow the children."

Zeb gave her one last lick before loping to Peter's side.

Rose followed the stone path to the road. Leaning against the fence, she watched until the children and the dog crossed a small hill and stepped out of sight.

She would never know the man Peter became.

She would never bounce Emma's babies on her knees.

Footsteps kicked up a dust near her left side.

"Good morning."

She looked up into Charlie's concerned eyes. "Charlie. You startled me." She turned to brush tears from her cheeks. "How does this morning find you?"

"I'm a mite worried about a friend. I don't know if I can ask what ails her, but I sure wish she'd tell me."

His kindness broke the dam, and she sobbed. The final goodbye with her children had destroyed her.

Charlie put a fatherly arm around her and guided her up the porch stairs to a pair of chairs. He sat beside her, patting her hand from time to time until she gained control.

Finally, she forced a smile. "Women sometimes have emotional days."

His eyes pierced her pain. "Happened to my Esther. Mostly when she was expecting."

That was the last thing she needed to hear. There'd be no babies for her. Not ever. She rose to her feet. "Charlie, will you do something for me?"

"Name it."

"Take me to the depot?"

Her friend stared at her long and hard.

The chickens clucked. The cows lowed. But the silence

between them stretched.

Slowly, Charly stood. "If you're sure that's what you want."

Words of agreement stuck in her throat. It was the last thing she wanted. "Can we leave in an hour?"

Keen eyes searched her face. After a pause, his glance fell. "I'll ready the wagon."

Charlie made his slow way across the road, his shoulders stooped lower than she'd ever seen them. How she'd miss the only father figure left in her life.

After the breakfast dishes were washed and put away, she dragged her trunk to the front door. Her few pieces of furniture, along with her mother's dishes, which were still packed in a barrel, would be left behind. She imagined Samuel would send them after she settled into a new home. He'd probably be glad to be rid of any memories of her.

Harvest money filled the cup hidden on the top cupboard shelf. She counted out a portion equal to the sale of her house and left the rest. A few bills were tucked in her reticule. The remainder went into her trunk.

She packed a sandwich, two boiled eggs, crackers, cheese, apples, and two bottles of water. This food must stretch until she found a job.

Lying on the dining table was her letter to her husband. She touched the page. "Goodbye, Samuel. Maybe someday, someone will fill that void in your heart."

A tear smudged the ink on the single page. She turned away. She would shed no more tears for the man who'd never loved her and never would.

Her gaze caressed the house she had called home. No place on earth could ever be as precious.

Though she fought against it, the wedding portrait drew her gaze like a bee to honey. The couple had been as 'happily ever after' as any fairy tale. Samuel had lost the love of his life that February day.

"Please, God, allow him to find that kind of happiness again."

Her glance fell on the radiant bride. "Samuel took the right girl to that picnic all those years ago. You made him happy."

Her gaze moved with an aching heart to the smiling face of her husband. "I love you, Samuel. You'll never know the truth, but I love you." Sorrow dammed her heart. "Had you wanted it, my love would have been strong enough and deep enough to take us through the years." She swallowed hard, refusing to let any more tears fall. "You never misled me. You told me from the beginning that you'd buried your heart with Ginny. I suppose even spinsters have dreams. Mine were foolish ones, to be sure.

"You married me for the sake of your children. Forgive me for failing you and them. You wanted to be the one to comfort them and listen to their problems. Perhaps if you had trusted me with them, our relationship might have blossomed."

Closing her eyes, she gave her head one slow shake, then another.

"One day when the part of your heart not buried with Ginny mends a little, you'll find that special woman. She'll be beautiful and kind." Rose touched her own soft cheek, wishing for the kind of beauty that appealed to her husband. "I made things harder. I should have realized all you needed was a housekeeper. Now you'll have the trouble of dissolving our marriage, but Mr. Sawyer will assist you." Bitterness crept into her voice. The Sawyers had been right about her, but they'd been hurtful as well. "I never put that joy on your face, but someone will. You're not meant to be alone."

Sadness drove her to Peter's room, where his sheet and quilt were strewn across the bed in disarray. Rose smoothed the bedding one last time. "I love you, too, Peter. Things will be hard around here again, and a little messy until your pa hires a housekeeper. I'm sorry."

Emma's room was next. It was tidy, as Rose expected.

Emma's doll, wearing the dress Rose had sewn for her birthday, lay against the pillow. She touched the dress's tiny pink folds. "I love you, Emma. You're a sweet, kind girl. I'll miss you and your brother."

The clip clop of horses' hooves and the rolling of wooden wheels against the dirt road carried through the walls of her home. *Their* home. She drew back her shoulders. Time to go.

Resolutely she picked up her basket, her carpetbag, and her reticule. She opened the front door without a backwards glance and placed them outside. Then she began dragging her trunk down the steps.

She and Charlie lifted the trunk into the wagon. The silent journey to the depot ended all too quickly. With little traffic on the streets, not even the city fought to bind her there.

The decision of where to go loomed over her. She didn't want to head south to the big city of Cincinnati. Village life suited her better. Or a farm. Like the one she'd lived on for months.

Rose went inside the station while Charlie saw to her luggage. Fighting melancholy, Rose searched the northern destination chart on the wall. Since she'd never been north of Hamilton or south of Cincinnati, she had no idea where to go. One of her students had moved to Harrison from Piqua. It seemed as good a location as any, and it was little more than a sixty-mile journey.

Charlie crossed and uncrossed his arms as he arranged for her trunk to be loaded on the train.

That done, he shuffled to her side. "Piqua, huh?" His hands trembled. "Rosie, are you sure about this? You leaving like this don't feel right."

"Samuel will understand." She hugged the dear man who seemed as distraught as she felt. "Thank you for the ride. I won't forget."

"Repay me by writing real soon to let us know you're

settled." Charlie took her hands.

"I promise."

She mounted high metal steps and sat in a forward-facing seat. If only things had turned out differently.

Charlie stood alone on the wooden platform beside the locomotive. She waved goodbye.

He lifted his hand. Worry lines etched deeply on his face, and for once, the twinkle was missing.

Her abrupt departure had done this to him. She regretted involving him. His forlorn figure grew smaller as the train pulled away.

The chugging motion coupled with black smoke gave her a queasy stomach before she'd traveled three miles. Constant stops made it worse. The conductor offered a dipper from a water bucket. After drinking her fill, she doused one of her handkerchiefs with the water and held it over her nose and mouth to block out nauseating fumes. She leaned her forehead against the cool windowpane and closed her eyes against the curiosity of surrounding passengers.

Why was nothing easy?

CHAPTER 28

A restaurant owner bought six bushels of apples without quibbling over the price. The entire wagonload sold before nine o'clock. Even though Samuel dreaded an unavoidable conversation with Rose, he made it home an hour before the children were due that crisp, sunny afternoon. It would give them time to talk in private.

He definitely owed her an apology, but he didn't know how to explain Ginny's hold over his heart, his guilt for falling in love with Rose. He lingered over rubbing down his weary horses and providing generous portions of oats and water. Though he was no closer to finding the right words, it was time to talk.

He stepped inside the kitchen. No stew bubbled on the stove. No delicious aromas wafted from the oven. He looked around, but Rose wasn't in the bedrooms or the attic. Was she at Hazel's house? She always left a note on the table.

Ah, there it was. He snatched the paper from the smooth surface. His heart pounded at the first sentence.

Dear Samuel,

By the time you read this letter, I will be long gone. I realize my leaving creates a hardship in caring for the children and the home. I know now that you only needed a housekeeper. Our marriage happened much too soon for all of you. Pauline was wrong. You didn't need a wife, at least not right away.

I tried to care for your family's needs without overstepping the boundaries given me. I've often felt like someone you had to tolerate in your home but didn't want. Although I believed the situation had improved, I now understand my mistake. I tried to take Ginny's place, but everyone understands I am nothing like her. You acknowledged as much to Peter last night.

I'm certain Mr. Sawyer will still be willing to prepare legal documents to dissolve our marriage. I heard him make the offer months ago. I will sign anything you wish.

Selena Harris from church needs a job. She's young, and her sparkling personality will appeal to the children if you decide to hire her as a part-time housekeeper. She has fallen in love with your city and needs a job to remain there.

Please say my goodbyes to the children. I know you married me to take care of them. I deeply regret disappointing you. I do love Emma and Peter, and it breaks my heart to leave them. But it was breaking my heart more to stay. I'm certain they will grow up to be strong and faithful, like their father.

Very truly yours,

Rose

She was gone. Without saying goodbye. A chill spread across his chest. He'd failed her and his children. And himself...though that hardly mattered now.

The page crumpled in his fist. He sank to his knees. She was gone.

Peter's agitation last night had overridden a nagging insistence to clear the air with Rose. He'd comforted his son and neglected his wife. Again. How many times had he done that in the past months? Focused on Emma and Peter. Ignored Rose's needs. He'd used his grief as a shield to keep her away. To protect his heart from falling in love. How many times had he hurt her in his selfishness?

Last night hadn't been the cause. Last night had been the last straw.

What a fool he'd been. She likely construed his silence as rejection, when it was far from it.

Yet words had seemed inadequate. An apology hadn't seemed appropriate because he hadn't been sorry he kissed her. An explanation? Yes, he owed her that because he shouldn't have embraced her until he'd worked through the pain of losing Ginny.

The shattered pain in Rose's eyes haunted him.

He rubbed his hands through his hair. How was he to manage without her? He didn't realize her importance to his happiness until he'd read her note.

She didn't deserve any of this.

The door opened and Charlie, looking as if he'd aged ten years in one day, stepped inside. He closed the door. "Son, I got some hard news."

~

*R*ose clutched the railcar's iron railing on wobbly legs at the landing in Piqua. Exhaust smoke swallowed her up, but at least the ground didn't move. Or did it? Nausea made it difficult to be certain. The train ride had been torturous, especially since she had no place to go.

She arranged for her trunk to be held temporarily, and then toted her basket and carpetbag to the station. Despite the cool afternoon, every window inside the building was open. The cross breeze provided the fresh air her body craved. Finding the women's waiting area deserted, she slumped onto a bench until her stomach eased. Then she strolled with other pedestrians on the bustling city street.

Soon she was back at the depot purchasing a ticket. There were no jobs nearby, but a cook was needed at a restaurant in Bradford Junction, a nearby railroad village. *Please, Lord, let it be a short ride.*

An hour later she stepped onto the railroad town's platform, her stomach protesting as if she'd traveled an extra sixty miles instead of ten. Her stomach balked at any further travel today. Job or not, she'd spend at least one night in the village.

"Ladies and gentlemen, you have twenty minutes to eat supper." The conductor consulted his pocket watch. "Remember, only twenty minutes, folks."

A few travelers from the crowded platform rushed into a nearby restaurant. Others crossed the track toward two other eating establishments. Some entered a white frame building, Mrs. Saunders' Eatery, the one she'd heard required a cook.

Rose sank onto a bench outside the busy depot to wait for the restaurant to empty. A half dozen men worked around the station's roundhouse. A burly man loaded her trunk into the depot's baggage section.

Everything had a dreamlike quality. Her heart cried out for Samuel, Peter, and Emma.

"Ma'am, please." A young woman carrying an infant displayed her basket's contents. A little girl around four years of age clung to her Mama's arm. "I have a roasted turkey sandwich, fried peach pies, boiled eggs, and sliced bread. And those apples were picked fresh this morning."

"Smells delicious." Although Rose's stomach lurched at the aroma of peaches, this mother's eyes pleaded with Rose to buy her food instead of eating at an overcrowded restaurant. "I'll take a fried pie. I haven't eaten peach pie in a long time." Apple pies were another matter.

The brown-eyed girl tugged on her mother's skirt. "Mama, she likes peaches. Just like me."

"What about that, Liza Jane?" Her mama set her basket on the bench. "Remember we asked God to help us sell everything in our basket? See, He always takes care of His children."

Liza Jane beamed at Rose.

Her own hungry days after Papa died hadn't been so long ago that she didn't remember them. Here was a family down on their luck. "Do I see two slices of bread? And I can't resist freshly picked apples—I'll take two of those." As she spoke, she covered the apples in her basket with her carpetbag. She had only been able to force down a few crackers all day.

"Thank you, Ma'am."

Rose paid what she asked.

Two men gaped at them from the roundhouse entrance. Rose ignored them, turning her attention to the conductor. He entered the restaurant and quickly exited to cross the tracks for the other restaurants. A crowd followed him outside like ducks in a row. A boy not much older than Peter stuffed biscuits into his pocket.

A middle-aged couple bought two peach pies from the persistent mother. A husky farmer bought the turkey sandwich.

The triumphant look on Liza Jane's face warmed Rose's heart. They left the platform as the train pulled away. Black plumes of smoke wafted over, reigniting a bout of queasiness. It eased after she ate the hearty bread she'd just purchased.

Best get this job request over with because she must find a place to stay. Whispering a prayer, she gathered her basket and carpet bag and crossed the track to the smaller restaurant.

Inside, a boy and girl with the same dark brown hair and eyes cleared dishes from a dozen tables inside the spacious dining room.

Rose tried to catch the eye of the girl, who was perhaps fourteen and wore a checked blue apron over a green calico dress. In vain. The siblings were too busy to talk, which was a promising sign.

"Pardon me." She blinked at their similar looks. "You're twins. I had two sets of twins in my class."

The girl continued to stack dirty plates, but the boy turned to her.

"I was a teacher." Rose's voice trailed off. "I heard you need a cook."

The boy pointed to a closed door. "Mrs. Saunders is in the kitchen. She hates doing all the cooking."

Rose knocked. Receiving no answer, she pushed the knobless door open. A short woman with gray-streaked brown hair peeled potatoes at one of the long tables lining the inside wall of a kitchen three times the size of the farm's.

"Mrs. Saunders?"

The plump woman didn't even glance her way. "Restaurant's closed until the next meal train."

"I need a job."

Her head shot up, and her dark eyes took her measure. "Can you cook?"

"I've received compliments."

"Humph." The shorter woman set her knife on the table. "Another train of customers will arrive in about an hour. The previous crowd ate the last of the soup and most of the sandwiches. If you can prepare enough soup to feed at least fifteen people and prepare ten roasted beef sandwiches by the time they get here, you're hired."

"What kind of soup?"

"Vegetable. Carrots and celery are already in there. There's the rest." She nodded with her chin.

Potatoes, onions, and tomatoes were strewn haphazardly about a large work table. Jars of seasoning were arranged on a shelf above. Rose shoved her belongings under a table and grabbed an apron from a wall hook. "Consider it done."

Mrs. Saunders watched her dice potatoes into bite-sized pieces and toss them in the huge pot already on top of one of the stoves. "It'll take a full pot. Meat in the icebox is ready for slicing." The twins brought in an armload of dishes. "That's Cora and John."

They exchanged greetings. John disappeared into the dining room while Cora washed plates in a deep basin without the convenience of a pump handle. It surprised Rose how accustomed she'd grown to indoor water.

Eighteen sandwiches adorned a platter by the time the train whistle blew. She dished up fragrant, bubbling vegetable soup and then helped the others set hot bowls in front of each chair.

The hungry crowd rushed in. Cora plopped a plate in front of a burly customer. "When we serve soup and sandwiches, we're supposed to have everything on the table when the guests arrive. Tea, coffee, or milk is in the kitchen. Ask which one they want. Mrs. Saunders collects money at the beginning while we keep each table's bread baskets filled with biscuits or cornbread. Everyone gets one bowl of soup, one sandwich, and one piece of pie, unless they pay extra."

Twenty minutes flew. The conductor opened the door. "Train leaves in two minutes. Two-minute warning, folks."

Mrs. Saunders locked the front door after the last man exited with half a sandwich in his hand. "That's the last meal train today. John, Cora, eat supper before cleaning up."

The children served themselves then ate as if starved.

Mrs. Saunders looked at Rose curiously. "What's your name?"

"Rose Walker."

"Is there as Mrs. in front of that?" She glanced at the ring on Rose's left hand.

She lowered her eyes. "Yes." How did one explain leaving one's husband?

"Humph. My husband died at Gettysburg. Won't ask about yours if you don't ask about mine. Hate thinking about it and that's a fact. Well, Mrs. Walker, I reckon you're hired. You'll get one free meal a day plus your wages." She named a weekly salary almost double her teaching salary. "Bradford Junction is a meal stop. We serve three breakfasts, at least two dinners, and two suppers daily. The schedule changes. You'll cook all meals, six days a week."

No wonder she paid generously.

"I help with meal preparations. Mrs. Wendy Mobley bakes pies, cakes, breads, and such daily. Cora washes dishes. John does everything else that needs doing. Does that sound acceptable?"

"Yes." She dared not refuse the long hours.

"I'll call you Rose. Supper is your pay for today. You start tomorrow morning at five-thirty." She scurried from the room.

Rose wondered if the harried woman rushed everywhere or if today had been a particularly trying day. She carried a bowl of vegetable soup into the dining room to sit with the siblings. "When do you two go home for the day?"

Cora lowered her head.

A whistle blew, and John stared out the window. "Ain't got no home."

Rose spilled a spoonful of soup onto the table. She wiped up her mess with an unused napkin. "Where do you sleep?"

"The kitchen," he answered gruffly.

"Where are your parents?"

Cora told the story. "Pa was a brakeman. He slipped on ice and fell off a train. Broke his neck."

"That was two years ago." John shoved his half-empty plate away. "Ma took sick last fall. No money for the doctor. We buried her next to Pa in the churchyard."

Two other children, Peter and Emma, crowded into her thoughts. Her heart ached. Suffering in children always hit her harder than anything else. Her troubles shrunk in comparison. "Did you find this job immediately?"

"Bank took our house since we couldn't pay the mortgage. Mrs. Saunders gave us a job and a place to sleep. Been here ever since." He shoved the last bite of the sandwich into his mouth.

They'd suffered more than she could understand. "Do you attend school?"

John snorted. "Ain't got no time for school."

Her eyes widened. "Are there boarding homes with a vacancy nearby?"

Cora raised her eyebrows. "Don't you have no place to stay neither?"

"No, I don't have a place to stay yet." The schoolteacher in her couldn't refrain from correcting Cora's grammar after trying to ignore John's butchering of the English language.

Her brow puckered. "Maybe Mrs. Westlake's. She used to speak to Mama at church. She lives in that big white house down the street. We can show you after we clean up."

"I'll help." The offer elicited smiles from them.

It was fully dark when they walked down a quiet street. Rose and Cora tugged their cloaks closer in the brisk breeze. John turned up his collar.

A five-minute walk led to a two-story clapboard home. A thin woman in her fifties answered their knock.

"Mrs. Westlake?" Rose hoped to avoid traipsing all over town in search of a room.

"I am. I don't believe I've had the pleasure." The unsmiling woman's eyes narrowed.

"My name is Rose Walker." She raised her chin. "I accepted a job as cook at Mrs. Saunders' Eatery and wondered if you have a boarding vacancy."

"Is that the Welch children with you?" Mrs. Westlake's tone remained frosty.

"Yes, I'm grateful John and Cora showed me where you live. I'm new to the village."

"Follow me." She picked up a glowing lantern.

She stepped into a spotless hallway with the front door facing a staircase, the children following. An open doorway to the left revealed a long dining table. A sitting room opposite provided ample seating for at least a dozen guests.

Wooden stairs creaked. Rose held onto the oak banister as she and the twins followed Mrs. Westlake to the second floor.

"All rooms on this floor are occupied. There's one room available." She unlocked a door with a key from her pocket and climbed a small, enclosed set of stairs leading to a long attic room with slanted walls. There were three beds in the first section with a heat stove, a small table, a spindle-backed chair, and a waist-high chest with a pitcher and a bowl on top. A lantern sat on a bedside table. A narrow aisle in the middle with windows on either side of a corridor led to an open room, identically furnished.

"I rent this room to families, railroad men, anyone who needs a place to stay."

It was much too spacious. "All I require is a single room."

"This is my only available room, Mrs. Walker." Her stern face showed no signs of softening. Did she ever smile?

"Room and board are the same low price, no matter how many people occupy the room." She named a figure that her salary would more than cover. "Breakfast is served promptly at six, dinner at noon, and supper at six in the evening."

"May I eat breakfast early? I have to be at work at five-thirty."

"Six o'clock. No earlier. Tardiness won't be tolerated."

"I'll only eat lunch here on Sunday. Will you lower the price?"

"That's not possible. The first week must be paid in advance." She extended her hand.

Rose paid her and received a key. "My trunk is at the station."

"I'll fetch it for you," John said, his voice timid, probably due to the woman's forceful personality.

"Thank you, John. I'll walk with you."

She settled in thirty minutes later, having given a generous tip to John and Cora. She yawned. Her sleepless night and stressful traveling day had drained her energy.

Once a fire blazed in the stove, she changed into a flannel nightgown.

Samuel had surely discovered her note by then. Was he upset? Surely the children would be fine once they adjusted to a new routine. Their father had never allowed them to need her, anyway.

Floorboards creaked. Wind whistled outside the window. She crawled into bed. All houses made sounds, but this one seemed noisier than most. And lonelier.

Would Samuel follow her? No. Even if he wanted to, she wasn't in Piqua, as Charlie had no doubt told him was her destination.

She'd write to him of her job and her new boarding home so he wouldn't worry. It was time to begin a new life without her family...even if her broken heart never healed.

CHAPTER 29

*S*amuel, frantic to hear from Rose, rode his horse to the post office every day for a week before finally receiving the letter that Charlie assured him was coming. It wasn't like Rose to worry him. Then again, none of this was like her. He'd prayed for her safety as often as he'd prayed for her broken heart. A beautiful woman, all alone...well anything could happen.

She wasn't the only one with a splintered heart—and not just his own, but his children's.

Trotting home to read the letter in privacy, he considered Peter's and Emma's sadness, hurt, and confusion over their stepmother's absence. He had taken them aside as soon as they arrived home that first day. They asked lots of question about when Mama Rosie was coming home. He couldn't answer. Emma sobbed on his shoulder. Peter curled up on his bed. The chaos of the kitchen and piles of laundry was beginning to remind him of the days before Rose came. Peter missed his stepmother's cooking. Even Samuel was tired of his own burnt meals.

But he missed so much more than the surface things. He missed her gentleness, her cheerful demeanor. Her confidence in tackling every task. Her compassion for their grief that rose up at unexpected moments. Her laugh and her sense of humor that invited them all to see the funny side of a situation.

The finality of Rose's note had scared Samuel. Her suggestion to dissolve their marriage had been as startling as everything else she'd done. She had even suggested hiring a part-time housekeeper, of all things.

He didn't want a housekeeper. He wanted a wife. He wanted *Rose*, but he'd made so many mistakes that hurt her. He saw that now.

Charlie told Samuel about Rose's brokenhearted sobs when she left. He'd wanted to follow her to Piqua, but Charlie suggested giving her a little time.

He looped the horse's reins to a fence post, rushed inside his house, and broke the letter's seal.

Dear Samuel,

I'm sure you'll be happy to discover that I found both a job and lodging in Bradford Junction, Ohio, a small railroad village west of Piqua. I work as a cook at Mrs. Saunders' Eatery.

John and Cora Welch, a couple of orphans, work here. They sleep at the restaurant because they have no home. I can't understand why someone hasn't adopted them. The fourteen-year-olds have been a tremendous help to me. I love them already.

I sleep in an attic room at a boarding house down the street from the depot and restaurant. The huge room with six beds was Mrs. Westlake's only vacancy. The proximity to my job is convenient, as I walk to work before dawn and return after sunset.

I hope Peter and Emma are doing well and like Selena. She'll take good care of them.

I am writing to both Richard and Celia. I don't want anyone to worry.

Please forgive me for leaving without saying goodbye.

Very truly yours,

Rose

She found a *job*? His head reeled.

She didn't plan to return. And she believed this was happy news to him.

It felt as if she'd traveled thousands of miles away. She'd begun a new life that didn't include them.

He crumpled the letter. Stopped short of tossing it into the fire. She clearly didn't want anything from him.

A cold draft blew through the room, and he turned to find that Peter and Emma stood at the door.

He knelt and held out his arms. They ran into them. With a heart heavier than a pail of milk, he asked them to sit and prepared to read Rose's letter aloud. How he wished to protect them from another loss. Again he considered going after her, but something held him back.

A knock at the door a moment before Charlie entered.

"You may as well hear this, too," Samuel said. "Join us at the table." He waited until his friend settled into a chair and folded his hands expectantly. "I've heard from Rose."

Emma clapped her hands.

Peter straightened in his chair.

Charlie's expression managed to be both wary and hopeful.

"When will Mama Rosie be here, Pa?" The joyful, expectant look on his daughter's face broke his heart.

Samuel's heart tumbled to his toes. "She's not coming, Emma, at least not yet."

Color ebbed from her face.

Taking a deep breath, he read the letter aloud. Silence followed.

"Who are John and Cora?" Emma asked.

"Orphans who work with her."

"She loves them." Her voice was filled with hurt.

"That's what she said."

"Doesn't she love us anymore?"

Peter's shoulders stiffened. His head went down, his expression hidden.

Samuel pulled his little girl onto his lap. "She loves you and Peter." He rocked her, trying to comfort despite the loss in his own heart. He met Charlie's troubled gaze, silently pleading for guidance.

The older man cleared his throat. "Do you know what I hear Mama Rosie saying?"

Emma sniffed. "What?"

Peter looked up hopefully.

"She wants us to pray for her." Charlie fiddled with his hat.

"She does?" Emma titled her head.

"We pray for the people we love, don't we?"

She nodded.

"Mama Rosie is far from her family." His gaze darted to each face. "She's bound to be sad. Let's pray God will keep her safe until we see her again."

"I will," Emma said.

Charlie patted her shoulder. "Good girl. Want help stabling Midnight, Samuel?"

He had forgotten the saddled horse tied to the fence. "Yes, thank you."

The two men crossed the yard to the barn silently, Samuel leading his horse.

"She's got a job, Charlie."

"I heard."

In the barn, Samuel lifted off the saddle. "She thinks I'm happy about it."

"Think so?" Charlie leaned against the stall.

"That's what her letter said."

The older man sighed. "I reckon you're angry."

"You saw Emma's tears. You bet I'm angry. Running away never solves problems." He led the horse into the stall.

"Reckon that's true. So, you planning a trip to Bradford Junction?"

"Not yet. I've got children to care for, animals to feed." He brushed the horse's side. It rankled that she'd started a new life. Without him. He needed to do some thinking. "Looks like I'll be hiring a housekeeper."

"Do what you think best. Just remember what I said to Emma. I'll pray for all of you." Charlie sauntered away.

Samuel leaned his forehead against a post. Now that he knew Rose was safe, his fear for her ebbed away, making room for anger that grew. She'd forced her stepchildren to lose two mothers in the same year.

Nightmares had haunted Peter's sleep almost nightly since she left. Emma wore Rose's simple dresses and played quietly with her doll. The merry mood created by Rose's presence had vanished. She'd maintained a calm, cheerful demeanor, quietly caring for the family and the house without fuss or complaint. She'd brought a positive change he hadn't fully realized until she was gone.

Life with Ginny had been far more complicated. She'd never enjoyed living on a farm, but her attitude had worsened after she'd befriended Lily Ann. When she wasn't in town visiting the ladies, or inviting them over in the guise of working together, she'd create excuses to keep Samuel from working because she didn't enjoy solitude.

Rose hadn't demanded the same attention. She hadn't demanded anything.

He slammed his palm onto a wood post. If she was unhappy, she should have told him. He couldn't read her mind.

And here she figured he'd jump at the chance for an annulment. For an intelligent woman, she sure neglected the brains God gave her sometimes.

She evidently needed time away from the family. He was happy to grant it. He needed a chance to simmer down himself.

Charlie was right about one thing. He must pray soon. For now, there were chores to do.

~

A half-moon peeked between the branches of a barren tree. Rose pulled her cloak closer to her body to shield against the cool night air. She was too late for supper at Mrs. Westlake's again.

For someone earning a living as a cook, it surprised her how challenging it was to find time to eat. Her employer watched every penny. Rose elected to eat breakfast as her free meal and purchased lunch from Liza Jane's mother. She'd made a friend of the spunky little girl.

More often than not, Mrs. Saunders asked her to remain and serve supper. The first night she'd been too late to eat with the other boarders at Mrs. Westlake's. After that, she'd demanded a free supper if working late. Her boss grudgingly agreed. Other than that, Rose didn't mind the work. Long days gave her more time with the twins, who were learning to trust her.

Wendy Mobley commandeered one large stove while Rose cooked on the other. The short, auburn-haired widow had an infectious laugh and friendly manner. The restaurant kept sandwiches and pastries on hand to serve customers between serving hours and on Sundays. Rose prepared full meals for the railroad's daily meal stops.

Two weeks had flown—at least the days. Nights were another story.

Stars lit up the clear night sky. A train whistle blew, a

familiar sound she heard day and night. A need for fresh air had driven her to stroll around town before returning to her lonely room.

Almost November. Undoubtedly, Samuel had received her letter. Thanks to her foolish heart, she searched every train arriving from Piqua for sign of him. John walked to the post office daily.

But there'd been no letters. No telegrams.

Youthful, vivacious Selena would help Peter and Emma through any rough spots caused by Rose's departure. They'd only relied on her for meals and clean clothes anyway.

She stumbled on the dark street. Did Samuel miss her?

Unlikely. The longer she was gone, the less she believed she'd ever see him again.

~

"Will you teach me to make your Baked Chicken Pie?" Cora stood beside Rose at a worktable three days later. "It's my favorite."

"I'll do better than that." Cora would wash dishes all her life unless she learned a new skill. "I'll teach you to cook."

"I'd love to learn but"—she frowned at the dirty dishes lining the counter—"there isn't time."

Cleaning this restaurant was a full-time job. "I'll help when you get behind."

"You will?" Her eyes widened.

"Certainly." Rose selected a cookbook from her basket. "I use this book, *Directions for Cookery*, by Eliza Leslie. My father bought it for me after my mother died."

"You lost your Mama, too?"

Rose touched Cora's shoulder. "As a little girl."

Cora turned her gaze to the book. "Is it difficult to make?"

"I'll show you." Rose hugged her. "We'll make supper together."

Cora showed a surprising knack for cooking over the next few days.

Both children needed to attend school, but they'd remain there unless a loving family offered them a home. It was a shame no one helped them.

~

A dreary rainy day became a drearier night. No stars peeked through that gray blanket. It felt too cold for the second Friday of November. Rose trudged through dead leaves toward the boarding house, too weary to care about the weather. Another day had passed without a letter from Samuel.

He hadn't bothered to write.

After Papa's death, the future had appeared bleak and dismal. This heart wrenching loneliness surpassed even that miserable time.

Rose had written Celia, who'd asked her to come live with them, but Rose refused to burden her friends.

Richard's latest letter ordered her to return to her husband and children. He claimed that it didn't matter that Samuel didn't love her. She'd turned her back on the safety of a home, Richard said. Now she had nothing.

The truth of his words stung. She truly had lost everything, but there was no going back. She didn't compare to Ginny. No denying that truth.

Her best hope was to find a teaching position. Unfortunately, the annulment would squelch that possibility because a teacher's reputation must be above reproach.

She bore the blame for her mistakes. Samuel, in the throes of grief, hadn't been thinking clearly when he'd proposed. It had been up to her to carefully evaluate his proposal. Her desire to marry him had clouded her judgment. Sorrow was her consequence.

She shouldn't have allowed the Sawyers' disastrous visit to shut down communication with Samuel, because she saw now she had unfairly transferred their total disregard for her feelings onto her husband. She should have been honest with him about things that hurt her, like his insistence on being the sole comforter when the children's grief got the best of them.

Instead, she allowed that wedge to remain and separate them. Why? Because she'd seldom been valued for her own self.

Unhappiness clung to the orphans, too. Mrs. Saunders gave them a place to live and generous meals, but she paid little money. They slept on bedrolls in separate kitchen storage closets.

They were good children. Didn't God care about them either?

The thought stilled her steps a few feet from the boarding house porch. Was that what she had been thinking? That God didn't love her because Samuel didn't want her?

Disturbed by the direction of her thoughts, she continued up to her room. No sooner had she hung her shawl on the wall hook than she acknowledged the truth—she did *feel* that way, even though it went against all the teachings of the Bible. Intellectually she knew God loved her, John, and Cora. He had proven it by sending His Son, Jesus, to die on a cross for their sins. She'd attended church all her life and learned that God loved all people and had a purpose for each life, including hers.

Her mother had read her wonderful stories from the Bible. As a child, Rose had loved Jesus, the One who welcomed little children, with all her heart. She'd known He loved her and always would.

Her brain acknowledged a truth her heart no longer felt.

She prayed for Samuel and the children every night. She asked God to give John and Cora a loving family. She'd prayed, but she hadn't touched her mother's old Bible in a long, long time.

She heaved open her trunk and took out the heavy black book with creased, worn pages. Opening to the book of John, she began reading.

CHAPTER 30

*W*hen Rose arrived at the restaurant's kitchen the next morning before dawn, Cora launched herself into Rose's arms, almost knocking her down.

"What's wrong?"

Sobs were her only answer.

Rose guided the distraught girl to a chair. She met John's troubled gaze as he hovered over his sister. Wendy hadn't arrived yet, and Mrs. Saunders usually didn't descend from her second-floor apartment until the first breakfast train was due.

"What happened, John?" Rose asked. The twins had no parents, no one to battle for them. She'd fight for them if necessary.

"Mice ran over her face while she slept." He pointed to the closet closest to the outside wall. "Critters weren't a problem until it got cold, but we gotta get used to it. Ain't got nowhere else to go."

Tears drenched Cora's red, blotchy face. "I can't sleep there. I can't."

"I'll switch with you." John patted her shoulder awkwardly.

"What is it?" Wendy, a petite redhead, entered the room and knelt beside Cora. She pressed a handkerchief into her hand.

Rose quickly explained.

"I'll get a batch of biscuits in the oven and then collect my cat." Wendy stood. "I thought something scurried around yesterday. Any mice Harry doesn't catch will be too frightened to return."

Cora stared with empty eyes.

"That'll help, won't it, Cora?" John knelt beside his sister.

"Maybe." She swiped her cheeks with the handkerchief.

Rose watched them, a wild idea growing. What prevented her from raising the twins? Once the annulment went through, her ties to Samuel would be at an end. He didn't want or need her. These orphans did.

Why hadn't she thought of this earlier? Too mired in her own sorrow. Not a good quality. She'd make up for it now. She'd never been so happy to be overpaying for a family room. She'd tutor them at night until they were able to attend school.

If they wanted her. "John. Cora. Why don't you two come live with me?"

The twins looked at each other and had a conversation nobody else could hear.

When Cora turned back to Rose, hope glimmered in her eyes. "Until the mice are gone?"

"For now." This seemed an answer from her prayers last night, but she'd made too many mistakes by leaping ahead without seeking God's guidance. And she was still married. Samuel had a say in any larger commitments Rose might consider.

Cora burst into noisy sobs.

John extended his hand. "We accept."

Rose clasped his calloused hand. Cora clung to her.

John wrapped an arm around both of them.

"Can't anybody else get a hug around here?" A tearful Wendy

tapped John's shoulder. "I can't think when I heard better news."

Cora giggled, and it was the first time Rose had heard her laugh.

The breakfast train was due in thirty minutes. With everyone's help, sausage, gravy, and biscuits were ready on time.

Mrs. Saunders raced in as the whistle blew to announce the train's arrival. "Where are the scrambled eggs?"

"Oops!" Rose winked at John and Cora. "We'll have eggs ready for the next meal train."

The twins grinned back. They were in this together.

❧

*R*ose postponed a difficult conversation with Nora Saunders until the beef was roasting in the oven and the asparagus soup simmered. Nora had given the twins a room —such as it was—and board, along with a pittance to work for her. After today, that cost was going up. Rose, knowing how Nora watched every penny, every mouthful, dreaded arousing her anger.

After whispering a silent prayer, she motioned for the twins. "Mrs. Saunders, John and Cora are moving into my boarding house today."

The older woman glanced at them as she sliced carrots. "They don't have enough money to live there."

"They'll live with me from now on." Her body tensed.

Mrs. Saunders' dark eyes snapped. "They live with me."

Rose drew a deep breath. "They sleep in storage closets. I have beds for them."

"I gave them a roof when they had nowhere to go." Though her chin was high, color drained from her face. She sank into a nearby chair.

Rose's heart softened. "And they've been grateful."

The twins exchanged a glance.

Rose put her hand on Nora's arm. "You took them in when no one else did. That's a wonderful thing. Now I want to give them a home."

"I thought *I* gave them a home. Three hot meals a day." A big gray cat entered the open closet. "Guess I was wrong."

"I guess, like me, they'll receive one free meal daily from now on." Rose broke the uncomfortable silence. "They won't board here so their pay will increase."

"Outrageous." Mrs. Saunders leaped to her feet. "I've a good mind to fire all of you."

How quickly anger replaced compassion. "If that's your wish, we'll leave right now." She met her boss's blazing glare, even as she wondered where they'd go. Had she provided them a home only to get them dismissed?

John inched closer. Cora reached for Rose's hand and held on.

"Fifty cents extra a day for each." Her lips set in a thin line.

"If they work past six, their supper is free." Rose must say it all now or she'd lose her courage. "With Sundays off. They haven't been to church since they started working."

Hands on hips, Mrs. Saunders's angry face seemed set in stone. "Any more demands, Your Highness? If not, get back to work. I expect this place to be spotless before you leave tonight." She walked out, and the dining room door crashed into the wall.

Cora shook with fright.

"We still have jobs." Rose laughed a little, impressed she hadn't backed down.

Mrs. Westlake was next.

Rose brought the twins for the conversation with Mrs. Westlake, who had promised "one low price no matter how many people shared the room." She was also as stern as Rose's worst teacher as a child. After the angry scene with Nora, Rose didn't look forward to the discussion ahead.

John, chatting nonstop, carried a box containing everything

they had saved from their parents' home, including kitchen items and the family Bible.

Cora's carpetbag occasionally brushed the road. Everything they owned fit in two containers.

Rose paused at the bottom of the stairs leading to the boarding house door to whisper a prayer for courage.

Inside, Mrs. Westlake stepped from the sitting room. Her eyebrow lifted.

"Good evening, Mrs. Westlake. Might I speak with you?" She hoped her face didn't betray her anxiety.

"You may." She led them to the vacant sitting room. "I see you missed another meal tonight, Mrs. Walker."

How the woman expressed disapproval without using any inflection marveled Rose. "My apologies."

Mrs. Westlake gestured for them to be seated.

"John and Cora will be living with me from now on, Mrs. Westlake." Something about this woman caused Rose to feel like an unruly student.

"I see." Her frosty glance took in the fidgety twins. "Your weekly rent will double."

Must she fight everyone to take these children under her wing? "No, Mrs. Westlake. You told me when I arrived that room was the same low price no matter how many people stayed there."

"So I did." She pursed her lips. "How kind of you to remind me. Very well. They may stay, but the cost of meals will now be tripled."

Rose stood, shaking her head. Confrontations always challenged her, and this day had been full of them. "I informed you weeks ago not to make breakfast or dinner for me except on Sundays due to my work schedule, yet you never reduced my board. I only eat ten meals weekly at your establishment, yet you charge for twenty-one. These children work with me and will only eat ten meals weekly here also. Charge me the normal room rate plus ten meals apiece for each of us or I will find a new place to live."

Mrs. Westlake stood. A brief gleam lit her stern features. "I didn't know you possessed such a stubborn streak, Mrs. Walker. Very well. Your charge will go up the amount of nine more meals. I'm agreeing because I remember their mother." Her expression softened as her gaze rested on the orphans. "She was a good woman who took you to church every Sunday. I'm sure you'll do well with Mrs. Walker." She quoted a price in such a harsh tone that Rose accepted immediately. Her pay covered the increase with precious little left. She thanked her and ushered the twins upstairs.

"Which bed is mine?" asked Cora after Rose lit the lanterns.

"I sleep in the bed closest to the door. John, your room is at the end of the hall."

"My own room?" He picked up a second lantern and raced down the narrow corridor.

Cora jumped onto her bed. "This feels like heaven. I haven't slept in a bed since we lost our home."

Rose's cheeks burned for being too engrossed with her own sorrow to help them. She reached into the wood box for kindling. "No more sleeping on floors." There'd been enough of that.

Cora rubbed her arms. "It's freezing up here."

"I'll soon have a warm fire." Rose lit a match to a twisted sheet of newspaper and tossed it into the grate.

John plopped onto the last empty bed in the main room. "Last night my bedroom was a supply closet. Tonight, I have three beds. I'm gonna sleep on a different one every night until I figure out which I like best."

"Understandable." Rose laughed. "We'll attend church tomorrow. Shall I launder clothes tonight?"

Cora twisted her apron, looking more nervous that pleased. "I ain't been to church since Mama died."

"Can we go to our old church?" At least John was excited. "The one near our old house?"

"Of course." Rose sat on the corner of Cora's bed. "Is something wrong, Cora?"

She averted her eyes. "Folks don't wear aprons to church."

"Not usually." Her brow furrowed.

Cora glanced at her brother.

"John, will you build a fire in your room?" Rose asked. "Then unpack your belongings while Cora and I talk."

He left with the bag.

"What's bothering you?"

Cora's face flamed. "This is the last dress Mama made me. I have another one, but it won't button anymore." She removed her apron.

The fabric stretched across the bodice too snugly for modesty. No wonder she always wore the apron.

Rose understood. The fourteen-year-old had developed after her mother died. "Cora, our bodies change as we grow older. That's the way God designed us. All you need are dresses to fit you." She opened her trunk and selected a pink floral calico. "Do you like this one? Try it on. If it fits, I'll hem it tonight."

The girl fingered the dress.

Rose pulled out a white shirtwaist and a blue skirt. "I have several plain skirts that I wore to teach because dark colors don't show dirt. That's why I wear them at the restaurant. I can alter two to fit you so you can work in them."

Tears chased each other down Cora's cheeks as she rocked on the bed.

"Please tell me why you're crying." She gave her a handkerchief from a bedside table.

"It's been so long since I had a new dress." She blew her nose. "I love them all. Pink's my favorite color."

"It'll look beautiful on you." Rose held it up against Cora's dark hair. "Let's see how it fits."

CHAPTER 31

$\mathcal{A}$ t church, Cora's cheeks matched her pink dress. The siblings blossomed under the congregation's loving attention.

One white-haired woman drew Rose aside to say she often prayed for the Welch children. She called Rose "an answer to prayer."

"Can we show you around town this afternoon?" asked John as they strolled home for dinner. "We'll take you to our old house."

"I'd love to see it. Let's dress warmly." Wind whipped her skirt around her ankles. "Those gray clouds might hold the season's first snowfall."

"We don't have to work today. I can't remember the last day we ain't worked." John tossed a pebble over the railroad tracks into a vacant field.

"Thanks for demanding Sundays off, Rose." Cora frowned. "It doesn't seem right to call you that now. How should we address you?"

Thoughts of another little boy and girl brought a familiar ache for them. How she missed Peter and Emma. It took a minute to rein in her emotions. Miss Rose didn't fit since they'd called her Rose since the beginning. She wasn't adopting them, but she was taking them into her home. "How about Mama Rosie?"

~

*H*is fourth Sunday without Rose. Samuel kept busy during the week and tried to dismiss her from his thoughts. He'd dealt with the gruesome task of slaughtering his pigs for market this week. Now the fire must stay lit in the smokehouse to cure the meat. After that, the attic demanded his attention.

But Sundays were a day of rest, with too much time for thinking.

Friends at church asked about his wife's absence. The first week Charlie took the children to church while he remained at home. That didn't feel right, so he didn't stay home again, but the questions were tough to answer.

Mrs. Bradshaw had cornered him inside the church building two hours ago.

"Have you heard from Rose?" She gripped his arm, preventing him from following his children out the church door.

He had sighed. "Not since the letter I told you about."

"When will she return?" Her blue eyes pierced his facade.

"I don't know."

She poked his chest. "Go after her."

He folded his arms. "I can't spare time away."

"Humbug. Hazel and Richard will watch the children."

This woman never gave up. "I'm sure they're willing, but I'm too busy."

"If you're not careful, you'll lose Rose for good. Isn't she worth fighting for?"

She was. No doubt about it. That didn't mean he wanted to hear it right now. He left the building in a huff. Hazel took one look at him and offered to keep the children the rest of the day.

Long strides took him home in record time, battling his inadequacies.

As Rose instructed, he'd hired Selena, who worked three days a week and remained until the supper dishes were done. The children got along with her better than he did. Burnt meals didn't bother him as much as her flighty ways, and her bubbly laugh grated on his raw nerves.

Nothing amused him these days. In fact, he barely tolerated his own company. He had nothing to say, couldn't force himself to speak past the emptiness Rose's leaving had caused.

Rose had chosen to leave. He ground his teeth, tempted to travel to her and demand an explanation. She seemed to resent being different from Ginny. Didn't she realize no two people were identical? He loved both of them. Couldn't she understand how guilty he felt for loving her? But he'd never told Rose in so many words that he loved her.

He hadn't prayed. He didn't exactly blame God for his misfortune, but it was difficult to discuss the situation with his Maker.

Donning a warm coat, he wandered out to the apple orchard in the falling temperatures. He plopped to the ground where that disastrous argument about Ginny's parents had taken place.

The Sawyers had written upon learning of Rose's departure. Solomon volunteered to handle the annulment. Orange flames had devoured that letter, turning it into flaky cinders.

But Rose deserved a response. She must wonder how he felt about her new job, her new home.

Angry, disappointed, hurt. Scared that he'd lost her. He wanted her home. Their marriage recorded in the family Bible proved her place was with him and his children.

Didn't she even miss the children? Her brother? Her niece and nephew? No, for if she did, she'd be on her way home.

Fluffy snowflakes fell as he stalked back to his warm house to write a letter.

~

*R*ose laid awake a long time after she blew out the lantern.

The snow had fallen to an inch deep during their jaunt around town. The twins showed her their school, the bank, the stores, and friends' homes. The mood became playful when John hurled a snowball at his sister. She fired back. Soon all three scrambled for enough snow to pelt one another, the hilarity a healing balm for all of them.

Supper was a much livelier meal than usual with John's high spirits. Three railroad men from the second floor chuckled at his exaggerated description of the snowball fight. Rose marveled at his knack for storytelling.

After heating water in the kitchen for all three of them to have a nice long soak in the tin tub, Cora pleaded to go first. Rose didn't begrudge her a bath that lasted three quarters of an hour in the downstairs room set aside for this purpose.

When they all settled in the room, Rose broached a topic near to her heart. "You must return to school. I brought my teaching books. We'll work in the evenings to get you caught up. Maybe by spring I can afford to let you quit your jobs so you can go to school."

John looked at his sister. "Mama Rosie, we'll add our money to yours and save until we return to school."

Rose's eyes misted at their wonderful attitudes. "That helps, especially since you need clothes immediately."

John owned two sets of clothing that were frayed, snug, and exposed his ankles.

"I'll sew a long curtain to hang in the hall for privacy. The heat stove has a flat burner, perfect for heating water or coffee or soup."

Cora's dark eyes had grown huge. "We really do have a home now, don't we, Mama Rosie?"

Now, listening to the fire crackle in the darkness, she considered Samuel's reaction when she wrote about the twins. Their marriage wasn't annulled yet, after all. He, with his compassionate character, would approve of giving them a place to stay, but she'd done it without consulting him. He had a right to know.

A locomotive chugged into the station. How she longed for a train to bring him to her. Of course, that wasn't going to happen. But a letter wasn't too much to ask.

Please write to me, Samuel, even if it's just to say goodbye.

So much for listening to her heart. Jeremiah had warned that the heart was deceitful above all things. It had been a mistake to allow her emotions to make the decision to marry.

But had all those years of only making sensible, practical decisions made her happy either?

No. She sighed. It seemed best to use a combination of heart and mind to reason things out when making decisions. What a mess she'd made of her life.

But she must stop believing she had no worth if a man didn't love her. Her self-esteem had taken a beating. Yet God had created her in the first place and loved her still, even with all her flaws, as her daily Bible reading had reminded her. He was right here with her, even in her darkest hour.

Her heart ached for Peter and Emma. They'd suffered too much already, and her leaving must have brought another heartbreak, which she sincerely regretted. If they only knew how much she missed them.

She knelt on the cold floor and asked God to help Samuel

through his grief. She prayed for Peter, Emma, John, and Cora, who had suffered so much sorrow at such young ages.

She prayed until her legs went numb and her spirit emptied of words.

A semblance of peace pushed past the emptiness of losing Samuel and the children. She wasn't alone in her struggles.

≈

*R*ose refused to allow the twins to work twelve-hour shifts, heightening tension between her and Mrs. Saunders, who balked at hiring new employees. They compromised—the siblings would get an hour off every morning and two in the afternoon.

They became students again when Rose assigned work from her cherished Ray's Arithmetic and McGuffey Readers. They studied during breaks.

After the twins had lived with her a week, Rose sent them to the store with a list and cash. They returned with ready-made clothing, shoes, stockings, and fabric. She'd altered a shirtwaist and skirt for Cora. John's new shirt was next.

"There was a letter at the post office for you." Cora laid it on the kitchen table.

Her heart leaped at the sight of Samuel's handwriting. She shoved the precious letter into her skirt pocket. "Thank you. Please take the purchases home and be back in half an hour."

They scurried away. Wendy had already left for the day. Mrs. Saunders was at the grocery store.

Rose broke the seal.

Dear Rose,

I don't understand why you left so suddenly. If there's something to talk about, you don't run away like a child. That never solves anything. I understand needing time to think, but you took a job?

Heat flooded her face. He thought her behavior childish?

I'm sorry I didn't write sooner. I'm preparing the pigs for the meat markets. The smokehouse is already half full. It's a busy time of year.

I hired Selena to keep house for us in your absence. As you predicted, the children like her. They keep asking when you will return. I don't know what to tell them. Perhaps you can enlighten me. When will you come home? I don't know what to think anymore.

Very truly yours,

Samuel

If her job bothered Samuel, he'd be even more hurt about her taking in the twins. She reread the letter. No mention of annulment. His tone sounded angry, confused, frustrated, but the last paragraph gave her hope. He expected her to return on her own.

Was she willing to sentence Samuel to the emptiness of a loveless marriage? That's why she left in the first place. But none of that was Peter or Emma's fault. Their sadness wrenched her heart. Her broken heart would remain broken whether she remained here or went back to the farm. Perhaps for their sake she could return?

The twins deserved a home, a real home. If she went back and Samuel decided they could adopt them, John and Cora would have a father, a brother, a sister, an aunt, an uncle, and cousins.

Here they only had Rose and each other.

No, she wasn't about to make big decisions affecting so many lives without seeking God's guidance. Never again. She'd learned that lesson, at least.

She traced his signature with her finger, foolishly wishing he had personally delivered the message. Foolishly, her yearning to see him remained unvanquished.

~

"*Mama* Rosie, who wrote that letter?" Cora looked up from a book that evening while John wrote in a new journal at the table in their room.

The question she'd dreaded. Rose's fingers shook as she pinned sleeves onto John's shirt. "Samuel Walker. My husband."

Cora gasped.

"You're a widow." John's brow furrowed.

"No, my husband is alive." Rose laid the cloth aside. "I married Samuel in May. His first wife died in a tragic accident. Samuel needed a wife to keep house and care for his sweet children."

"How old are they?" Cora laid down her book.

"Peter is seven. Emma's six." She crossed to the curtainless window to avoid their eyes. A train's bright headlamp lit the tracks as the engine chugged into the station.

"Why did you leave them?" Cora's tone sharpened.

"It's difficult to explain." Every part of her heart willed Samuel to step off that train and come for her. "I loved Samuel when I married him, but he didn't love me. He still misses his first wife."

Cora jumped to her feet. "You left children who needed you because he hurt your feelings?"

Rose flinched. "It's not that simple—"

"Did you consider their feelings? Now they've lost two mothers." Scarlet flamed Cora's cheeks.

True, if her stepchildren cared for her. Rose covered her hot cheeks with icy hands. "No, they never let me get close—"

"Will you leave us, too?" Cora asked.

Rose gasped. Her motive had been to free Samuel to annul a marriage he regretted, not to harm the children.

The truth struck with the swiftness of lightning.

Peter and Emma *had* relied on her, and she'd abandoned them. His letter had said as much.

Rose stumbled to her bed. Held onto the wooden headboard as if it were a lifeline. She, who had always put children's needs above her own, had failed them. Cora was right about her selfishness. Samuel had said the children wondered when she was returning. She'd trampled their security.

John knelt and pressed a clean handkerchief into her hand, compassion softening his dark eyes.

She dabbed her tears. "It's true. I failed them."

"No, I was wrong." Cora sat on the bed beside her. "It just reminded me how I felt when Mama..." Sobs halted her words.

Rose gathered her close.

John's shoulders heaved. Rose pulled him up and placed her other arm around him.

Stormy weeping finally passed. Rose fished clean handkerchiefs from her trunk for them. "My dearest wish is to return to a farm in Hamilton that has room for all of us. Whatever my future holds, you both will be part of it as long as you desire to be."

The twins exchanged a look.

John squared his jaw. "We'll go if you go."

"Let's pray for the future like Mama taught us," Cora said. "When she died, I prayed for a family. God sent us to Mrs. Saunders while we waited for you to come. Now, I'll pray that your husband wants all of us."

"Yes, let's leave it in God's Hands." Rose, humbled by Cora's simple faith, fought for control. "He knows best."

~

*S*amuel pulled up the collar of his coat against the cold and stepped off his back porch. The children were tucked in bed for the night.

Samuel shoved his hands in his pockets and gazed up at the moon. Was Rose staring at it, thinking of him as he thought of her?

He dusted an inch of snow from the frigid log. Four weeks ago, he'd enjoyed a picnic here with his wife. On that magical day, he'd glimpsed a special glow in her eyes—for him, a feeling he'd reciprocated. But she'd bolted when he almost kissed her. He'd violated their marriage of convenience. His broken promise had upset her.

No, that wasn't true.

Not long after that, he'd kissed her, and she'd reciprocated.

His inability to express his love for her had upset her. He shouldn't have stuffed the pain of Ginny's loss so deeply.

Reminiscences of the early days of his first marriage rushed back. Their excitement the day they discovered they'd be parents. The day he'd held Peter in his arms for the first time, a baby boy who depended on him. Then Emma completed their family. Precious, indeed.

Other memories weren't as joyful, tense days that all couples experience. Even that last morning, they had argued over Ginny's latest purchase. Another fancy new dress she wanted to order from her seamstress for an upcoming party at Lily Ann's —this when he struggled to put food on the table. He'd refused to buy on credit. She told him she was going for a ride. He'd imagined when she didn't return soon that she'd needed a couple of hours away, never dreaming he'd find her unconscious less than a mile from home. That terrible sight was forever imbedded in his heart.

Samuel stood and strode for the next hour among the apple orchard that had been Ginny's dream.

The old maple tree beckoned him as he strolled back toward the house. Somehow, he felt Rose's calming presence there. She had brought peace and comfort to his family. He had believed he was the strong one. He hadn't realized how much he'd relied on her strength until she left.

His love for Rose had grown without his permission. He had appreciated her love for his children from the beginning. This fall, he'd courted her while the children were at school.

Shoving his hands into his pocket, he sat under the tree where they shared that last picnic. Barren branches now, but the leaves had been a beautiful shade of yellow that last day with Rose, offering shelter from the sun and rain.

There was no shelter now. He rubbed his boots back and forth over muddy, soggy leaves.

He wanted Rose home.

Samuel stood suddenly and cracked his head on a sturdy branch. Wincing, he saw stars of a different kind. He held onto the branch until dizziness passed.

Nothing had gone right in the past month. Not one thing since Rose left.

Something held him back from going after her. Guilt. Over being untrue to Ginny.

How was he to overcome it before he lost Rose forever?

CHAPTER 32

On Saturday afternoon, November twenty-fourth, Mrs. Saunders entered the kitchen where Rose peeled potatoes for supper. "You have a visitor. A man."

Rose's heart skittered. Samuel had come. With annulment papers? To see how she fared? She glanced at the ashen twins, surely wondering, as she did, what was about to happen. "Everything will be fine." She untied her apron. "I'll speak with him and return to work directly."

"Be certain that you do." Nothing mattered more to Nora than customers. "The first supper train will be here in less than two hours."

"Beef is roasting in the oven." Rose patted her hair with shaky hands.

"Humph. Reckon I'll slice onions." Picking up a knife, she set to work.

"Thank you." Gathering her courage, she pushed on the dining room door with a racing heart, but the man waiting for her wasn't the one she'd hoped for. She tamped down her disappointment. Samuel wasn't coming. The next time she'd see her husband would to be to sign annulment documents. "Richard. Why are you here?"

Wearing a brown coat with a leather bag at his feet, Richard held out his arms. "I might ask you the same thing, Rosie. I missed you."

His welcoming hug thawed the icy hurt caused by his letter.

"Can we sit and talk?" He indicated a table closest to the fireplace in the empty room.

"Only for a few minutes. I have cooking to do." She eased her tired body onto a wooden chair. "We'll eat supper here after the last crowd leaves. You can buy a meal from Mrs. Saunders, the owner. That will put you on her good side."

"I will." He draped his coat over a chair before sitting next to her. "I won't leave until tomorrow. That gives us an opportunity to talk."

Her spirits lifted. "You'll love the twins."

"I got your letter. I'm eager to meet them."

Though dying to know how Samuel and the children were coping, she asked about Richard's family first.

"Heat from the fire still bothers Hazel, but the doctor says that's normal. Polly caught a cold, but otherwise everyone is healthy."

She had to know. "And Samuel and the children?"

Richard sat back in his chair. "Well, now, let's see. Peter and Emma don't know why their stepmother up and left. They're unhappy and confused."

Her hands quivered. Cora had assessed their feelings correctly.

A log shifted in the fireplace.

"Samuel is as cross as a hungry bear. The children have stayed at our home every weekend since you left. Everyone is happier that way, believe me."

Neither the anger nor the longing for solitude sounded like Samuel. Her heart sank.

Richard's brow furrowed. "A lot has happened."

"For you or for me?" More difficult news?

"Maybe for both of us." He stared at his clasped hands. "We will talk more later. But first, will you forgive me for that awful letter I wrote?"

The words had slashed through her. "You wrote what you felt was right."

"I was upset." He leaned forward. "I had no call to say it. Hazel told me not to write to you while I was angry. I'm sorry."

"She *is* your better half."

"Don't I know it." Dark circles shadowed his brown eyes.

His regretful sorrow touched Rose. "Did you come all this way to apologize?"

He nodded. "I couldn't stand to have such rough words between us. You're my sister."

"Thank you." She covered his hand with hers. "That means a great deal."

"Will you burn that awful letter? Tonight?"

She laughed. "I promise."

Smiling, he patted her hand. "I'll find a place to stay." He put on his coat.

"Stay with us. We have the attic room at Mrs. Westlake's boarding house just down the street. Pay for your Sunday meal as soon as you meet her. She'll be happier." Strolling with him to the door, she extracted a key from her apron pocket. "Drop your bag off there and come back."

"I'll return as soon as I'm settled."

She smiled. "Knock on the kitchen door, and I'll bring out fresh coffee. Wait to eat with us."

He agreed and left with a lighter countenance. Rose's heartache eased. She really did love her brother. His apology paved a way toward healing the hurt inside her.

Back in the kitchen Cora and John looked up. "My brother is visiting. You'll meet your Uncle Richard tonight."

~

*A*ny awkwardness of meeting their new uncle for the first time dispelled under Richard's teasing manner. John told him over supper about growing up in the railroad town and losing their parents. He explained how they came to work and live at the restaurant. Cora took up the story with the day they moved in with Mama Rosie.

Rose was thrilled that Richard listened with a compassionate expression. As much as she hated to acknowledge it, he'd been self-centered in recent years. That wasn't true today. Something was different.

Later, the four of them strolled through town. Candlelight shone through the windows, brightening dark streets. A thousand stars lit up the night sky. When Cora complained of numb feet, they headed back. The exhausted twins were soon in bed. Rose, sewing basket at her feet, sat with Richard in the deserted sitting room.

She stitched while Richard spoke of his positive impressions of the twins.

"Your decision to invite the twins into your home concerned me." He stared into the crackling fire. "I saw it as another obstacle between you and Samuel. After hearing their story, I understand."

"Thank you." His affirmation lifted a load from her shoulders. If only her husband would agree.

"I'll try to make Samuel understand." He rubbed his fingers across his forehead. "Sis, there's something else that needs saying."

She placed the shirt in her sewing basket. "I'm listening."

"It will make me seem like a jealous bum, but here goes." He scooted a chair closer and sat facing her. "When Papa left you the house, it felt unfair. You received the more expensive item."

He patted his chest. "I received tools I'd never use. I sold them immediately with no consideration for sentimental value."

"I was all alone when Papa died." She closed her eyes as the grief and loneliness of that time washed over her anew.

"I realize that now—and I sure didn't need another home, but Pa's decision simply seemed a sign of greater favor for you. I resented it." He clenched his fists. "I never even acknowledged it to myself. But when you married Samuel last spring, that resentment resurfaced. You had a forty-acre farm, which is more than I'll ever own. You sold Papa's house and then were hurt when I asked for my share. Samuel had never been so angry with me. I didn't understand." He lowered his head. "Then you left him. Left behind a thriving farm, a good husband, a fine family. It made no sense."

Rose stared at him, a hundred pieces falling into place. It explained why their relationship had remained at surface level for years. Why he didn't help her pay Papa's debts. Why he felt he had a right to her inheritance. "I never knew."

He strode to the fire and stared at the flames. "I didn't understand it myself."

"There won't be another payment for a few months. Celia wrote that Fred had to hire a housekeeper when the doctor recommended she rest." She joined him beside the fire. "She thinks in the spring—"

"Keep it. If you return to Samuel, that money belongs to both of you. If not, well, you'll need it even more."

"I will." Even as she acknowledged that sad truth, something mended in her heart. How she'd longed for a closer relationship with a brother. "Because that house was his way of caring for me after he was gone. He gave me security. It was a wonderful gift."

He patted her shoulder. "Took a while for me to realize it. I've been a fool, Rosie. Forgive me?"

"Of course." She hugged him. "When I got that letter, I was so afraid I'd lost you too."

"Never happen." He grinned. "Want to come to the house for Christmas? Bring the twins."

"I can't. We'll have to work." That wasn't the only reason.

She'd never return to Hamilton again unless Samuel wanted a true marriage.

CHAPTER 33

A colder than normal November led to a blustery December. The twins worked hard at their lessons. John demonstrated writing skills while Cora showed an interest in history.

"I can't believe the change in these children." Nora sliced a loaf of bread for the sandwiches the first Friday in December. John and Cora walked to the post office for some exercise.

Rose was glad that Nora had noticed their contentment, too. She sliced ham as thinly as possible, a skill improved by recent experience.

"John used to be quiet. Land sakes, but that boy talks a mile a minute. And I heard Cora singing while she washed dishes. *Singing.* It's the first time I've heard her pretty voice." Nora paused regretfully. "I failed them."

"No." Rose set down her knife. "Do you know what Cora told me?"

Nora shook her head.

"She said, 'God sent us to Mrs. Saunders while we waited for you to get here.'"

"Well, I declare. That is a nice way to look at things." Nora's fingers touched her parted lips. "Thank you for telling me."

Rose's thoughts turned to her brother's visit last month. It gave her high hopes for Samuel's acceptance of the twins. She'd written him of her decision and how their personalities blossomed in her care.

Samuel replied that he spoke with Richard. The children were getting along well in school. Selena kept up with household chores. Charlie had taught him soup recipes. The letter ended with his usual question—when did she plan to return?

No mention of the twins. How did he feel about them living with her?

Jealousy surged that Selena had taken over her job. She searched the letter for hope of a future. He didn't close the door, but he wasn't coming through it to fetch her.

Did he miss her or her housekeeping skills? Hard to say.

⁓

The second week of December brought a dusting of snow. Unless Samuel missed his guess, those dark, gloomy clouds held more.

That Tuesday, his pockets bulged with cash from his last delivery to the meat market, his most profitable year. And his most heart wrenching.

Samuel was glad to prepare his own lunch. Eating a simple sandwich was preferable to Selena's company. He squirmed when he was alone with her. He'd never felt that way with Rose. He'd always anticipated their time alone together.

Horses neighed in the corral, the mournful sound piercing his sadness. He stared out the window at them. Midnight and Star had been fed and groomed. But he never called them by name any more, never spoke to them. Midnight, Ginny's horse, had survived when she died. A part of him blamed the horse for unseating her.

He strode to the corral fence and stood with one boot resting on the lowest rung. "It wasn't your fault, boy." Midnight whinnied and lowered his head for Samuel's gentle hand. "An icy patch. Not your fault."

"Well, now, that's what I've waited to see."

He turned, startled at Charlie's voice. "What do you mean?"

"You speaking kindly to Ginny's horse." He stroked Midnight's glossy side. "Seemed like you blamed him all these months."

He rested his cheek against the horse's mane. "I didn't realize it."

"I figured. But there's nothing to forgive. He came for you when she fell off. Did the best he could to save her."

"You're right." He looked at Midnight. "Sorry, boy."

"You went out this morning." The older man's engaging grin warmed his heart. He hadn't realized he craved company.

"Just got the last of the meat to the butcher." Star, at Midnight's side, neighed for his share of attention. Samuel stroked her mane.

Charlie rubbed his hands. "Feels like winter done got here."

Samuel contemplated an overcast sky. "More snow on the way."

"December eleventh is awful early for our third snow, even if it hasn't amounted to much. You hear from Rose?"

Samuel wished he had apples in his pocket for his horses. "You mean after the letter about the twins living with her?"

"Yep."

He opened the gate and rested a hand on Midnight's mane, leading her toward the stable. Charlie led Star. "Heard from her last week. Seems pretty happy up there."

"How so?" Charlie followed with Star.

"She went on about John and Cora. She's getting along better with her boss." He led Midnight into a stall. "She did ask about Peter and Emma. Nice of her to remember them."

"Sarcasm don't impress me none." Charlie closed Star's gate.

"How am I supposed to feel?" Samuel rested his cheek against Midnight's mane. "She's more interested in John and Cora than her own stepchildren."

"Hogwash."

Samuel closed the stall. "She left without saying goodbye. She found a job and a *new family* in Bradford Junction. She doesn't care about us anymore." He leaned his forehead against a support pole. "If she ever did."

"You know better." The older man's tone grew stern. "Rosie loves all of you."

"She has a new family."

Charlie's gaze traveled to the white house visible through the open barn door. "Oh, I expect your house has room for more children. It would have all come about in due time, anyway. More children, I mean."

"Babies. I expected babies some day. John and Cora are almost grown up."

"Kids of all ages need loving care." His tone sharpened.

"I know that." Samuel sighed. "Want coffee?"

"Thought you'd never ask."

A few minutes later they sat at the table with steaming cups in front of them. "She's never mentioned a desire to come home."

"Son, she's waiting on you."

"Me? I've asked repeatedly when she's returning."

"You gotta go get her."

Samuel stared at orange flames in the fireplace. He'd have pursued her the day she left if he'd been certain of her love.

Charlie rubbed the back of his neck. "I don't believe I ever told you about Ramona."

Samuel turned his attention back to his friend, trying to

conceal his impatience. He wasn't in the mood for one of Charlie's stories. "Who's Ramona?"

"My wife."

Samuel shook his head to clear it. "Your wife's name was Esther."

"Ramona was my first wife."

Charlie had been married twice? That captured his attention.

His neighbor ambled to the front window and stared across the dirt road toward his white farmhouse. "I was just a kid when I married Ramona. Her best friend was my little sister. One day I looked at her and realized she had grown up. We were married a year later.

"We bought our farm and moved into the home I helped build. This place was further outside the city in those days. We were happy, what with owning our own place and expecting a baby and all. But something went wrong when it came time for the birth. I lost them both."

The gray-haired man gripped the window sill. "I wanted to die with them." His voice rasped with pain. "There wasn't nothing left to live for. I didn't care about my farm if Ramona couldn't watch things grow with me. For a long time, I thought I'd die. I hoped I'd die.

"Then I met Esther. There was something about her. I couldn't stop thinking about her, but I had a problem. I felt disloyal to Ramona, like I wasn't being true to her." Charlie looked over his shoulder at Samuel. "Maybe you know how that feels."

His words struck like a punch in the breadbasket. "I think I might."

Charlie looked out the window again. "It took a while to work through my guilt. I could've lost my chance with Esther, but she was patient. Finally, I realized I'd never forget Ramona.

She was the first woman I loved. But I realized my heart found room for somebody else."

He rejoined Samuel at the table. "I was married to Esther for thirty-seven years before the Good Lord called her home." His voice roughened. "We grew old together, raised a houseful of children. Now those children have children. I grew to love my Esther as much as I loved Ramona. Maybe I loved Esther more, since we weathered the trials of life together. I sure never thought that was possible at the beginning."

Slowly, Charlie stood and crossed to the door. He shrugged his arms into his coat. "I told Rose about my two wives back in the summer when Ginny's folks were staying with you. Her spirits were pretty low that day." He opened the door. "Just thought you might like to know. I've wanted to tell you about Ramona since Rose left. You've been too angry to listen."

An icy draft hit Samuel in the face as Charlie left. He grimaced as he drained his cold coffee. After crossing to the stove, he poured another cup.

Setting his cup on the hearth, he sat cross-legged in front of the fire. A tremendous weight tumbled from his shoulders. How had his friend known what he most needed to hear?

Because Charlie had suffered the same guilt. He understood.

Ginny had been an insecure woman, requiring lots of attention. He'd lived with her possessive attitude a long time. It still bound him to her, but should it?

For the first time, Samuel glimpsed the problem through Rose's eyes. He'd held her at arm's length long enough. He'd focused on their old friendship in the beginning, which had been quickly reestablished. Ginny's parents brought with them their own disaster. Looking back, he saw that they'd tossed many wedges between Rose and him—indeed, the whole family —and Samuel's focus on his children afterward had been to the detriment of his marriage.

The time of waiting was over. Charlie was right. He must go

to her. Beg her forgiveness and tell her he loved her. He'd encourage her honesty and listen to whatever she wanted to say. Then if she wanted an annulment, Solomon Sawyer would be all too happy to oblige.

First, he must face his pain.

He finally did what he should have done in October when he found Rose gone. He knelt in front of the dying fire and poured out his heart to God.

CHAPTER 34

Since Christmas had been especially difficult for John and Cora last year without their mother, it was important for Rose to make it a meaningful celebration for them.

Four days before Christmas, Nora granted permission for her to shop while the twins struggled with arithmetic. Brisk wind stole her breath on her way to the mercantile. Holding up her skirt, she stepped carefully to avoid the worst of muddy, slushy roads. Black soot from the locomotives spotted the few patches of snow remaining on the grass, one of the disadvantages of living near a train depot.

Rose hadn't shopped for months, and it was fun searching store shelves for gifts. A cookbook, *Buckeye Cookery*, was perfect for Cora. Milton Bradley's Checkered Game of Life, which contained nine different games, was a fun choice for John, and she imagined playing the game with the twins on winter evenings.

Anticipating her brother and his family's visit on the Saturday after Christmas, she purchased Quiz, a winding toy, for Clay and Spilikins—jackstraws to Rose—for Polly.

Enough peppermint sticks for everyone went into the growing pile.

There were two more children to consider. When would she see Peter and Emma again? Samuel wasn't going to come for her. She'd accepted that. But it didn't seem right not to buy gifts for her stepchildren. She selected a wind-up train for Peter and puzzles for Emma.

What about Samuel? A pocket watch similar to one her father owned caught her eye. She rubbed her finger over the smooth metal. Samuel's watch had broken last summer. If she splurged on this expensive gift, her surplus cash would be gone, excluding the money for three train tickets to Hamilton stashed in her trunk. She knew that Samuel wanting her back was a vain hope, but the money would stay locked away anyway.

Months might pass before she saw her husband again. Lost in indecision, she studied the watch.

The storekeeper cleared his throat.

Heat filled her face. "I'll take this watch as well."

Her words surprised her as much as they did the portly man behind the counter. She'd carry it in her pocket as if she carried part of him with her, even if he had no knowledge of the gift.

～

*A*n eight-foot evergreen tree adorned the sitting room in the boarding house. That evening, Mrs. Westlake invited John and Cora to decorate with her. They accepted enthusiastically. Rose sipped tea as the others hung candles on the tree. They sang Christmas carols while tying pinecones to branches with red yarn. After a festive evening spent stringing popcorn and munching sugar cookies, they all slept soundly.

The next day at the restaurant, Nora consulted with Rose about the work schedule for Christmas Day. Trains ran daily, despite the holiday, which meant customers. They'd all work until mid-afternoon. Rose was to prepare a big breakfast and a lavish dinner. Anyone coming later would receive soup and leftover turkey sandwiches.

Townspeople unable to afford a big meal at home also dined at Mrs. Saunders' Eatery. There was no schedule for them.

Rose surveyed the restaurant's dining room in advance of Christmas. Greenery and holly berries on the dining room mantle created a holiday atmosphere for guests. What did the farmhouse look like with a Christmas tree near the front window? She'd never know. Her heart ached for Samuel, Peter, and Emma. If her husband cared for her at all, he'd have come by now. Hope had died a painful death.

On Christmas Eve, Rose attended services with the twins. The simple yet meaningful service bolstered her faith. She sang "Silent Night" and thanked God for the love He gave the world that first Christmas even as loneliness for her family in Hamilton chipped at her heart.

Cooking began early on Christmas morning, and four mince pies baked in the oven by mid-morning. Rose swiped a trembling hand across her brow at memories of baking for Samuel. The past must remain in the past. While slicing pumpkin pie, she glanced at Cora's happy face. The twins needed her for the next few years. After that? Rose resolved not to think of growing old alone.

Flurried activity of cooking for and serving guests soon pushed aside melancholy thoughts. The whistle blew, announcing the arrival of another locomotive. Early again. They didn't have food on the tables yet.

Everyone scurried to serve the meal. Nora collected cash from customers.

As Rose concentrated on balancing two steaming plates to serve to a family of three, she noticed a man's blue-checked shirt with a black coat. She had sewn Samuel a shirt in that same pattern four months before. Raising her gaze, she met the blue eyes she'd yearned for since the day she left Hamilton.

"Samuel." Of all the ways she'd dreamed of meeting him again, this had never occurred to her.

Searching her face, he stood. "Merry Christmas, Rose."

"Merry Christmas." She flushed. The children stared at her with wide eyes. She placed loaded plates on the table and crouched, hoping Peter and Emma would accept her hug.

"Mama Rosie." Emma threw herself into Rose's arms. "I missed you."

The precious girl had seldom called her by the name they'd all decided on so long ago. A promising sign. She picked up her precious stepdaughter and kissed her cheek. "I missed you." Emma clung to her.

When Emma's grasp loosened, Rose put her down and held out her arms. "Peter?"

The boy took two hesitant steps. Then he hugged her waist tightly.

"I missed you, too, Peter." Tears pricked her eyes.

"Then why did you leave?" The words were muffled against her apron.

Samuel placed his hands on Peter's shoulders and guided his son to stand in front of him. "We'll discuss that later, son. Rose, it's good to see you."

Did she see longing in his eyes?

Suddenly the clatter of silverware, the excited voices, the laughter faded away. She wanted to wrap her arms around him and never let go. Did he want the same thing of her? Fear of rejection kept her rooted to her spot. "What brings you here?"

"You. How long do you work? When will you eat dinner?"

Her stomach fluttered. "Perhaps in two hours. We'll eat after the next meal train."

"Shall we eat with you?" His hand fidgeted with Peter's collar.

"I'd love that." She smiled tremulously. "You can wait here or in the kitchen."

The muscles in his face relaxed. "Tell us how we can help."

They stowed their belongings under a kitchen table and then carried slices of fragrant pumpkin pie into the dining room.

Rose wanted to waltz across the room. Samuel had come. He'd brought Peter and Emma. Her gaze lingered on each face, drinking in their joy at this reunion. But there was something else too. An uncertainty, perhaps. Still, they were here. Rose served coffee and tried to slow the rapid rhythm of her heart.

She felt her gaze seeking out Samuel over and over—and found him looking back every time. Her prayer had been that he'd come and asked her to return. The way he stared at her—almost as if starved for the sight of her—gave her hope.

But it might not mean anything. She'd been wrong so many times. Even if he asked her to return, the twins also needed a home. What if he didn't want them? She braced herself for a painful discussion.

Cora and John shot Samuel worried looks as everyone but Nora pitched in to clear tables after the first crowd left.

"Everyone gather around." Rose beckoned them over to the welcome warmth of the dining room's fireplace. Samuel, Peter, and Emma joined her to stand on her right while the twins stood on her left. "Samuel, I wrote to you about John and Cora Welch. We work together and they have been living with me."

"Of course. I've looked forward to meeting you both." Samuel extended his hand in a firm handshake to John and then gave Cora a smiling nod. "I'm Samuel Walker, Rose's husband. And these are my children, Peter and Emma."

"It's a pleasure to meet you, sir. Merry Christmas to you all." But John's empty tone belied his words.

"Happy to meet you, Mr. Walker." Cora's gaze shifted to Emma. "I like your pretty dress, Emma. I had a cornflower blue dress with white daisies on it when I was a little girl."

"Mama Rosie made it for me." Emma held the skirt wide. "I wear it a lot."

"If you're done lollygagging, we've another meal to ready." Nora stood, arms crossed, at the door.

"Of course." Rose quickly introduced her family to Nora, and then scurried to the kitchen while the others finished clearing the tables. This wasn't a good place to stop, but they'd have to hurry to be ready for the next service.

In the next hour, Rose noticed that Cora's eyes lost their happy luster and John's grin seemed permanently broken. Did they wonder about the future, as she did?

After the last crowd they had to serve finally left. Rose and Cora set a large round table in preparation for their dinner.

Cora bit her lip and stared at her with a question in her eyes.

Rose lifted one shoulder. She couldn't comfort Cora because she didn't know if he wanted any of them.

They sat down with a grim-faced Nora for dinner. Samuel asked the blessing.

Rose twisted the napkin in her lap then tried to smooth the wrinkles she'd just caused. Good thing Nora had purchased sturdy linen.

Samuel smiled at Rose. "We're happy to share Christmas lunch with all of you."

Nora inclined her head. "I've been curious about you, Mr. Walker." Samuel's gracious words didn't warm her frosty stare. "We think the world of Rose."

His broad chest thrust forward. "I'm not surprised. We love her too."

Rose's fork clattered to her plate and bounced to the floor. She bent to retrieve it. What did he mean? Likely nothing. A general comment. She scooped mashed potatoes onto her plate as if the task required all her concentration.

"John, is your school far away?" Peter munched on a bite of turkey.

"Not too far." John indicated the kitchen door with a jerk of his head. "We don't go to school, so Mama Rosie teaches our lessons in the kitchen."

Emma gasped. "They call you Mama Rosie?"

Appalled at the color draining from her stepdaughter's face, Rose exchanged a startled glance with Samuel. "I told them they could call me that when they started living with me. I'm sorry, Emma. I didn't think about it troubling you."

The wounds she'd inflicted on her stepchildren piled up. What must be done to fix the damage? There was nothing she could do unless Samuel wanted her as his wife.

Samuel cleared his throat. "Rose mentioned you like to tell stories, John."

He shrugged, shoveling into his mouth a spoonful of mashed potatoes smothered in gravy.

"He tells wonderful stories." Rose wasn't accustomed to his rudeness. "John, tell us about the little boy you waited on last week, the one who only said one word the whole time he was here."

He crumbled a biscuit with clenched fingers. "I reckon all he wanted was pie." Crumbs tumbled down his chest.

Rose blinked. She'd laughed repeatedly at John's comic rendition about the little boy whose answer was "pie," no matter the question.

Something was wrong here. All four children fidgeted.

Peter and Emma stared at the older children.

"How are your reading skills, Peter?" Rose asked. "Have you advanced to the next level yet?"

He frowned. "I ain't in the next reader yet."

Had her departure adversely affected his learning? "And you, Emma? Do you practice your letters in the evening?"

The little girl shook her head. "Not anymore. I can write my name."

A skill she had mastered before Rose left.

Nora, tight-lipped, glared at Samuel.

He and Rose carried the conversation. She asked about the farm, Richard's family, their neighbors, and the church, more depressed than ever to have missed out on so much.

Samuel peppered her and the twins with questions about their job and Bradford Junction.

The twins relaxed with familiar topics. John even told a funny story about a howling neighborhood dog, grinning when everyone laughed. The atmosphere finally eased.

As soon as they consumed the pie, Nora stood and everyone followed her cue.

"Will you take us to your boarding house?" Samuel rested his hand on Rose's shoulder and looked into her eyes.

"Of course. We have to clean first." She shivered at his touch. At least he didn't want to hold their discussion, whatever the outcome, in a public restaurant.

The twins washed a mound of dishes. Samuel sliced turkey and ham for the sandwiches that Nora prepared. Rose prepared potato soup. The younger children wiped tables.

Afterward, they bundled up for a short walk to the boarding house. Bright sunshine had dried the formerly muddy road and warmed the day to a pleasant temperature, a welcome change from the past week.

Rose didn't know how to arrange a private conversation with Samuel. Emma held her hand and Cora claimed one of her arms as they strolled.

Samuel asked questions about the railroad. John gave short answers.

What had happened to the rapport they'd reached over dessert? Rose glanced at the tense faces of the children. All must wonder what tomorrow would bring.

Rose wondered that too. Only Samuel knew his intentions.

She introduced her family to Mrs. Westlake and the

boarders in the sitting room. Her landlady raised thin eyebrows and graciously invited them to tea.

Samuel declined for all of them.

John silently led the way upstairs to unlock the door. He pushed back the curtain dividing the room and then reached for kindling to build a fire.

~

*S*amuel, the last one to enter the spacious rooms, marveled that three beds in a sparsely filled attic managed to feel welcoming. Rose's touch. One of her many gifts.

He rubbed his hands together. Awkwardness put him on edge.

"Want to see the rest?" John asked.

"Yes, thank you." He, Peter, and Emma followed John down the hall to an identical room. "Cozy."

Some of the tenseness fell from the boy's shoulders. "I like it."

"Me too." Samuel clapped John's back, who looked up with a question in his eyes. It seemed they were all anxious about Rose's decision. She'd left him. Did she want to return? His chest tightened as he strolled back to his wife. "You've made a nice home for yourself." His tone sharpened despite his best efforts. She'd had a nice home on his farm.

Rose flushed and looked away. "Thank you."

"Not better than our house." Emma pouted.

"Emma, this is quite nice." Samuel tugged at his collar. He must arrange time alone with Rose, but how?

"I agree with you, Emma." Rose smiled tremulously.

Samuel raised his eyebrows. Her agreement boded well for their upcoming conversation.

"Won't you all sit down? I have gifts for everyone." Rose opened her trunk.

Emma, eyes shining, clapped her hands.

Perfect. The mood was already lighter. Rose always knew exactly what to do for youngsters.

She selected a package. "Merry Christmas, Emma."

His daughter tore into the brown paper to reveal new puzzles. She hugged them close.

The next gift went to Peter, who dropped to his knees and made engine noises while rolling his new train across the wooden floor.

Cora opened her package with slow deliberation. "I want to be as good a cook as you are." Her eyes shone. "Thank you for the cookbook."

John whooped at his game.

"I have one more gift." Rose turned to Samuel. "For you."

She hadn't known he was coming yet prepared a gift for him? An icy place in his heart began to thaw. He couldn't stop himself from putting his arm around her waist. Her startled gaze flew to his, and he regretfully removed his arm and stepped away. They had much to discuss before—

He reined in his thoughts. Best not get ahead of himself ,even though he wanted to take her in his arms and kiss her with all the pent-up emotions of worrying about her. Missing her. Loving her. "Let's wait a few minutes for that. I brought gifts too."

"How kind of you." Rose's words belied the worried glance she gave the twins, who stared at the floor.

Reaching into his bag, he pulled out a pink bonnet. "Rose told me about your dark hair, Cora. I hope you like it." He held it out to her.

"It goes with the dress Mama Rosie gave me." She placed it over her brunette braids with a happy smile. "Thank you."

"Glad you like it. John, I'll give you your gift later."

"That's fine." He and Cora exchanged glances. "Thank you, sir."

"Will you take your game downstairs and teach the other children how to play?" Samuel rested his hand on John's shoulder. "I want to speak to Rose privately."

"Sure thing." Game tucked under his arm, he glanced at Rose and then ushered the children out.

Samuel moved two chairs close together near the stove. He reached for her hand. She placed her trembling hand in his. "Let's talk." His fingers tightened around hers. He wasn't letting her go again. "A couple of months ago, you asked me a question. Perhaps I should begin by explaining my relationship with Ginny."

CHAPTER 35

*G*inny? After so many weeks apart, his relationship with Ginny was what Samuel wanted to discuss? Rose wrenched her hand from his. To cover her rudeness, she rubbed her arms. "It's chilly in here. The fire's burning low."

"I'll build it up." He squatted by the woodbox. When his back was to Rose, he started talking. "Back at school, all the fellas talked about Ginny's beauty. I never expected her to notice me. Didn't give it much thought. Then the school hosted a picnic."

Samuel felt he needed to go that far back? *Please, don't. Let it be.* Cheeks flaming, Rose busied herself with picking up after the children.

"That was just the beginning." With his back to her, he talked about his courtship with Ginny.

I was there, remember? Sitting between you at school. Trying not to see the personal messages on your slates. Soon a fire blazed in the grate. It warmed her skin but not her heart. Why put her through this?

"Ginny was so happy at our wedding." Samuel strode to the window. Lifting the curtain, he looked out toward the streets.

I know. Didn't I dust your wedding portrait weekly? He really didn't need to explain why a plain woman like herself didn't appeal to him. Sighing, Rose picked up brown paper fragments and smoothed wrinkles. This could be useful for wrapping future gifts. If she were going home with Samuel, she'd toss it in the grate.

Samuel's voice droned on. Like sentences with no periods, his words lost all meaning.

It seemed that she'd be supporting the twins on her own. She'd prayed for clarity, direction. Even a spinster with no knowledge of men understood this monologue. After months of rejection, this was no more than she'd expected.

But a whole lot less than she'd dreamed.

All the paper picked up, she cast her gaze around the room, looking for something else to do with her hands.

Why must he share so many details of his first marriage?

Because he missed Ginny. And Rose had never invited him to speak of her. That was one thing—maybe the only one—she could remedy.

Blessed silence. Finally.

"You were such a happy couple." Rose forced the words through stiff lips. How often had she wanted to speak to somebody about Samuel—her heart had nearly burst for news of him —and there had been no one to confide in? He needed freedom to speak, and she must give it. "A fairytale romance. Small wonder you miss her so much."

～

*S*amuel stared at her. Had she not been listening?

"Say whatever you like about her." Rose bunched the top quilt inside her fist. "I'll listen as long as you want to talk."

"I guess your thoughts took you elsewhere."

"I'm sorry." Her cheeks turned scarlet. "I'll listen now."

"My marriage to Ginny wasn't a fairytale romance." Slow steps took him to the bed where she sat.

"It wasn't?" Her knuckles turned white from wringing her hands.

"No." He sat beside her. Close enough that his thigh brushed against hers. "I expect that we had all the normal problems of every married couple. Like misunderstandings when talking about important matters."

She peeked at him without raising her head.

"Like you and me."

"Us?" Her voice squeaked. She cleared her throat.

He clasped her hand so that it was sandwiched between his. "You asked a question before you left."

❦

Rose covered her flaming cheeks with her free hand. "Please, forget I ever…I mean, I was…" No need to dredge up that painful scene. She yanked on her hand, unwilling to hear him reiterate the truth that he'd buried his heart with Ginny. "Let's just get to the task at hand."

"What task is that?"

"Deciding the future for these children we love." She tugged on her hand again, and he released her. Rapid steps took her to the window. Breathing hard, she stared out at the tracks across the street. Did he want them all?

"Agreed. We do love these children." Footsteps approached.

She tensed. No matter what he decided, she must not lose her composure. It was time for that sensible spinster teacher to take over. Her heart cringed to take up that bleak outlook, yet her dreams had betrayed her. There was no choice.

He stopped. A breath away.

Taking her by the shoulders, he turned her around.

She stared at the shirt she'd stitched for him. Her sensible side warned her to ignore the warmth of his hands, how good it felt to be close to him. Her heart longed to revel in his touch.

His hand moved to caress her cheek and tilted her resisting chin upward until she met his tender gaze. "If I tell you I love you, will you hear me then?"

Her jaw dropped "You love me?"

Joy lit his eyes. She gasped to see the same happiness on his face as had shown on the wedding painting. "Then why not tell me all those weeks ago? Why back away from me?"

Cupping her face in gentle hands, he drew her closer until their lips met. She wrapped her arms around his neck, returning his kiss with all the love and longing in her heart. That kiss led to another and then another. She leaned into him, finally home after being lost a very long time.

He led her to the chairs by the fire with an arm wrapped around her. "You asked why I backed away. If you keep kissing me that way, I might forget to answer."

Heat flooded her face. Smiling shyly, she nestled against his side.

"I loved you long before I kissed you." He gave her a lingering kiss. "Our solitary lunches this fall felt so precious. Like a courtship."

"For me as well." Her breath caught in her throat at the joy on his face.

"I realized how blessed I was that you married me. I hoped you'd eventually love me too. Sometimes, you looked at me and...well, I had my dreams." His fingers traced her jaw, stopping at her lips. "Yet those dreams tortured me. I felt disloyal to Ginny's memory. Did you know she was insecure?"

Rose's head reeled. That beautiful woman had lacked confidence?

"Most folks didn't. Ginny excelled at hiding such things. I'd rather not mention this but I suspect you're jealous of Ginny's hold on me."

His analysis shocked her. Jealous of Ginny? She'd simply thought of herself as inadequate and plain in comparison. She covered her burning cheeks with her hands, ashamed of her insecurity. Samuel was right. Maybe she had more in common with Ginny than she knew.

"She required daily assurances of my love, which I gave. But still she doubted me. I think her parents fussed over her looks so often that she imagined that the whole world required her to be beautiful every minute of the day." He clasped her hands. "Don't you see? I felt as if I'd betrayed her when I fell in love with you."

Rose's breath hitched at the torment in his eyes. "I didn't know."

"Rose, I love you." He tilted her face toward him with gentle fingers. "Your leaving angered me, but God brought good out of that lonely time. I needed time away from you."

Tears pricked the back of her eyes to remember dark days where she'd simply existed.

"I had to reconcile myself with Ginny's death before I could begin a new relationship on solid ground." His hands slid up her arms to her shoulders. "For weeks, I couldn't even pray. Then Charlie mentioned you knew about his first wife."

She nodded, remembering the pain on the old man's face. "Ramona." Compassion swelled for the fatherly man. How did one grow beyond such a tragedy?

"Then he met Esther."

Was it possible for Samuel's love to grow as Charlie's did for Esther? Hardly daring to breathe, she searched his face.

"I finally prayed. God worked pretty hard on my heart the past two months. He worked even harder the past two weeks. What better day to reconcile than Christmas?"

She leaned her head against his chest. A tear rolled down her cheek.

He lifted her face and caressed it, wiping away the tear with his thumb. "Do you think you could love me someday?"

"I do love you, Samuel." She stroked the strong hand that cupped her face, smiling at the sparkle in his blue eyes. "As strong and deep as you can ever desire."

"When did you fall in love with me?"

"I was about sixteen the first time."

His jaw dropped. "Sixteen? You loved me before I courted Ginny?"

She nodded. "I buried my feelings before your wedding. Later, I only remembered our high school friendship. When you proposed last spring, those memories flooded back."

"You agreed to marry me under difficult circumstances because you already loved me?" His intense gaze held hers.

She clasped his hand. "I dreamed a big dream."

He stood and raised her to her feet. "Let's make a pact: no more secrets."

"No more secrets." They sealed the agreement with a kiss. She rested her face against his chest. The thud of his heart thrilled her senses. "Samuel, what about the twins? I told them they'd always have a home with me."

"And so they will, in Hamilton with us." His arms tightened around her.

"I'm sorry I didn't discuss the matter with you first—"

"Richard explained. At first, your decision just erected one more barrier between us."

"I'm sorry." She caressed the wrinkles from his brow.

He kissed her fingers. "I like the twins, and we'll get to know one another."

She pulled away. "There's another matter we must correct."

He quirked an eyebrow.

"You must trust me with Emma and Peter."

"I do."

"No, you don't." She stepped back. "You insist they turn to

you for everything. You even chastised me for comforting Emma."

"That was wrong. I wanted to shoulder the brunt of their grief. I had the best of intentions, thinking you had enough responsibilities. You weren't used to parenting. I was. I regret it. And unfortunately, their grandparents had convinced me that it was my duty and mine alone. Please forgive me."

"You see, I want more than a place at the table." She took a step closer. "I want a place in their lives. Their hearts. If you continue to push them away from me and always toward you, that will never happen."

Looking at her with troubled eyes, he rubbed his jaw.

She waited. This was too vital to brush aside. He must realize the damage that could occur if he insisted on being their only shelter.

"You're right. I hadn't looked down that road far enough to contemplate those consequences." He looked at her. "That wasn't my intention. I merely tried to protect them from that terrible grief."

"But you don't have to protect them from me." She reached for his hand and brought it to rest against her lips. "I love them too."

He enfolded her in his arms. "I'll do better."

"Thank you." A huge weight dropped. John and Cora would have a real home again, and Samuel would allow her to love Peter and Emma.

"Peter has been anxious to see you. I believe he'll cope better now if he sees me hug you or kiss you."

"Good." That had been a niggling worry.

"I want a promise from you." He cradled her against his heart.

"What is it?"

"That you'll never leave again."

She tilted her head to gaze into his eyes. "I'm sorry for

leaving you and the children. For not being honest about my hurts, my needs. For putting you all through this heartache. Never again."

"I'll hold you to it." He sealed the promise with a long, slow kiss. "I have some news."

"Oh?" She nestled against him.

"I finished two attic bedrooms"—he grinned—"along with the storage room you suggested. Seems like I got them completed just in time, because you and I will be sharing the big bedroom."

The look in his eyes brought a heated flush to her cheeks. She was ready for a real marriage. "Whatever you say." He pulled her closer and she kissed him. Then she drew back, embarrassed. "I'm sorry."

"I'm not." He kept his arms around her. "In fact, I think you should do it again."

She complied, her confidence growing. "Let's tell the children our news."

"We will." He kissed her again.

"Wait—I have a Christmas gift for you." She stepped back.

Samuel picked up his bag. "Me first."

"All right." Excitement took over as he fished a brown package from his bag. She stared at the first gift he'd ever given her, and then tore it open, exclaiming over the delicate blue shawl.

"I hope it matches your fancy blue dress. It's a pretty color on you."

"Samuel, it's perfect. I will wear them both for Christmas supper. Thank you." She reached into her skirt pocket. "My gift isn't wrapped." She set the pocket watch into his palm.

He rubbed a finger over it. "How did you know we'd come?"

"I didn't. Even if I never saw you again, this gift felt important. It's been in my pocket since I purchased it. It was almost like having a part of you with me."

He caressed her face. Dreams of the days ahead filled her thoughts. The future, which used to loom like a dark shadow, now beckoned her. She began to plan. "Our room and board are paid through the end of the week. Mrs. Westlake won't mind our leaving."

"Probably not." He kissed her cheek.

She pulled back from him. "Nora will lose three employees. I can't leave her."

"Oh, yes, you can."

His kiss left her no doubts about where she wanted to be.

"We can leave in the morning."

"Please, Samuel, can I give her notice? At least two days?"

He sighed. "I can live with a delay of two days. Today is Tuesday. Charlie's taking care of the animals for us. He's quite worried about you. I'll send a telegram to ease his mind and ask him to show it to Richard."

"He's bringing his family on Saturday."

He shook his head. "No, he's hoping to see us in Hamilton for an even bigger celebration. Staying until Friday gives me an opportunity to consult a lawyer here about adopting the twins. Then we're all going home together Friday morning. I'm not leaving you on your own again."

"It's a good thing there are extra beds in this room." She laughed. "You can't know what a blessing this room has been."

CHAPTER 36

$\mathcal{M}$rs. Westlake had moved the children to a small parlor with a table off the main hall to play their game. When Rose arrived with Samuel, they put the game back in the box and watched the couple with fear in their eyes.

"Did you like the game?" Samuel asked.

"Yes, but"—Emma tugged on Rose's hand—"are you coming home with us?"

"I am." The little girl's shining eyes warmed Rose's soul as much as the small arms wrapped around her waist.

"You won't leave again?" Emma asked.

The question pierced her heart. She crouched down to Emma's level. "I'm sorry I left the last time. I'll never leave again."

Peter moved closer. The twins backed away as if to give them privacy.

"Polly told me you're really nice, but Peter said you tried to make us forget Ma."

Rose sat on a chair and leaned forward so she was eye level with the little girl. "Emma, keep remembering your mama. I lost my mother when I was young. No one made me forget her. I loved her so much. You love your mother, too, don't you?"

Emma nodded, tears filling her eyes.

"And she loved you." Rose pressed her cheek against Emma's. "You'll see her in heaven someday. I'll take care of you until then."

Beside Emma, Peter sniffed.

She extended her hand.

He shuffled over and grabbed it.

"I'm not perfect," Rose said. "I make mistakes, but always remember that I love you."

"You don't want us to forget Ma?" Peter chewed on his lip.

Rose shook her head. "Never ever." She opened her arms and cradled the precious boy to her shoulder. He heaved a great sigh and rested against her.

Samuel knelt beside them. The children threw themselves into his arms. He held them a moment before tickling their waists. They laughed and tickled him back.

Rose looked up and caught Cora's ashen face. She stood and rushed to her. "Honey, what's troubling you?"

The corners of her lips turned upward. She only managed to look more forlorn. "I guess you'll go home soon. We sure appreciate all you've done for us, giving us a place to live and all. I slept in a bed for almost two months."

"Thanks for the Christmas gifts," John said. "I'll think of you when I play the games." All animation drained from John's face, making him look as lost as he had in those early days.

"But you're coming with us." They believed she planned to leave them behind. She'd been so concerned with the younger children's feelings that she neglected to share the news.

"John, I didn't give you my gift yet, though part of it is still in Hamilton. I'm glad I remembered to get this out of my bag before we came downstairs." Stepping closer, Samuel reached into his pocket. He placed a fish hook on John's open palm. "I'll give you the fishing pole when you get to the farm."

John stared at the shiny metal. "I love fishing."

"I hoped you did. And we've got two empty bedrooms just waiting for someone to occupy them." Samuel grinned.

John looked up at Samuel with wonder in his eyes.

"Yes, Samuel has built new attic rooms." Rose touched John's arm.

Cora covered her face in her hands.

Rose placed an arm around her shoulder with a glance at Samuel. "The two of you will attend school in Hamilton. How does that sound?"

Cora peeked through her fingers at her brother.

"Please live with us." Rose's heart plummeted. "Samuel will speak with a lawyer about adopting you."

"We've got a dog named Zeb." Peter tugged John's sleeve. "He's a pretty good dog. I taught him a trick. He fetches a stick when I throw it."

"We have chickens. I'll teach you how to feed them." Emma stood beside Cora. "You can be my sister. I don't have one of those yet. I've got a cousin and a doll, but not a sister."

"There, how can you refuse an offer like that?" Samuel rested a callused hand on John's shoulder.

"You really want us?" John's voice squeaked.

"Absolutely. And that new fishing pole I left at home? We'll use it often. Together."

John's face relaxed into a grin. "I never could turn down a day of fishing."

"Good. We leave Friday morning."

"We accept." John extended his hand to Samuel, who clasped it in a firm handshake.

Emma tugged on Rose's sleeve. "But do you really love all of us?"

She laughed and slid a finger down the little girl's pretty

nose. "Emma, I had twenty-one students last year and loved every one of them. My heart is big enough to hold all of you."

As she looked at the happy faces of the four children, she realized God had answered her prayers beyond her imagination in spite of all her failures. Had she not left on that northbound train, she wouldn't have met the twins. In the midst of her troubles and mistakes, God answered Cora's prayer for a loving home while allowing Samuel time to work through his grief.

She extended her hand past Peter and John to Samuel, who gripped it as if he'd never let go. He reached around Cora and Emma to grasp her other hand enclosing their precious children in a circle of love.

Did you enjoy this book? We hope so!
Would you take a quick minute to leave a review where you purchased the book?
It doesn't have to be long. Just a sentence or two telling what you liked about the story!

Receive a FREE ebook and get updates when new Wild Heart books release: https://wildheartbooks.org/newsletter

Don't miss the next book in Second Chances Series!

A Not So Persistent Suitor

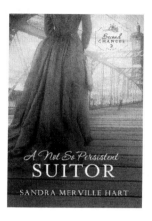

Chapter One

CINCINNATI, OHIO
FRIDAY, SEPTEMBER 14, 1883

Cora Welch swiped a dainty pink handkerchief over her damp forehead. The thought of a two-mile walk in the unseasonable heat of the mid-September afternoon decided her. She'd spend a precious nickel on the horsecar fare back to her boarding house home in the city. It was but a five-minute walk downhill to Oak Street from her school to pick up the car.

"Cora?"

She turned at the familiar voice. "Olivia?" She hadn't seen Olivia Farnsworth since June, before Cora left to spend the summer at her home in Hamilton. Olivia attended the same Cincinnati church as she and her brother, John. "How lovely to see you again. What are you doing in Walnut Hills?"

"Good afternoon." The tall blonde lifted the hem of her stylish blue dress off the dirt path as she quickened her step to match Cora's. "I've just come from a pleasant visit with my aunt. I imagine you had classes today."

Cora was a second-year student at the Cincinnati Kindergarten Training School. "My final year just began." Cora shifted a basket, heavy with two textbooks, to her other hand as they walked. The horsecar couldn't arrive soon enough. It had been a long, exhausting day. "The first week of classes just ended. If you're interested, there may be time for you to enroll for the current term."

"I see you are still recruiting for more kindergarten teachers."

Cora laughed at Olivia teasing smile. "Guilty. It's just that I've seen the overwhelming need for teachers for these little ones. If you could see their faces light up with joy when I'm reading to them or singing with them, you'd understand my enthusiasm." The desperate need for kindergarten teachers, a new field, had changed her college choice from teaching history. She was hopeful of a job back in Hamilton, where her adoptive family lived. Sallie, her five-year-old sister, would be in kindergarten now if there was a class for her to attend at the local school. There'd be a place for her three-year-old brother Aaron to attend if Cora had anything to say about it.

"I'm certain of it. I've no ambition to be anything other than a wife and mother. I don't want to waste my parents' money and my time to go to school."

Cora squelched a sigh. Olivia's feelings were common. The women who continued to teach school after marriage were rare. Mama Rosie, her adoptive mother, was a great example, for she hadn't returned to teach after marrying Samuel. Not that Cora would ever be the talented teacher that Mama Rosie had been, but she planned to wait two or three years to marry and then teach until her first child was born. Then she'd return to her teaching when her youngest child reached four years of age, old enough to attend kindergarten. Goodness, but she was getting ahead of herself. Ben Findlay hadn't even proposed yet.

The ladies reached the stop to the sound of clopping hooves.

"I've missed you at church." Olivia reached into the reticule hanging from her wrist as a horsecar pulled by four horses stopped at the corner of Oak and Hunt streets. "Though your brother only missed one Sunday service all summer."

"I spent the summer with my family, but John stayed in Cincinnati because of his job." John worked in the composing room at the *Times-Star*. Cora made a fuss of searching for a coin from the pocket of her pink gingham dress to avoid Olivia's gaze. She'd long suspected her friend's romantic interest in her twin and didn't want to encourage it. In fact, John avoided Olivia, and since Cora sat with him and Ben, she tended to do the same, so the two of them remained casual friends. Cora's protective instincts for her brother's feelings prevented anything more.

Rennie Hill, their Hamilton neighbor, had a better chance of winning her brother's heart than anyone she knew, yet there was some trouble between them that neither had shared with her.

A mother holding a sleeping baby led a little boy to the empty horsecar. Smiling, Cora waved to the boy too young for school then she stepped aside for the little family to go in first. She paid the conductor on the back platform.

Olivia sat beside Cora in a middle seat. No breeze stirred inside the hot car despite every window being open. Still, the roof brought immediate relief from the hot sun beating down on her straw hat, which was threaded with pink ribbon to match her dress.

"It's impressive that John wants to be a reporter." Olivia's brown eyes gleamed.

"He's long been a teller of tall tales." Cora remembered the family's laughter around the dinner table at John's embellishment of daily events. He was more suited to writing novels and short stories, in her opinion.

"I suppose that many reporters begin their careers by learning how to print the newspapers," Olivia said.

"No doubt." As the horses ambled down Hunt Road toward Cincinnati, the car's rocking motion relaxed the day's tensions from Cora's shoulders.

"Perhaps his friendship with Ben Findlay has given him opportunities at the *Times-Star.*" Olivia gave her a side glance.

"Possibly. John met him outside the newspaper's building. Ben put in a good word for him, which was probably one of the reasons John was offered the job." Cora's heartbeat quickened at the mention of her beau's name. How she had missed him over the summer. She and Ben had often included John in their outings last spring. Or was it more correct that the twins included Ben in their plans? Either way, all the evening strolls, Saturday outings, and Sunday afternoon dinners spent in the man's company had started her well on her way to falling in love with him. "Ben started out as a newsboy, selling papers for *The Cincinnati Enquirer.* He worked his way up to the composing room. The *Times-Star* hired him as a reporter three years ago."

"I attended a banquet at the Burnet House this summer. I saw him there."

"Oh?" Cora was surprised. A banquet at one of Cincinnati's best hotels was quite an occasion—and far above his means. He must have been an invited guest instead of a paying customer. "He didn't mention it when he and John accompanied me to Sunday dinner at my boarding house." She hadn't seen Ben since. She imagined he wanted to give her time to settle back into her routine of school, student-teaching, and her job at the sweet shop. He would call tomorrow and escort her on an afternoon stroll. One of their favorite destinations was the big fountain on Fifth Street. Afterwards, he often treated her to a lemonade or an ice cream. Anything was fine with her as long as they were together.

"I'm not surprised." Olivia fingered a fold of her dress.

Cora raised her eyebrows. "Why? Is it a secret?"

"I don't know if I should tell you."

"You've already started." Why wouldn't Olivia look at her? "You may as well finish the story."

"He escorted another woman." The words came out in a rush.

Cora gripped the basket's handle. Surely, she had misunderstood.

"I don't know her name." Olivia finally looked up. "It upset me for your sake. I didn't know that your courtship with him had ended."

"It hasn't." The words came out in a whisper. "I mean...I thought he was interested in renewing our courtship when I returned from my parents' farm." That could explain why she'd only seen him once since returning to the city a week ago.

"I thought so, too. I've seen the way he looks at you."

"H-how does he look at me?" Cora hated the way her voice shook. How could she survive losing another person she loved?

"Like he's never seen any woman as lovely as you." Olivia gave her a sad smile. "You and John are undeniably twins. You share those dark good looks."

"I hardly think that's what he thinks." Cora didn't believe it, especially given that Ben's attention had wandered over the summer. She brushed back her dark brown hair, which was parted in the middle and gathered into a bun at the nape of her neck. Her mother believed that her best feature were her brown eyes framed by black lashes. "I've got a mirror. My looks are as ordinary as most."

"The woman he escorted wasn't nearly as pretty as you." Olivia patted her hand.

As if that made a difference. What mattered was that Ben was courting another woman.

"Do you think Ben intends to tell you about her?"

Perhaps that was reason for tomorrow's stroll. "I don't know. I wonder why John didn't mention it."

Olivia shrugged. "Maybe he didn't know. John wasn't there."

Cora assumed Olivia had looked for him. She was often looking for John.

"He did go to Hamilton for your sister's birthday, right?"

"Emma turned twelve last month. Mama Rosie—Mama, that is—celebrates each child's birthday with either a party or a special supper. John came home for a few days to join the fun." That explained her protective brother's silence—he didn't know. They'd endured many hard times together, and they watched out for one another. "Did you talk to John often at church? Seems you are fairly well-informed about his activities." Cora hoped to steer the conversation away from herself, for she needed time to think. She counted Olivia as a friend, but not a close one.

"Well, as to that..." She studied her clenched hands.

Olivia's blush confirmed Cora's suspicions about her interest in John. She ached for her friend's sadness—and her own. "What about you? Is anyone courting you?"

"George Randolph escorted me twice to supper this summer. He's the one who took me to the banquet where I saw Ben." Her shoulders slumped. "I just can't get excited about George."

"I'm sorry. The right man will come along for you." Cora's spirits plummeted. What about the right man for her? She had thought Ben was the one she'd someday marry. Had he lost interest in her?

Ben Findlay tipped his bowler hat at an acquaintance without missing a step toward Dan's Sweet Shop, where Cora worked from three o'clock to six o'clock Monday through Friday. Though his work day had technically ended, Ansel

Bridges, his boss and editor at the newspaper, had told him when he hired him three years before to always be on the alert for a story. Observing that his editor never relaxed, Ben had resolved to follow his footsteps.

Mr. Bridges seemed to take him under his wing early on... not so much in the past few months. At least one man had taken the time to teach him. Ben's own father had never possessed the patience to talk with him. Robert Findlay's years fighting with an Ohio regiment in the War Between the States had stolen something from him that Ben and his ma couldn't restore.

Bad memories. He had other things to think about this afternoon and no thoughts to spare on his absent pa.

Truth to tell, Mr. Bridges had also disappointed him. He had invited Ben to a fancy supper attended by many city leaders. Rival newspapers were sending their best reporters, and the editor had wanted Ben on the team of *Times-Star* reporters representing the paper. Of course, his most-experienced reporters would be assigned the best stories from the occasion, as always. Yet his boss enumerated the benefits of meeting prominent political leaders. It had been Ben's first invitation to such a gathering. Corruption among some politicians and attorneys had fostered a disrespect in Ben for them. He didn't know who gave favors in return for bribes and didn't search for the information. Politics didn't interest Ben because he'd seen enough to suspect the city's various wards were controlled by ward bosses, but advancing his career did.

His boss's one stipulation was that Ben escort his daughter Felicia to the banquet. By the time his boss mentioned Felicia, Ben had wanted to go so badly that he'd made only a feeble protest about courting Cora. Mr. Bridges waved this protest aside, saying that this was a business dinner and his girl would understand.

Ben hoped that was true. He'd shaken the hand of the mayor for the first time that evening. He'd met wealthy citizens and even carried on conversations with a few. He'd written four articles about the evening that had printed in their paper—with Ben's byline.

Mr. Bridges had been right about the event boosting his career.

Unfortunately, Felicia had not understood. She had blushed and batted her eyes at him and seemed to believe that evening had been the beginning of a courtship. After the fact, her father proudly beamed that Ben could scarcely find a finer woman.

Ben felt like he'd crawled into a kettle of day-old raw fish. The whole situation stank. Worse, John had been away from the city when it happened, and Ben had been too ashamed to admit to his friend—Cora's twin—that he'd accompanied another woman to the event.

Now that Cora was back, he'd have to tell her. Not tonight, though. This was a surprise visit. They wouldn't have enough time alone. He'd escort her to her boarding house and, if he was invited, join her for supper. He had enough money to pay Mrs. Baughman, who owned Cora's boarding house, for his meal.

This evening, he just wanted to enjoy her company for the few minutes she could spare before her nightly studies. They had all day tomorrow. Though he dreaded it, he'd tell her then.

"Ben?"

Startled, he looked over his shoulder. His heart sank to see Felicia close the door to millinery shop. "Miss Bridges." He tipped his hat.

"How lovely to see you again." She stepped toward him, clutching the strings tied around a hatbox. "You agreed to call me Felicia at the banquet." Her tone was a lighthearted rebuke.

"So I did." His face flushed from more than the sun's heat. He had managed to avoid her since that evening. Something in her possessive hold on his arm as he escorted home at the end of the event warned him to stay away. It wasn't the tall brunette's rather plain looks that made him reluctant to talk with her.

Felicia possessed a pleasant personality. She was twenty-four, his age, and he had no doubt she'd make some man a fine wife. Just not him. Cora so filled his heart that he couldn't consider courting another woman. "I see you've been shopping."

"Yes." She lifted the brown hatbox. "My mother dropped me off earlier and took our buggy with her. I told her I'd enjoy a stroll home. You recall meeting my mother?"

"Of course." Besides sitting opposite Mrs. Bridges at the banquet, he had met her on two other occasions. "Lovely woman. How is she?"

"Quite well, thank you." Felicia shifted the box to her other hand. "I misjudged the weight of my purchase. I fear this will grow heavy before I reach the next corner."

His discomfort deepened at her hints. It was difficult not to carry her package. His mother had raised him to act as a gentleman. "I'm afraid I am expected elsewhere..." The words died on his lips. Cora didn't *know* he planned to escort her home from work, though either he or John made a practice of it whenever possible because of the taverns along the route. "My apologies for my inability to assist you."

"Don't give it another thought." Her smiled widened as she touched his sleeve. "I'm certain you'd escort me were you free to do so. Until next time, then." Long curls fell across her shoulders as she tilted her head up at him.

Ben didn't have a lot experience with women—his courtship with Cora was the longest in a handful of relationships—yet he understood Felicia's veiled invitation to call on her. He tipped his hat and turned on his heel, vowing to take a different route to Dan's Sweet Shop next time.

Cora wiped spilled soda from the long marble counter separating servers from customers. Three other ladies, wearing white frilled aprons like hers over their dresses, served soda drinks to guests who sat on spindle back chairs lining the counter. On the opposite side of the aisle stood shelves with attractive displays of various kinds of candy, including peppermint and chocolate. Cora was glad other workers helped customers with those purchases because the candy tempted her far more than the drinks. The small café with its small round tables in back invited guests to enjoy their treats on the premises.

Despite the heat driving in a steady flow of customers for a cold, refreshing soda, the afternoon had dragged. All she wanted was to talk to John and see what he knew about the banquet. She didn't like to think badly of Ben. Surely Olivia had been mistaken. Ben probably had shown polite interest in a young woman's conversation, someone he happened to sit beside during supper. His innate kindness was one of the things she loved about him.

She bent over the counter lest someone notice the sudden blush in her cheeks. She'd only acknowledged her love for him to herself. She certainly had never spoken of it.

Neither had Ben.

A bell jingling over the door drew her eyes. Disappointment filled her when a stranger strode in and stopped at the front table where soda water was purchased from the owner or his wife.

"Ben coming to escort you home this evening?" Cindy Tomlinson, a pretty brunette in her mid-twenties, walked behind Cora balancing a tray of dirty glasses.

"I don't know." Cora strove to keep a light tone. She wasn't sure she wanted him to walk her home tonight. What if he didn't tell her about the other woman? "We have plans tomorrow."

"Good." She added the dirty glasses from Cora's station to her tray. "You leave in fifteen minutes. I imagined he'd be here by now. Doesn't he usually come early and have a soda at your counter?"

That brought a smile. "He buys me a soda, too, unless we must leave promptly at six." That was last spring. Had everything changed?

"Did you try the week's specialty yet?"

"Dan created a licorice soda this time." Cora shuddered. Her boss's concoctions sometimes missed the mark, but he kept trying. "No, thank you. I'll enjoy my licorice in a stick of candy."

"Agreed." Cindy laughed. "This one was a failure to me too. Better luck next week." She toted the dirty dishes to the kitchen in the back, past the café set up for customers preferring a relaxed, more private atmosphere to enjoy their drinks and candy than the seats at the counter provided.

The door opened to a tingling bell. Cora looked that direction, and her heart skipped.

Ben's brown eyes sought hers as he removed his bowler hat. He smoothed back his blond hair parted on the side. She loved his clean-shaven look when many men preferred mustaches or beards. His beige-colored coat half-hid a white shirt yet did nothing to mask his tall, broad-shouldered frame.

He strode to her counter. "Sorry I'm late."

"You're not late." Cora wondered at the strain on his face. A difficult day at the *Times-Star*? Or was it guilt? "I wasn't certain you were coming."

"I haven't tried the flavor of the week." Ben slid onto one of the spindle-back chairs lining the counter in front of her. His fingers drummed against the counter. "Do we have time?"

"We can stay after my shift ends to finish if you like." Cora could pretend the situation between them was as it used to be until they were alone. "I'd prefer the lemon soda myself. You can try the licorice."

"Licorice?" He chuckled. "Fine. Let me go purchase them from Dan. You can make them if you like."

Cora nodded to Mae, her coworker. "I'll get this one."

"I figured you would." With a nod, Mae returned to her conversation with a customer.

Two squirts of flavoring were enough for Ben's drink. She added the soda water with a grimace. At least it smelled delicious. Both drinks were ready when he returned.

As soon as he resumed his seat, two couples came in. Several others followed. All four servers behind the counter rushed to fill drink orders. Only three of the twenty chairs were empty by the time everyone had been served.

By then it was after six. She leaned across the counter to Ben. "Sorry about that."

"Think nothing of it." He grinned. "I knew I was taking a chance on getting to talk with you here. Want to sit in the back to enjoy our drinks?"

She nodded. There were two couples and a family sitting in the café. No fear of a private conversation with strangers nearby. "Do you like it?" She gestured his glass.

"Delicious."

She laughed with him as the bell tingled.

Her brother gave a little wave. "Is there time for a soda? I'm parched."

"If we hurry. We'll sit at the tables. Licorice or lemon?"

Her landlady stopped serving supper at seven. Her brother's presence, while welcome, put off her questions for either of them.

"You kidding? I'll try the licorice."

Laughing, Ben picked up her glass and his while John paid. "I'll wait for you at the table."

Cora forced away her worry for the moment. It was better to learn the truth directly from Ben. If he didn't bring up the topic tomorrow afternoon, she intended to ask.

ABOUT THE AUTHOR

Sandra Merville Hart, award-winning and bestselling author of inspirational historical romances, loves to discover little-known yet fascinating facts from American history to include in her stories. Her desire is to transport her readers back in time. She is also a blogger, speaker, and conference teacher. Connect with Sandra on her blog, https://sandramervillehart.wordpress.com/.

ACKNOWLEDGMENTS

This story has special significance because it was the first story I showed to my agent, Joyce Hart. She never gave up on it through the many edits because she liked it from the beginning. Thanks to Joyce for her perseverance. That this story has not only found a home but also become a series brings us both peace.

What a joy it is to work with Misty Beller, Robin Patchen, and the whole team at Wild Heart Books. Publishers, editors, and authors work as a team, and I appreciate their hard work in helping to make the book the best it can be. I look forward to working with them on the next book in the series. I want to give special thanks to Robin for her patience and perseverance with this story, because her editing skills and eye for detail definitely made this a better story. I gave her more of a challenge on this one than I intended. You're a marvel, Robin!

I was inspired by a visit to the Hamilton Lane Library and couldn't resist using it in my story. Thanks to Brad Spurlock, a Reference Services staff member, who found the name of the Lane librarian in 1877 and a bit about her so that I could include her name in the story.

Thanks to family and friends for their continued support.

Thank you, Lord, for giving me the story.

AUTHOR'S NOTE

I am from Ohio, and it was a joy to write this story set in three of that state's towns and cities in 1877—Harrison, Hamilton, and Bradford Junction.

Readers of my other books will not be surprised to find a bit of Civil War history in my story. Morgan's Raiders came through the village of Harrison in July of 1863, terrifying its citizens. Confederate General John Hunt Morgan's troops burned the bridge over the Whitewater River on what was then known as Main Street and now is called State Street. Union soldiers in pursuit came into Harrison later the same day, after Morgan's Raiders were gone.

I visited the Hamilton Lane Library to utilize the excellent research resources available for local history and was so inspired by this historic building and the wonderful books it contained that I had to include this beautiful, octagonal building in Rose's story. Thanks to Brad Spurlock, a Reference Services staff member, who found the name of the Lane librarian in 1877 and a bit about her so I could include her in the story.

Our fictional family's walk to Lane Library enabled me to show readers the growing city of Hamilton in 1877. For instance, the Hamilton House (also known as Hamilton Hotel) had a stagecoach office where the stage received a fresh team of horses while passengers enjoyed refreshments.

Bradford Junction (now known as Bradford) was a village in 1877. It was a railroad town and meal stop for trains. Arrival times varied because time was not yet standardized.

I hope you enjoyed this story set in three Ohio locations in 1877. I invite you to read the next book in the series, *A Not So Persistent Suitor*, to discover what happens to our characters in Cincinnati in 1883 and 1884.

Sandra Merville Hart

If you love historical romance, check out the other Wild Heart books!

Marisol ~ Spanish Rose by Elva Cobb Martin

Escaping to the New World is her only option...Rescuing her will wrap the chains of the Inquisition around his neck.

Marisol Valentin flees Spain after murdering the nobleman who molested her. She ends up for sale on the indentured servants' block at Charles Town harbor—dirty, angry, and with child. Her hopes are shattered, but she must find a refuge for herself and the child she carries. Can this new land offer her the grace, love, and security she craves? Or must she escape again to her only living relative in Cartagena?

Captain Ethan Becket, once a Charles Town minister, now sails the seas as a privateer, grieving his deceased wife. But when he takes captive a ship full of indentured servants, he's intrigued by the woman whose manners seem much more refined than the average Spanish serving girl. Perfect to become governess for his young son. But when he sets out on a quest to find his captured sister, said to be in Cartagena, little does he expect his new Spanish governess to stow away on his ship with her six-month-old son. Yet her offer of help to free his sister is too tempting to pass up. And her beauty, both inside and out, is too attractive for his heart to protect itself against—until he learns she is a wanted murderess.

As their paths intertwine on a journey filled with danger, intrigue, and romance, only love and the grace of God can overcome the past and ignite a new beginning for Marisol and Ethan.

~

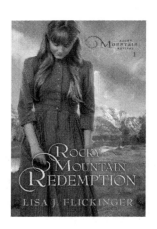

Rocky Mountain Redemption by Lisa J. Flickinger

A Rocky Mountain logging camp may be just the place to find herself.

To escape the devastation caused by the breaking of her wedding engagement, Isabelle Franklin joins her aunt in the Rocky Mountains to feed a camp of lumberjacks cutting on the slopes of Cougar Ridge. If only she could out run the lingering nightmares.

Charles Bailey, camp foreman and Stony Creek's itinerant pastor, develops a reputation to match his new nickname — Preach. However, an inner battle ensues when the details of his rough history threaten to overcome the beliefs of his young faith.

Amid the hazards of camp life, the unlikely friendship growing between the two surprises Isabelle. She's drawn to Preach's brute strength and gentle nature as he leads the ragtag crew toiling for Pollitt's Lumber. But when the ghosts from her past return to haunt her, the choices she will make change the course of her life forever—and that of the man she's come to love.

~

Lone Star Ranger by Renae Brumbaugh Green

Elizabeth Covington will get her man.

And she has just a week to prove her brother isn't the murderer Texas Ranger Rett Smith accuses him of being. She'll show the good-looking lawman he's wrong, even if it means setting out on a risky race across Texas to catch the real killer.

Rett doesn't want to convict an innocent man. But he can't let the Boston beauty sway his senses to set a guilty man free. When Elizabeth follows him on a dangerous trek, the Ranger vows to keep her safe. But who will protect him from the woman whose conviction and courage leave him doubting everything—even his heart?